Night Swimmers

Night Swimmers

Roisin Maguire

—

First published in Great Britain in 2024 by
SERPENT'S TAIL
an imprint of Profile Books Ltd
29 Cloth Fair
London EC1A 7JQ
www.serpentstail.com

1 3 5 7 9 10 8 6 4 2

Typeset in Tramuntana Text by MacGuru Ltd
Designed by Nicky Barneby @ Barneby Ltd

Printed and bound in Great Britain by Clays Ltd, Elcograf S.p.A.

A CIP catalogue record for this book is available from the British Library.

HB ISBN 978 1 80081 674 9
TPB ISBN 978 1 80522 121 0
eISBN 978 1 80081 675 6

FSC
www.fsc.org
MIX
Paper | Supporting
responsible forestry
FSC® C018072

Part One

—

Chapter 1

———

SHE HEARD THEM BEFORE she saw them, a cluster of brightly coloured chickens, fussing at the water's edge, flapping and clucking.

'Silly bitches,' she said.

Treading water, blinking the salt from her eyes, she watched them for a moment. They were folding towels, stowing phones in yoga-bags, pulling off sandals. They were toeing the water, expressing dismay at its temperature. They were coming in, now. She could hear the giggles and the tiny little screams of surprise as the water met their smooth white feet. They wore dinky little swim-hats and their shoulders were hunched and pale and narrow.

She flipped herself over and ducked down, down, down under the surface, letting the sparkle of her bubbles soothe her, feeling the cold rush over her skin, her belly, her thighs. A cool hand. She felt the tick of her pulse grow heavy as she dived into the dark, but kept going, kept swimming and wriggling downwards until her heart became a knocking in her throat and temples, forcing her to turn back, push to the surface again, pull fresh air in and blink and drip and breathe and look out to sea and try to pretend she was on her own.

'What the hell are they doing here?' she grumbled, lying

back crossly and kicking great columns of water up into the air, letting it rain down again, delicious. She could have stayed for ages longer but the shrieking and splashing carried out across the still plane of water in the bay – her bay – and jangled her, spoilt it all. No one ever came all the way around here, to this pebbly, inhospitable place. They put up their windbreakers and their deckchairs and the rest of their shit back around the corner on the main beach where the sand lay golden and inviting and cool and bright, and left this place for her.

Bugger, she thought.

She rolled over, disgruntled, looking out to where the grey sea met the grey sky and disappeared, feeling the depths beneath her dangling toes, dark and heavy and beautiful. It was maybe fifteen, twenty metres deep out here, just at the edge of OK, just before the currents began, those whip-strong lines of muscle from east to west, those unstoppable forces, those dangerous beasts. She could see them from where she was, juddering the water ahead, as if freight trains ran just underneath the surface and dragged the sea along.

She swam away, just to be sure, swam a little distance in, towards the shore.

They were still in a tight group, the other women, but they were in the water properly now at last. Their red and green and blue and white heads bobbed up and down as they sketched a communal breaststroke around and around in tight circles, up down, up down, up down, like that fabulous fairground game where you got to hit rodents with a mallet. She wished she had a mallet, now, she surely did.

They'd be there for ages on her beach, she grumped, even after they'd got out of the water – swaddled in special swimming robes and taking photos of themselves, drinking hot things that steamed from shiny metal cups. Adventurers, all. Triumphant explorers of the deep on social media.

She'd have to go in, then. Get it over with.

Damn.

She headed back, slowly, like a schoolchild at the morning bell.

The dog saw her coming, jumped up from the shelter of the dark rocks, and started barking as it always did.

'Good lad,' she said, and smiled a little, felt a teensy bit better.

The dog came to the edge of the water, barking, barking, barking.

The chittering and bobbing stopped among the swimmers, and squeaky wondering began.

'Oh my god, look at that thing – I wonder where its owner is.'

'I wonder if it will come in? D'you think it will come in?'

'Oh god, Ellie, I hate dogs, you know I hate dogs. I hope it doesn't come in.'

'That's not a dog, that's a monster.'

Nervous giggling, swivelling of bright heads.

'I'm getting a bit cold. I'll really need to get out, in a minute.'

'How can we get out, if it's there, like that? I wonder how we can get out?'

Their voices, rising, travelled faster over water than on land. She could hear every word, their clear assertive diction shining through.

'Oh my god, look! There's someone way out there – I bet it's their dog.'

'Where?'

'Where? I can't see anything.'

'They haven't a hat on, or anything. Look – miles away – that black dot, there, see?'

Pause. Everyone looking.

She felt like waving, but didn't.

Dog, barking and barking.

Barking and barking and barking.

Paws in the water now, barking and barking.

She imagined its mouth open, doing that frothing thing by now, all the teeth jangling in there, sharp in its blunt ugly head.

The heads turning to her, to the dog, to her again.

All standing now, pimpled and chilly no doubt, their silly orange tow-floats dangling, staring out along a pointing finger to where she swam.

'Unless it's a seal?'

'Oh god, Ellie, I hope it's not a seal. I hate seals.'

She obliged, with a flip of her feet, ducking under, hearing a shriek before the water bubbled over. It was a pity, she thought, in the murky white of it, holding herself down by letting breath stream out. It was a damn pity she wasn't a seal. Seals could submerge for six minutes or more. Fantastic creatures, altogether. She could have swum right past them, right in to shore, invisible; lolloped out and up the beach and away, before they knew it.

As it was, she thought, bubbling slowly to the surface, she'd have to go past them.

She began to swim again.

She used long, strong, steady strokes, forgetting the others briefly in the tick-tock-tick-tock of it, loving the stretch and the pull of it, loving the slip-slap of it on her face as she turned to snatch a breath, then turned to swim again. She saw the sleek dark rocks slip past, marked her progress on the familiar spikes and lumps of them, felt herself getting close to shore.

'Excuse me! Hey, excuse me!'

She kept swimming, tick-tock-tick-tock.

'Hi!' On two friendly notes, '—Excuse me, is that your dog?'

Dog barking and barking and barking.

Its stump of a tail would be whacking back and forth now at the sight of her approaching head. All four legs would be bouncing on the sand at once, as if she'd been gone for a fortnight – stupid thing.

Tick-tock-tick-tock.

Bark, bark, bark, bark.

'—Hello? Excuse me?'

'He won't answer. Why won't he answer you, Kate?'

'Rude thing. Horrible, like his dog.'

'Honestly!'

She must be almost level with them by now.

She could see the seabed, rippled and light, within a toe's reach below her.

Tick-tock-tick-tock-tick-tock.

'Hey! Can you call your dog, please?'

The voice was bawling now.

'—You shouldn't just let it run loose like that, you know. Scaring people. Hello? Hello?'

She paused in the water, blinked it out of her eyes and found her feet on the sand. It crisped nicely between her toes like a welcome home. She looked at them, standing there. The woman stopped shouting. Moderated her tone. Straightened her bony shoulders.

'It's – your dog's being a nuisance! Look! It won't let us out of the water!'

Behind her, the other women closed in, a line of faces with knitted eyebrows, nervous eyes.

Bark, bark, bark, bark.

The leader's swimming-hat was a deep purple, no doubt she'd say it was mulberry, with daft little rubber flowers dotted around the edge. Grace knew that if she ripped it off, the hair underneath would be long and shiny and perfumed and smooth. She didn't, of course. She flicked her own wild seaweed lengths back over her shoulder instead, and let the woman register several things. Then she stood up slowly. Felt gravity pull everything back down, that had floated so nicely before. Watched the woman's face go slack with surprise. Smiled.

'Good god, she's got nothing on.'

'Oh my lord, I wish I had my phone.'

Tittering behind Purple-hat, who didn't seem to know where to look.

Bark, bark, bark, bark.

'Em,' the woman lowered her head and shook it, as if trying to get rid of the image she'd just seen '—your dog—'

'Not my dog,' said Grace briskly, heading for shore with great long strides, hearing snickers and snorts behind her, 'never seen it before in my life.'

Chapter 2

———

'WHAT SORT OF A NAME'S that? English?'

The man leaned on the wall with a big elbow, and his belly swelled out in profile as if he were being slowly inflated. Evan made himself smile and meet the man's eyes.

'It's Welsh, I think, actually.'

'You Welsh then?' The voice was marginally friendlier. 'You boys can play rugby, I'll give you that.'

'No,' Evan answered quickly with a little laugh, 'I'm from Belfast.'

'Oh right, so who d'you play for then? Cooke?'

'Eh, no. I don't actually play rugby, at all, I'm afraid.'

'Oh.' The big man nodded, with some disappointment, and kept his steady gaze on Evan who was standing on the step of the little house with the heavy cardboard box in his arms. It sagged at one end, wetly, and he realised the milk must be leaking inside. He shifted it a little, taking the damp weight onto his forearms to stop the bottom dropping out. The morning sun was strong on his face, glancing sharp off the water, and he felt a prickle of sweat in his armpits, as if he'd been caught doing something he shouldn't.

'—I used to climb a bit, though, when I was single, and do some mountain biking too,' he heard himself say loudly, and there was a little sharpness in the tone, a bit of the old fire. The man stared back as if it were a school-yard contest, his face blank and expectant like a great big dog. A reek of fabric conditioner wafted across the little garden wall between them and Evan had a sudden image of the man's vast white polo shirt hung out on a washing line somewhere, flapping in the bright sea breeze, and the man himself naked from the waist up beside it, waiting for it to dry, that wide inscrutable face staring out any curious passers-by.

'The wife not down here with you then?'

Evan blinked. 'Eh, no. No. Not this time.'

'Aye, well. It takes a wee break sometimes, or you'd have them strangled, I suppose.'

Evan looked at him, and the man looked right back.

'You don't sound like the Belfast ones we get around here, so you don't.'

Evan smiled apologetically. There was a tickle of liquid at his elbow. 'Well,' he said, 'I'd better—'

'—It's a big box, that.'

Evan nodded. 'Yes, it is. And heavy too.'

'You here for a while, then?'

'Just the week. Airbnb, you know?'

The big chin lifted as if to say is that right? and Evan couldn't think of anything else to do but smile and shrug and start to move backwards, already feeling the dark and gloomy interior of the cottage as a sanctuary to be gained.

'Well. It was nice to meet you . . .?'

'—Frank,' the man said, and nodded back over his shoulder where the little lane wound up and around, away from the beach and towards the little village. 'Live back round the corner, there. Coastguard houses.'

Ah, yes, he'd noticed them on the way in, last night, a snug little row of white cottages, creeping their way down the hill, hunkered down against the sea storms that must batter the place in the winter months.

Evan nodded. He was being vetted. Being checked to see if he'd be any trouble. Midnight parties and skinny-dipping, that sort of thing. What the other Belfast ones did, maybe.

'Well, I'm just here for a wee break, just a week, Frank. Nice and quiet. Bit of photography. That sort of thing. You'll have no trouble from me, I promise.'

The silence buzzed in the air between them, at one with the gentle rustle of the waves just a few steps beyond the lane. The tide was right in, it seemed, filling up the whole of the bay, sneaking towards them as if eavesdropping.

The milk was still dripping.

'Well, it's nice meeting you.' Evan gave a last friendly nod of farewell and pushed the door with his elbow so that it swung wide behind him, the little house cool and dark and private.

'Christ!' he said quietly, to the solid, dark wood.

It was a relief to turn and set the soggy box on the little table and shake the milk from his fingers. The carton had fallen over inside, and the lid was loose. Going to the thick white sink under the window he found a dishcloth and wiped the stuff from his arm. It had run all down the side of his t-shirt too, leaving a splodge the shape of Ireland, but he didn't change it. It didn't matter.

Through the window a tall dark hedge loomed, full of bald places and gaps where the leaves had failed in the salt wind and a ragged plastic bag clung limp to its topmost branch.

Seven days, here. He looked around slowly. Seven days.

His stomach growled and he lifted a loaf from the top of the box and ripped open the flimsy plastic wrapper. Pulling out the end piece, the heel, he bit into it. Anything would do. He chewed in the dark and quiet room, and the bread was dry and soft and thick and good.

'How long d'you need?' he'd asked her quietly, yesterday. She'd been perched at the very edge of the big soft chair in the sunroom, where Jessie had died, and her hair was knotted up in a rough pile on the top of her head, dry and straggly, a funny colour at the roots, and she was engrossed in whatever she was doing on the laptop on her knee.

She hadn't looked up at his question, and her fingertips flew across the keyboard in hot communication with someone other than him. He looked over her bent head out through the big bay window into the bright green of the garden full of spring birdsong, where the sycamore's thick trunk curled and curved into branches heavy with new leaves.

'Lorna?'

'Oh my God, Evan. *I* don't know.' She'd twisted her face up and away from the screen in his general direction, but hadn't looked at him. Not really. She never did. Her shoulders were hunched up against him, and there were dark lines down the sides of her mouth where she held herself tightly in.

'A week? Would a week help?' he'd ventured. 'I mean, tell me what you need, that's all.'

She'd looked back down where her hands rested on the keyboard and made that long sighing sound that meant he was being obtuse again – stupid, thick, impossible.

Her shoulders were thin where he stood behind her. He could see the sharp lines of them through the blouse she wore, and he thought she must be cold, but he knew better than to mention it. One long elegant finger tapped a key as if eager to be off again, making words for someone else to see.

'Whatever,' she'd said, finally, as if realising he was still standing there. 'Yeah. A week. *Fine.* Christ.'

Her shoulders had that tension, that last-minute holding before she snapped.

'All right,' he'd said quickly then. 'All right. I'll go. It's fine. I'll get somewhere to stay, today, this afternoon, leave you in peace—'

'Evan. Could you just – fucking – stop – talking?'

He could hear her teeth through all the words, clenching. As he watched, she shook her head slightly, as if to rid it of a buzzing thing, an irritant, and her fingers started dancing again, speaking to someone else – anyone else other than him.

She'd sat there, typing, as he left the room, went to the car for his iPad, started searching for somewhere not too far away, but not too close, either, for one person, for a week. She hadn't looked up to say goodbye, even when he hovered at the door with his bag on his shoulder – or watched him drive away down the street and out of the city and away from her, from Luca, from home, from everything.

The bread stuck in his throat and made him gulp, hard, to shift it.

He looked down and saw he'd eaten several slices without noticing, but he felt a bit better. There was butter in the box somewhere, too, he remembered, and jam, so he pushed aside pasta, bacon, tinned soup, and that little bottle the weird shop assistant had made him buy.

Hand cleaner or something.

'You'll be glad of it, so you will,' she'd told him firmly, nodding hard as he tucked the little bottle into a corner of the cardboard box on the counter. 'It's on the news, you know – it's a pandemic coming, so it is. Won't be able to get the stuff in a day or two. Honest to god. And are you sure you've enough pasta, there? That one bag won't do very long, will it?'

'Eh, yes,' he'd said. 'Thanks, it's plenty – I'm only here for a few days. There's only me.'

There'd been a distinct thumbprint on the lens of her glasses as she'd looked up at him, passing him the change, sizing him up. He would have dearly liked to take the glasses from her and give them a good wipe, the way he did to his own, but of course he didn't.

Seven days, here. Seven days.

He wanted a drink. He took a deep breath and held it.

He'd have water.

There was an ill-assorted array of glasses in the cupboard over the sink, and to his surprise they sparkled brightly, spotlessly clean. He took one down and creaked the tap into action, letting it run a little before risking a fill. He was suddenly terribly, horribly thirsty, the cold water sliding down his throat and into his stomach. It was cold, and exactly what he needed. As he refilled the glass and drank again, the branches of the straggling hedge outside the window were lit up by the sun breasting the ridge of the little house, and became a little brighter, a little less dusty.

Inside the place was even darker, now that the sun was shining outside. The walls were papered with woodchip, grey with age, and the surface undulated in and out, the ancient stones behind the paper shifting with the passing of the years. A stern, dark dresser stood against one wall, stacked with ill-assorted things, and bookshelves were shoved here and there into alcoves and corners, bursting with paperbacks and tattered magazines.

A large and sagging sofa of indeterminate colour squatted in the middle of the room, and this was where he had spent the night, restless, tangled in woollen blankets and throw-rugs and cushions, rather than face the bedroom where things scuttled and squeaked after dark.

There was the skull of a little bird on the shelf over the fat and ancient TV set, sharing space with a few dog-eared novels and a battered box of Connect-4 and a couple of tattered packs of cards, all forgotten as families packed themselves up and left for their real lives, squabbling and hustling and shutting the door behind them, leaving the dark and the quiet for him, all alone, all alone.

'Right!' he said brightly to the empty space and to himself, clacking the tumbler down onto the counter. 'Let's get this place a bit more comfy, shall we?'

He put what was left of the milk, the butter and the eggs into the rumbling old fridge that squatted under the counter, finding it pristine on the inside despite its yellowed door. The cupboards too, although battered and faded on the outside, were solid wood – good-quality old stuff that you couldn't get any more – and thoroughly clean. He arranged his bare rations neatly on one shelf and folded the soggy cardboard box ready to wedge it into the bin.

Bin.

He looked around, opened a few cupboards, but realised it must be outside.

The back door was a half-door, like a stable, and it took a bit of shoving and cranking and scraping of bolts to get both halves opened together, but at last he stood blinking in the light. A few steps away, a row of great big man-sized bins stood in varied colours.

He had a sudden vision of himself, tiny as a stickman in a child's drawing, fastened to the earth by the soles of his shoes, and the whole thing – air, sky, space, universe, galaxy, everything – spinning out and spinning out and spinning outwards and himself only a speck there, indistinct and irrelevant, being spun.

He was crying again. He thought he was over that nonsense. He put his hand up to cover his mouth and felt his face all wet, but there was nothing he could do about it. He let his shoulders shake and the tears run, and just waited.

Must get the camera out, set it up, he thought, after a while. That'll help.

He rolled his shoulders, several times, and felt them loosen up, drop down.

He began to move his hips in big wide circles, like at that yoga class the one time he went, where he'd hidden, mortified, behind Lorna at the back of the grubby hall, and watched her stick her lovely arse up in the air, and bend her tight body around and around, her face blank and still as a geisha's, looking through him even then.

'*Aaaaahh!*'

It was a long, loud sound, and he drew it out as slow as he could, still rotating those hips, still watching the pink skin of

15

his inner eyelids lit up by the sun. Then something rustled, and his eyes snapped open.

There was a face in a spindly gap in the hedge, shadowed by an immense hat like one of those the Australian cowboys wear, without the corks. Two grey eyes were staring at him, from a face that was either shockingly dirty or extremely tanned. It was impossible to tell.

Evan froze, feeling his mouth open and close, searching for words, but nothing came. His face flooded hot. Neither spoke. The face looked at him without expression. It was like being watched by a cat, inscrutable and detached; and then it was gone. It moved backwards, suddenly, and disappeared.

He held his breath, his skin prickling, his ears hissing.

There was the sound of feet scrunching over an uneven surface behind the hedge, and dappled light as the stranger trudged steadily away, the sound gradually fading, fading, and then gone.

'Shit!' he said, sagging, to the garden, to the hedge and the bins and the sky, and it came out angry. 'What the hell's *wrong* with these people?'

After a minute he stooped like an old man to pick up the cardboard and stuffed it deep into the bin with more force than was actually needed.

It was going to be a long week.

Chapter 3

––––

GRACE CLIMBED THE STEEP BANK behind the cottages and the dog lolloped beside her, its tongue hanging out. For the last few steps she had to push hard on her thighs to keep moving, and she sucked each breath in deeply, right down to her belly, and her legs wobbled a bit. Came with getting older, she supposed, but it was a bollocks, altogether. Once upon a time, she could have sprinted up here, no trouble, turned right, and run all the way to the village on the narrow path without stopping – 10p in her hand for a mix-up and five Refresher chews.

At the top of the bank she paused to catch her breath and the dog ran yipping in crazy widening circles, as fresh as a daisy and as ugly as sin, hot on the scent of something wild and unlawful on its territory. She let it go. She looked out at the sea instead, her hands on her hips.

It was different every single day. Every single hour. She never tired of looking at it. They said it was the cure for sorrow, to look into water, and for all the troubles of the heart. Today it was beguiling, at its most duplicitous. Feathery little waves danced up the beach, coaxing the foolish for a swim or a paddle, biting their skin with tiny knives when they dared. She huffed a laugh, thinking of the women and their stupid hats and their scandalised expressions. Only the hardy could swim this water, year round. Only the insane and the hardy. Only the damn bloody-minded and the insane and the hardy.

Only her.

The dog came to her heel, panting, with mud on its twisted snout.

'What's wrong with you? Not fit, or something, you ugly fucker?' she asked it kindly. 'Look at me, I could run all day.'

The dog shook itself hard, unimpressed, and a long string of drool whipped around its ears.

Grace stood a while longer, looking down from on high.

She could see her own house far off to the right, tucked away back around the corner, the last outpost before the cliffs and the wilderness of the coastal path. There was the rental cottage down below too, of course, and the lane winding around from it towards the main beach, and the coastguard houses running alongside, now almost empty except in summer, and then the hill got in the way and the few scrubby trees and grassy banks were all she could see to the left. The whole panorama of home, as familiar to her as breath.

Below her, the squat, dark shape of the rented cottage – her parents' old place – sat at the edge of the narrow bay, its little garden a green margin around it, its low front wall touching the lane. When she was growing up, there had been a wide expanse of sour grass and scrub where the little pebbly beach was, now, and they'd kept a goat, an emaciated thing, on it for years. Gone, now, that particular goat – and grass, of course, eaten up by the sea and by time. She shook her head and her hat loosened.

The man had gone inside. Back inside and closed the door. No more weird gyrations on the back doorstep. No more crying in the garden.

She hadn't liked the look of him. Not at all. Not one bit, she hadn't.

The dog sensed her sudden tension and whined, so she

shook herself a little and turned towards the village. She'd check in the shop that there had been no trouble settling him in. They were a stupid lot, she'd found, these townie tenants, and even though the instructions were spelled out on the website – 'collect the key from the village shop, park your vehicle at the top of the hill where the road ends and the lane begins' – they invariably got in a tizzy searching for little code-boxes that didn't exist, or trying to drive their immense 4x4s down the tiny lane anyway, with forty surfboards tied on top or a million bikes or something else flashy and ridiculous.

She tended to let Big Frank wander down, suss them out, spend an hour or two of his long, lost days now he was retired from the building site. He'd see them passing by, looking everywhere, rubbernecking as they went, and he'd set out after them, rubbing his hands and telling Maggie Hitler that no, he'd behave this time, he'd be nice.

Like hell.

The dog had its head stuck in a rabbit hole now and was snuffing loudly and wiggling its sad stump of a tail, thrusting with squat hind legs in an effort to push itself further in.

'Come on, before you get your fat head stuck! Come on, Dog!' she told it, and waited until it withdrew, shaking its head free of dry earth and dust and looking at her with its tongue out, panting. She pictured the sweet little rabbit family deep down inside, blessing her, and cuddling close, and she smirked.

'Gettem next time, lad,' she said. 'I'll bring the stick, I promise, and we'll have stew.'

The village was as still and quiet as ever as she strode down the last mucky bit of the path and onto the cracked tarmac of the street. Everyone lived somewhere else now, in smart new farmhouses and ugly white bungalows, and the shop and the pub and the old empty church were like tethers, keeping them all from flying away altogether, and bringing them back now and then, to make contact with one another, to bring temporary life to the stone and the brick of the place. There were a couple of cars parked in front of the pub, but no one stood outside having a smoke, and the door was closed against the warm spring day.

She took a frayed rope from her pocket and strung it around the dog's neck as a token of compliance, before hooking the loose end around an old broken fence post beside the shop. The dog sat down and looked at her as if butter wouldn't melt in its mouth.

'Fucker'll be gone before you step one foot in through that door,' laughed a voice behind her.

It was old Thompson. Harmless enough, but with an unhealthy addiction to the performance statistics of horses and dogs. Cost him his farm and everything in it, over time, the stupid bastard.

'Bit of luck, it'll get fucking run over,' she answered pleasantly. 'I can get a good-looking one instead, then – a bit more like meself.'

She liked Thompson. He'd carried her off the rocks that time – when she was younger, of course and a good bit lighter – and had called to the hospital in the town to visit her, too. Had stood, smelling of cows and shite, at the foot of her bed, and she hadn't known what to say, so hadn't said anything at all, and after a while he'd gone away again and she'd stared dry-eyed at the ceiling and felt her legs itch in their stiff new plaster and heard her ears buzz with the stretched-out silence of loneliness and living.

Becky was stacking old newspapers when she jangled in through the shop door.

'Got a right weird one this time, have I?' Grace asked without preamble.

The girl looked surprised. 'What makes you say that? I thought he was sweet.'

She bound the papers with twine and humped them down onto the floor behind the counter with a grunt.

'Aye, well, you like dozy fuckers like Paddy Murphy so . . .' Grace didn't wait for an answer but looked along the shelves for something nice for after dinner.

Becky said nothing, but she was smiling. Grace could feel her doing it without even looking.

'Paddy's hardly dozy with a Master's degree, Grace.'

'Fucking Master's degree doesn't say he's got any brains – will you catch yourself on? Any dozy bastard can buy themselves one of those.' She brought a packet of apple pies to the counter and set them down, fishing in the deep pockets of her coat for coins. 'What was it in, again? Horse racing? Liqueurs?'

'Shame on you, Grace Kielty. You know rightly it's a proper Master's in Philosophy he's got. He says he's not going to be a barman all his life, that's all, and fair play to him. Stop winding me up.'

She held out her hand for the money.

'And we'll be going contactless over the next few weeks, too, Grace. Because of this pandemic, so it is. Just so you know. So you can get organised. Do you want some hand sanitiser? I've only a couple left.'

Grace snorted, counting coins in her hand. 'Contactless? What's new, around here?' she retorted. 'Although the word is, Miss Breen, you're well into the contact yourself, recently. You were seen at the beach corner, so you were. Just so you know.'

She nodded slowly and fixed the girl with her best stare, holding out a cupped hand full of small coins at the same time.

Becky propped her hands on her hips and regarded her, laughing, 'Well, I didn't have you pegged as a gossip, Grace, and that's for sure. What are you like?'

Grace didn't answer, but smiled back, looking knowledgeable.

Becky took the money with prissy-tight lips and tipped it into the till without checking it. '—D'you want a bag?'

Grace shook her head, and the box of pies disappeared into the loose folds of her coat. 'They won't be as good as Our Abbie's, but beggars can't be choosers,' she said.

'Och yes, Abbie. How's she doing up at uni? Any word from her?' Becky asked brightly. She and Abbie didn't get on, so they talked to and about each other like women out of washing powder adverts.

Grace shook her head and turned to go. No word. She didn't care. Girl could do what she wanted.

'Anyway, why d'you say he's weird?' Becky called after her. 'Your new one? What did he do to you? He's not even here a day yet.'

'Just looks weird, that's all,' Grace said over her shoulder. 'I don't like that tall, specky, gloomy type myself.'

'Just what kind do you like, I wonder?'

Grace swung around, to see the girl with her head cocked to one side, daring her to be angry.

'—You know, there's all types nowadays, Grace, that's all I'm saying. Someone for everyone, isn't that it? It's not too late, you know, to get it together with a nice wee farmer. You could shock us all and act normal.'

With a crack of a laugh Grace retorted, 'Hah! Normal!' and swung herself out of the shop and into the sunlit street where the old rope dangled empty from the post like a magic trick.

Chapter 4

———

THE HERON'S HEAD POKED FORWARDS, millimetre by millimetre.

It had its eye on something – the money-shot was coming any second – it'd strike, something would dangle and wriggle from that fearsome beak and the bird would shake its shaggy head to get it down and droplets would sparkle and it would be lovely, lovely – just hold it, any second now, *any second now*, he told himself grimly, his eye aching from squinting through the viewfinder.

But the sun had moved to a bad angle while he waited, and now it glared on the water in the foreground. It'd draw the eye away from the striking bird at the vital second – spoil the shot, he realised.

There was nothing fast about photography. All this staying still. Took stickability, concentration, patience – things he was only learning. The rocks underneath him poked steadily, painfully, into his belly, and his bladder was full and aching. Should he move? His mouth watered with the desire for a perfect shot, so he stayed exactly where he was, closing the shutter again and again to see the results, to predict the picture.

With infinite care, the bird raised one narrow foot and took a slow step forwards, dipped the foot down again into the water without a ripple, on the hunt for something only its sharp eye could see.

'Clever boy,' Evan breathed, holding himself taut.

He needed to change position to get rid of that glare, but that would certainly spook the bird, deny him what he'd been waiting so long for. His elbow and right knee were wet where the tide was creeping in over the rockpools, filling them up, and limpets stuck into him at all angles where he lay like a sniper among them.

'Come on, bird!' he muttered, suddenly impatient and strung-out and anxious all at once; the weight of the day's emptiness pressing down on him, his body deeply chilled.

Whiskey would slip down nicely now, it occurred to him.

A hot toddy.

He blinked the thought away sharply and concentrated on the heron, which was looking once again at the smooth surface of the water, waiting. Its leg was raised, fraction by fraction, and held there. One-legged yogi, it stood motion-less, its head and neck extended, pointing, its whole being projected down the long sharp length of its bill and focussed on what moved in the murky shallows beneath. He clicked and clicked again.

Then a dog yelped loudly and pelted slavering past him where he lay prone on the rocks and rushed on towards the water where it lolloped, barking and hairy and noisy and big. With a rough shriek the heron pushed out its great wings and lifted itself into the air, canting even as it rose, turning away from the dog and the sun and the camera, and flying out towards the little island ahead.

'Fuck!'

He shoved himself up to sit, his belly soaked and cold, feeling as if he'd been woken from a deep sleep, and grouchy with it.

He looked around. A group of people were spilling them-selves loudly down the little rockslide onto the sand, shouting their pleasure in finding this secret hideaway, this secluded place away from the hordes on the main beach.

'Here, grab them big stones, kids,' Dad was shouting, 'We'll make a wee fireplace, put the barbie on top, like a proper campfire, eh?'

The kids flew about the beach, climbing, digging, splashing, ignoring him, calling for the dog who ignored them in its turn, and the whole place was suddenly alive with noise and movement and ruckus, where before nothing had moved but the lacy waves at the very tide's edge.

One of the younger children noticed him there, lying low in the rocks in his camo-gear. She stopped running after her big sisters, toddled across the sand and regarded him with round blue eyes and the calm of the very young. When he raised his head from the camera she was just there, watching, and he found that he couldn't move under her still gaze. She was about two, maybe three. There were dimples in her fist that hypnotised him and suddenly he knew how she would smell, if he were to stretch out and lift her, feel her fuzzy cheek against his own. They looked at each other in silence for a moment or two. He was held by her presence – couldn't breathe, couldn't shift even a tiny fraction in case he spooked her and broke the spell. A hot wash of sorrow ran over him, and his eyes stung and shamed him.

Dad's eye was drawn to him by the stillness, by the child's quiet. He nudged Mum, who had carried chairs and windbreakers and cool boxes down the sliding slope like a pack animal, and was now wrestling with a fold-up seat, her mottled arms flapping in a vest-top. There was something feral in the way her head snapped up at the sight of him, sitting disguised on the rocks, and she called, '*Chelsea!*' in a guttural voice which cut through all the other sounds, and made every child on the beach stop and look around.

'Come here *nigh!*'

But the child remained, staring, and he had no choice but

to wriggle to the edge of the rock, stand up and wipe himself off as best he could, under the cold eyes of the other adults, the steady gaze of the little girl. Raising the camera, he waved it sheepishly at Dad, who took a few steps towards him.

'All right, there?' he asked loudly, from a distance, his hands on his hips.

'Eh, yes,' Evan answered.

There was a pause while everyone looked at one another.

'Photographer,' he said loudly, although he didn't have to. He turned to wave the camera where the bird had flown as if for corroboration, but of course there was nothing to see. The strap flapped wet against his hand. He'd have to be more careful of it.

'I was—'

But Dad was no longer interested.

'Go and play with yer sister,' he said to the little girl, who at last removed the thumb from her mouth and smiled a slow, wet smile at Evan.

'Go on, Chelsea!' Dad said, louder. 'Leave the man alone.'

As if he was doing something unsavoury, in the cold, in the wet of these rocks.

'*Angeline*, call Chelsea!' yelled Mum, flapping towels and looking towards the other children.

Like a flock of birds, the little girls gathered at the water's edge began to twitter, 'Chelsea, Chelsea, Chelsea, come on, come on, come on,' until she forgot the man in the rocks and turned and ran, fat-legged and frilly towards them, stumbling now and then on a worm cast or a pebble.

He made himself look away from her, to Dad who was still watching him, narrow-eyed.

A flare of anger made him say, 'You staying for the afternoon?'

'What?'

He gestured to the space, the beach, the water, the shrieking little girls now ankle-deep in the bright water.

'You here for the day?'

Dad kept his hands on his hips, square. Nodded at the woman and the bivouac taking rapid shape behind them.

'Yeah,' he said without apology. 'You?'

Evan angered himself by smiling and replying sheepishly, 'Nah, I'm soaked. Better go and get dried off.'

The man didn't smile, even then, and was clearly waiting to see him off the sand, to have this little lovely beach all to himself and his womenfolk and his horrible dog. Evan turned silently back to the rocks to lift his rucksack, the camera case – and for the first time saw something tucked in at the edge of the water, a fair bit off. Something that must have been there all along.

It was the man in the hat.

He was sitting in a hollow right where the sea licked the rocks, only the hat and the head visible, as still as the heron, and as silent. He was staring out to sea, but Evan could tell his attention was on the beach too, with all its noise and flurry. It was as if he were holding himself stone-still on purpose, like the heron, so as not to be seen, not to be discovered there, among the shining browns and blacks and greens of the little peninsula, where he'd nestled back into its arms out of sight.

Evan thought back to the morning, when he'd first arrived on the beach with his camera bag, drawn out of the dark little house and his own bad dreams by the dance of the sun on the water. He must have been there already, Hat-Man, sitting in the gap of the rocks over there, so still and quiet he hadn't been seen. Evan glanced down at his watch. Three hours ago. More. Wow.

Meanwhile, the Rowdy family had forgotten him and were coaxing flames from a small tin barbeque, so he took his own good time crossing the soft grain of the beach to the lane, and didn't look back to the rocks again.

*

27

Evan sat by the window in the battered old armchair, his phone bright in his hand, and empty.

'You go. Take the time you need, mate,' John had said that day three weeks ago, when he'd found Evan crying in the gents, unable to stop. They'd both been frightened, looking at each other in the mirror, at a complete loss. John had put an awkward hand on his shoulder and then let it drop again, stepping back when it made no difference. Evan had kept on crying, because he could do nothing else.

John had waited, fair play to him, looking at the floor, mostly. He hadn't backed up, gone out, shut the door, pretended he hadn't seen it. He'd waited.

'You should've taken time off after the funeral, mate. Don't know why you came straight back – like this,' he'd said. 'Jesus. Go on. No – go on, honest. Get your things. I'll let them know, see you're not disturbed,' and he'd clearly meant it.

That had been three weeks ago, and look.

Nothing.

He searched his apps with growing surprise. Not a dicky-bird, from any of them, on Teams, or Twitter or anything. Nothing.

He should be grateful. The workload had been immense, unmanageable. He hated his job.

He opened his personal mail, hit send and receive, and watched the little circle turn around slowly, as if thinking about it.

Nothing from Lorna, either.

He typed *LOR* and the machine auto-filled her address.

Hi, he wrote, poking awkwardly with tight elbows in the big soft chair.

Just letting you know I arrived safely. A weird little place called Ballybrady, right on the sea. I mean RIGHT on the sea. It's practically in through the door sometimes. I miss you. The house is OK, but it's small and dark and strange and I suppose Im not used to being on my own. I suppose you won't answer this. I think Im not supposed to get in touch. I don't know the rules for this. I miss you. And Luca of course. Hope he's behaving. I've booked the place for a week like I said, although Im only a couple of days in and it feels like Ive been away for weeks. Im counting the days, Lorna. Let me know . . .

He paused and fell into thought for a long time.

. . . what Im to do after. What you decide.

Im sorry about everything, Lorna.
Evan xoxox

Send.

The little circle took its own good time to rotate and then the message was gone.

He sat there in the fading light to see if she would reply.

At five o'clock he closed the device and got wearily to his feet, stretching slowly, before returning it to the bedroom, and closing the door on it.

Later, as he boiled eggs for a late supper on the ancient stove he heard the clamour and squabble of the Rowdy family going home, the clatter of plastic buckets and the whine of sugar-sticky, exhausted children, and the greater, heavier silence left by their passing, as he buttered toast loudly in the darkening kitchen and the last of the light went out of the sky.

Chapter 5

———

BY MONDAY HE WAS GOING CRACKERS.

'I'm going crackers,' he told the little bird skull on the shelf, and when its dusty eye sockets seemed to crinkle in agreement, he knew he definitely needed to go out for a while.

Outside, he shoved his hands deep into his pockets and looked around.

To his left, the lane ran back along the edge of his own little secluded bay and up a steep hill to the corner.

He took a breath full of salt. Right, then. He'd go up to the shop in the village and see if they still sold those things called newspapers, the flappy, paper kind where the print came off on your fingers.

His feet slipped and scrunched on the loose stone of the lane as he walked, and after a short march up the hill he felt himself out of breath. When he was younger, he'd have run every morning. His weekends had been spent on a bike in the mountains behind the city, or dangling from ropes on tricky rockfaces with John and the gang. Lorna was one of them at one time, of course – it was where they'd met.

Then when the kids came, when Luca came, to be precise, that all stopped. He'd still gone out on the bike once or twice after the baby was born, pleading a tough week and the need to blow it all away on a mountain trail, but he'd come back to Lorna's cold face and a day or more of the silent treatment, so had gradually let the gang slip away.

'Remember,' she'd said, holding the baby out to him like a sacrificial offering on his return, 'I used to do those things too. I used to love the mountains too.'

'I'll mind him, next week, then, and you go. We can take turns,' he'd offered naively, but she'd twisted her mouth up and held the baby out to him again.

'It doesn't work like that. It's time to grow up, Peter Pan.'

At the corner where the main beach ran away from the lane out to sea he stopped and looked around him to catch his breath. The sand was clearly visible today, the tide out and the place empty. He looked around again in some surprise. For such a lovely day, he wondered, where were all the people? The bright dots of children crouched intent on sandcastles were few and far between. Several dogs ran in the surf but their owners weren't staying, were striding along beside them, getting it done.

'Monday,' he said aloud. 'That must be it.'

Everyone else had work to go to. Except him.

The thought lightened him a little and he smiled to himself as he started on up the hill once more.

There was no one in the shop when he got there. An incongruous piano sonata tinkled away – but the space behind the counter was empty and there was no one among the shelves. No one stuck their head out from the little back room at the jangle of the bell. Shrugging, he gathered a few things that he needed. Eggs. Biscuits. Lamb chops that he hadn't known he wanted until he saw them lying red and bloody in a polystyrene tray in the fridge. A bar of chocolate, dark. The local paper, the only one on sale. Apples. He set the basket on the counter and looked around again, craning over the counter to see into the little room at the back.

'Hello?'

After a moment, he left the basket where it was and went back outside. Place was deserted. He went around the side of the shop building to where a long, high wall ran the length of what must be a back yard behind. The shop assistant was perched on top, her knees on a level with his eyes, sipping something from a thick white mug with a chicken on it.

'Lunch break,' she told him in a friendly way when she saw him. She waved the mug gently. 'I'll be back in ten minutes.'

'That's fine,' he told her. 'I'm in no hurry.'

He meant it. He wasn't.

She smiled, sipped from her mug and looked away again, over his head. He imagined she had a distant view of the sea from up there. He turned to go back around to the front of the shop. He'd seen a bench at the bus stop alongside. He'd wait there.

'D'you want a cuppa? It's green tea, just, but you're welcome.'

She was looking down at him like a friendly cat, bumping her heels gently against the old wall.

'Sure,' he said, suddenly thirsty. 'That'd be great.'

'Well, go on in, then. I can't get it for you, because of the virus, but there are mugs clean in the drainer and the teapot's on the stove.'

'How—?' he asked, and then saw a small door in the wall, ajar. He looked a question up at her and she nodded, smiled again, so he pushed it. Like everything else around here it was warped with the salt air and stuck a bit, but then it scraped open easily enough and he went through, looking around curiously.

He was on an old concrete path leading to an open door. To both sides of the path, the grass grew tall and snarled as high as his waist in tall humps and hillocks like wild beasts. Overgrown bushes and discarded metal junk were the skeletons; long, dry woven strands of grass the skin. He thought he could make out the shape of an old car in the thicket to his left, a tumbledown shed behind it.

'I know!' she called down, from the wall behind him. 'I've to take a machete to it every now and then just to get through. Watch you don't trip over *that*, by the way – it's in beside the door in the kitchen.'

He laughed and shook his head. His own garden was beautifully orderly, in neat stripes like pyjamas, but he suddenly liked this better, he realised – the craziness of it, the wildness, the fact that it didn't give a shit what the other yards nearby looked like, whether or not it matched.

'Could be a lion in here somewhere,' he called to the girl on the wall.

'Well, you know where the machete is, if you need it.'

The sound of her laughter followed him inside.

The little kitchen was austere and orderly, with white walls and a little caged window in one side, to let the light in.

'Tea,' he said, aloud.

He found it in a fat brown teapot on the stove, still hot to the touch, a mug sitting neatly on the counter beside it as if the girl had been expecting him all along. He'd never had green tea before, so he sniffed it cautiously as he took it back outside. It wasn't green, for a start. A pale golden colour. And it didn't smell like tea, either. Grass. It smelled like grass, he decided with a shrug. Couldn't be that bad.

The jungle in the back yard had been hacked back in one place to allow the girl to get from the path to the wall, and a precarious set of steps fashioned from old crates and large rocks. When she saw him coming, she budged along a bit, to let him up. He set his mug carefully on the flattest part of the wall that he could see, and climbed cautiously up the wobbly steps to throw one leg over, then the other. He hauled himself up, feeling clumsy, and felt her watching him with amusement. Everything he did seemed to make her smile. He grinned back. It was OK.

'Phew!' he said, wiggling himself comfortable and retrieving his mug. 'Haven't done that in a while.'

She waggled her eyebrows at him and pushed her glasses

back up to the bridge of her nose. He noticed they were clear of the large smudge which had bothered him the last time they'd met. Her skin was waxy and full of little blackheads around her nose, though, and he felt bad for remarking on it, even to himself. He sipped his tea. It tasted mostly of water, if he was honest, and definitely grass. A green taste. Not delicious but not too unpleasant either. He sipped again.

From their vantage point, a thin strip of blue sea twinkled over the tops of straggling thorn bushes. The ribbon of the main road ran out from the green spread a little further to the left, and disappeared again around a corner, heading elsewhere, out of Ballybrady.

'You can see the enemy approaching,' he said, nodding at the twist of the road.

'The only enemy is within,' she replied, and shook out the dregs of her tea into the wilderness behind her.

He looked at her and she nodded without looking back at him.

'It's what I believe. There is no earthly danger except that which manifests from within.'

'Oh. I see,' he said. 'Is that, like, Buddhism or something?'

'Yes.'

She didn't elaborate. He got the sense that she was waiting for him to poke fun, so he said nothing and drank his tea, enjoying the cool breeze ruffling the hair on the back of his neck. She kicked her heels a moment more, then stilled.

'I think it means,' she said, 'that, if you accept everything you perceive in the world around you to be a projection of your own mind, it's up to you to avoid making up enemies and difficulties and reasons for suffering. Stop making things bad when they're really not.'

'You think we make the whole world up? Is that what you're saying?'

She nodded, and looked straight at him, her eyes huge behind her glasses. 'Yeah. I do.'

34

He sat quietly for a moment. She thought he invented his own suffering. He saw Lorna's face, cold and set. He saw the baby's still features on that horrible night, oddly devoid of personality, dead. He saw Luca's eyes twisted up with rage and upset and dislike of him. He saw himself, useless and awkward and drained and unhappy.

'No. I don't buy that,' he said, a little loudly. 'Why would we decide to be unhappy?'

She huffed a little laugh, as if he'd asked the right thing. 'We don't. We just don't decide to be happy,' she said.

'How can you be happy if everything around you is shit?'

'But don't you see? It's not shit. We just *perceive* it to be shit.'

He shook his head. 'Right. So ... we could just as easily decide that, I don't know, our house falling down or something – that was OK? We could decide to be happy about that?'

'That's right,' she said in a warm voice. 'You've got it. Maybe it would be good to be rid of that house, you know? Maybe we'd be free then, to travel the world or relocate, or something. At the very least, we could decide, "So be it" – one less attachment to worry about, hurray! – and let it go.'

He laughed. He just came up here for a paper and some apples.

'Well, don't you see? That's why people are unhappy. That's why they suffer. They cling to things like – I dunno – houses and relationships and jobs and stuff, as if it'll all keep them safe. But these things don't actually stop the shit happening, do they?'

He shook his head again.

'So. Why hold on so tight to stuff like that? Why worry about shit that doesn't really matter? That's what I wanna know.'

She smiled at him, and her cheeks were pink. 'What's your name?' he asked.

'Becky. You?'

35

'Evan. I'm Evan.'

He put out his hand, awkwardly sideways on the narrow wall-top, but she shook her head.

'Can't. No hand shaking or anything like that for a while. But, pleased to meet you, Evan, anyway.' She nodded behind him, to the rickety steps. 'I'll let you get down first. Age before beauty, you know, and it looks like you might take a while.'

'Ha-ha,' he replied, shifting along and setting his mug down again to free up his hands.

'—You just think all that stuff up in your head, do you, about happiness and all?'

She nodded in a matter-of-fact way, collecting his mug as she shifted her broad bottom along the wall to the point of exit. He could see that she was gathering a lot of dust and lichen as she went but it didn't seem to bother her.

'Boyfriend did his thesis on it for his Master's degree. We ding-dong about it pretty much every night,' she said. 'Better than sex.'

He had been preparing to climb down, but missed his footing and slid in a heap onto the path and swore quietly.

She leapt nimbly down beside him, smiling as he wiped himself down and straightened his glasses.

'You are one surprising woman, Becky,' he told her, sternly.

'There's plenty of us about here,' she replied tartly, clacking the mugs together in her hand as she headed for the little kitchen. 'Better watch yourself, Mr Townie Evan. Let's get you sorted with your groceries and then you'd better get on home and batten down the hatches. There's something coming that we none of us will know how to deal with, I reckon.'

Chapter 6

———

'HOLY SHIT,' EVAN SAID, staring at his laptop. 'You were right, too, Becks.'

That SARS thing which had rumbled in the background of his own crisis had picked up pace while he was looking elsewhere, gathered momentum, begun to mean something to people – illness, ICU, death – and had finally tipped over into his own life with a messy thump.

They were calling it lockdown. What was locked? How had this happened?

Everything. Absolutely everything was locked down. No movement from here to there, or there to here, it seemed. No inter-household visits. No going outside. Until when? He read back and forth but couldn't see an end-date.

He brushed through the newspapers and clutter on the table to find his phone on its last bar of power, and scrolled shakily for Lorna's number. There she was, that lovely face, those slightly goofy teeth, the smile he loved first about her. He'd taken that photo, at the park. You could even see the trees behind her in the clipped-down icon frame, and she was really smiling, then.

He held the phone to his ear, aching to hear her voice. Why hadn't she called him, given him a heads-up, before it all happened, he wondered. Replied to his email, for god's sake? How was this the first time he'd heard about it properly?

The phone rang and rang and rang and he took it away from his ear to look at it in case it was broken. The smiling icon kept her white grin on, her crinkled eyes belying the ring-ring-ring of the unanswered call. He hung up and placed the phone on the table very gently, inserting the charger with the tips of his fingers as if it were a delicate thing.

He rubbed his hand over his face again and looked around at the little room, the doors opening off it to bathroom and bedroom and beach. Where he sat was dark and cluttered, the room untidy, too small for everything in it; a dusty, empty grate like a bad tooth in the wall, everything in thick cream paint or dark wood, the floor and furniture strewn with his things, cast willy-nilly with no one to chide him, because, after all, it had only been meant for seven days. Standing up he flicked the kettle on for something to do, and went across to the window, feeling confined already, gazing out onto the sand, the beach, the long string of sea at low tide.

He sat down again, and heard a loud ping in the quiet of the room as a message arrived. He pulled the laptop across the table, knocking magazines and empty plastic food packets to the floor as he did so. His eyes were terrible. He needed the laptop to see messages properly. This was not a time to make mistakes.

It was his first work email in three weeks, bearing it all out – John asking for his thoughts on a temporary closure of their business under the new government guidelines. Something called furlough. Sounded like an army term. He looked at it for a long moment, typed Lorna's email address instead, and then:

Please call me. Let me know you're all right. I need to hear your voice.

After a while he pushed himself up from the table with both hands and went slowly to the sofa, shoving sweaters and books to the floor to make space. He was suddenly freezing. He lay down and pulled himself into a tight curl and dragged a thick bright blanket tight around his shoulders. He closed his eyes and fell asleep.

When he woke there was the sense of evening in the room, and it was warm and soft inside his skin, so he stayed in a fizzing half-consciousness for a long time, thinking things over. Eventually he sighed and got up slowly, checked his phone for messages, and looked at the little button to make sure it wasn't set to silent.

OK. He stood up.

He'd make a plan.

First, provisions. There was hardly anything in the cupboards, although he ate like a bird anyway. He'd need to see if the little shop was still open, or pick up the car from the top of the hill and go to the town a few miles away, really stock up. Then, he'd contact the cottage owner, see if he could extend his stay. Then – well. He'd think about the rest later.

He had his jacket and keys in his hand, his phone in his pocket, when there was a loud *rat-a-tat-tat* at the door that made him jump. He blinked and waited a moment, as if he was busy, in the middle of something engrossing or important, before he went to it and lifted the clattering latch and scraped the door open across the uneven boards.

'Right, lad?'

It was big Frank, incongruous with a casserole dish wrapped in a tea towel. The wind was pushing at his thin hair, wisping it up and down again, but he was still in the white polo shirt bare-armed and unhurried.

'The wife sent me. Sent this. Just heard the news.'

He pushed it forwards and waited.

Evan was at a complete loss, standing there with his jacket and keys in one hand, holding the door with the other.

'She said wasn't right, you stuck all the way down here on your own and the shit hittin' the fan. You're not used to it, like. She doesn't want you going without, over this flu thing, she says. So.'

Evan looked at him.

'Here!' the man said, pushing it forwards again. 'She made it for you. You can throw the pan back when you're done, you know where we are, number seven, with the fake buzzard in the garden to keep out the seagulls.'

Evan roused himself to take the dish, horrified to feel the sting of tears in his eyes. It was warm and fragrant in his hands, a real kindness, a genuine surprise.

'That's – well. That's incredibly kind of her. Of you both—' he said, but Frank was already turning away.

'Shop up the hill is already out of bog roll,' the big man tossed back over his shoulder as he crunched up the lane. 'Looks like you'll have to use seaweed to wipe your arse. Can't help you there!'

Carrying the dish carefully to the worktop by the sink, Evan felt his mouth already watering with the aroma of roasted meat and gravy.

There was a ping in his pocket as the scattered Wi-Fi gathered itself for another surge and an email arrived.

Only John again. He'd closed the place down after all, the message said, following a further statement from the government. Couldn't wait around for Evan's response. Hoped that was OK. All happened very suddenly, in fact. Everyone had been notified, he'd set up answer-messages and updated the website. Just letting you know, he wrote, don't worry, it's all in hand, but take the break, get yourself together – you'll need to be back on form when this is all over, mate – we all will. Going to be one hell of a mess. He wished Evan good health, as if he were ancient and sickly, and signed himself briefly, busily, 'J.'

'What a guy,' Evan said to the empty eyes of the little skull on the shelf.

He tried Lorna's number again. No response. He wanted a fucking drink.

The scent of Frank's offering caught his attention. He lifted the warm dish closer and removed the tea towel. Thick, rich stew inside, carrots and onions and meat and potatoes. He fetched a tablespoon and dipped in, tasted.

Wow. The food was delicious.

His mouth ran with saliva suddenly, woken from a long drought.

Ping!

We're fine

Flat out with the crisis

Full time now at last

Julie takes Luca for me

Keep safe talk later

No emojis. Not even one.

Perhaps she was too busy. He thought about her – Lorna – clicking busily along in those sexy little shoes, the black ones, promoted at last from part-time flexi-hours to someone important. Even in his thoughts, she clicked on briskly down the hallway, shaking that hair behind her, and didn't look back.

Ping!

'Jesus!' he said aloud.

He looked at the phone darkly for a second, before lifting it and opening the new email.

It was from Airbnb.

A message from the property owner, signing herself 'Grace'. He pulled out a chair and sat heavily, picking up the spoon again, skimmed quickly down the message while he moved it methodically between dish and mouth, feeling the heat and weight of the food in his belly, the warm glow of meat and potatoes, spreading.

Due to the unforeseen circumstances, he read, he was to

stay in the property as long as he needed. There would be no further charge to pay. He was to make himself at home. Was he aware that there was a shed behind the property containing some gardening things? Perhaps he'd be good enough to tend to the grass, keep the hedge back, etc., etc., in return. Any problems he should just call. Then a phone number. He imagined her in green wellies, imperious in tweed.

So that was that, then.

He dipped again into the dish and heard a muted click as the spoon hit the bottom. Looking in, he was startled to see that he'd eaten at least half of the contents without noticing.

All around him the shadows grew, the sea just audible outside the window, the breeze gone with the dusk, but he barely noticed the heavy silence on the rooftop, the stillness all around, or the dark, dark room. Instead he lay, with his little daughter a hot weight on his chest, in a darkness just like this one. He felt the damp sweat of her drowsing, and saw again the dark shadow of her lashes on a pale cheek. He smelled the hot reek of her, lying curled in a heavy comma under his chin, exhausted with screeching, and brushed his lips gently against the tendrils of dark hair on the little head.

Tortured with reflux, she'd been, the poor thing. Night after night after night, screaming, everyone drained and black-eyed and spent. But now he remembered only the peace and quiet of them both as she slept at last, the calm after the storm. Lorna out catching up with some work, she'd said, some last-minute crisis that couldn't wait; him left holding the baby, his daughter, gladly. Half drowsing, it was as if he sat again on the big soft chair at home beside the French windows, the clean, safe scent of laundry all around them, the baby still at last on his chest.

Jessie, Jessie, Jessie, sweetheart, he remembered whispering, and then they had both fallen asleep.

He shoved himself roughly back from the table, shaking, and threw up in the sink.

It was very late. He saw through the big window across the room that the moon had come up with the tide, and it was a wonderful, round, bright circle in the black of the sky. He took a slow, shaky breath and went over to look out at the beach, the sea, the night sky, away from the pictures inside his head.

In the cold white light, a figure was crossing the sand, a black shape, moving steadily as if familiar with the route. At the edge of the water, where the moonlight made a yellow path, it stood still a moment, silhouetted against the sparkles, just looking out. Then it pushed off some footwear. Then it began to undress.

He watched the figure shrug off a large, loose covering, then smaller things, indistinct, standing one-legged like the heron. Its movements were slow and steady. It turned unself-consciously to put the things on a little rock away from the wet of the sand and he saw it had a woman's shape. She was naked. Long and lean. The moon gleamed on white-white skin and made the shadow very black behind her.

He shouldn't watch, he knew. He should scrape the old curtains across and turn on the TV, watch the white fizzing lights of it, or pick up a book.

The figure lifted her arms to the sky, stretching. She was tall. The moonlight gleamed on her, as if drawing her in. She placed a foot into the little waves. He could imagine the shock of the cold, but she didn't hesitate. She walked calm and slow into the water, and he saw it lick the skin of her ankles, calves, thighs, hips and secret places. He held his breath, impossibly moved, feeling everything intensely where he leaned on the wall by the window. Then she bent low and pushed her whole self into the gleaming oily gold of the moon-path, and he shuddered in sympathy, but she was in it now completely, part of it, swimming out with slow, languorous movements, a sensual breaststroke along the gold of the moonlight.

She was good at it.

With every outbreath, the head dipped down deep. With every inbreath, it rose, sleek as a seal and shining under the moon. He didn't know how long she swam, or how long he stood there, watching and breathing with her, up-down, up-down, up-down along the path of the moon on the water, but he forgot the pain in his chest and just watched her.

After a while, she turned back towards shore. She had no face that he could see, just a blank unearthly space where it should be. He shivered where he stood. After a time, he didn't know how long, she drew herself up to stand and left the water. Long silver streams ran from her as she walked onto the sand.

He watched her rub a large and floppy thing across her body, over her hair, and then drop it on as clothes. It reached to her knees. The other things were scooped up into her arms, and she scuffed her feet into what must be shoes or sandals at the little rock, and then she left, walking slowly across the beach in front of him, away from the lane that led to the village, away from Big Frank and his casserole wife – towards the darkness instead, and the waving night-time grasses on the dunes, and then she was gone, out of the light of the moon and out of sight.

Chapter 7

———

'YOU'LL NEED IT A BIT SHARPER than that, lad.'

It was Frank's voice, louder than it needed to be because of Social Distancing. He had announced this concept loudly on his arrival and repeated it often, like a mantra, when things got quiet. He would be observing Social Distancing.

Good, thought Evan.

Frank was behind him, darkening the inside of the rickety shed even further where Evan was poking about and wishing he'd thought to bring out a torch from the house. Things were scuttling about under his fingers.

He was looking for what Grace had called 'gardening things', and the closest he'd come was the pole in his hand, a long smooth 'C' of wood with a curved blade, that he'd found propped up against the door beside a rake and a bucket.

'Yep,' said Frank with some satisfaction. 'Wouldn't cut butter.'

'Is this for the garden?' Evan asked him, reluctantly.

'Aye. But no good to you unless you sharpen it. May as well use your toenails. Can't come in, like, to see better or Maggie'll kill me quicker than the fuckin' virus. I have to observe Social Distancing, like I say.'

Evan looked at the pole, flummoxed. It was a beautiful

45

thing in its own way, of course, an antique. But he'd imagined a mower, a Flymo maybe, for the tiny bit of grass at the back, and a strimmer maybe. Yes, a Flymo probably – light and floaty, the kind of thing a little old landlady like Grace would use.

'There'll be a stone somewhere for it, sharpen it. Grace is organised like that,' Frank said.

Evan waited a moment and let a silence grow. Then he gave in and asked, '—What exactly is it?'

Frank huffed a delighted laugh.

'That's a scythe, so it is,' he said, slowly and as if Evan were stupid. '—Works well on the long grass behind the bins, you see. Gotta keep that down in the summer or it's a hoor getting them out to the lane for emptying of a Wednesday.'

'There's no mower,' Evan said lamely.

'Sure, you're holding it,' Frank chuckled.

Christ, thought Evan.

He must have said it out loud, because Frank's belly in the doorway was wobbling as he laughed, and making the shadows dance. He was still laughing as he pushed himself off the doorframe and headed on down the lane.

Then something caught Evan's eye.

Away at the back of the shed, right in the corner, something long and broad and curved leaned up against the wall. He caught his breath, suddenly. There were planks and a broom or two parked on top of the thing he had noticed, so it was difficult to make it out properly, but his heart beat a little faster, just in case. He needed to get it out, have a proper look. Quickly, carelessly, he moved the junk from the top of it, throwing things to one side in a clattering heap until it was clear, and he could see that it was indeed what he had hoped for – a genuine top-notch ride-on kayak, no less. A solid plastic thing – proper – not one of those shitty inflatables they sold to simpletons nowadays. A bit faded, once bright blue and now grey in places. His heart soared. Just the look of it brought him back to his childhood, to blissful holiday afternoons alone on the shallow waters of Upper Lough Erne in its fibreglass equivalent, free from his mother's tight watchfulness, her nervous stewardship of him. The very sight of it meant freedom and escape.

It was beautiful and he took its weight respectfully, bringing it to lie on the dry and dusty floor of the shed. A kayak.

Taking his careful time he brushed the cobwebs from seat and sides, remembering what it felt like to sit down in the deep bucket seat and brace his feet against the ridges and ride the swell of the water as if it were a huge creature of sinew and muscle and he a gnat on its skin.

He jumped up and started to dig further into the darkness, hunting around for a paddle.

And there it was, sweet Jesus, tucked in behind the boat itself, hidden. His hand closed on it tight, and tugged it out for inspection. Both blades were sound, and a glance over his shoulder to the light showed him the same fine, still spring day that had seen him open the padlock, scrape back the doors earlier.

God, it had been years.

He went quickly to the doorway to check the distance to the water, because a kayak was heavy. First an easy drag across the stripe of grass, around the side of the house and onto the lane. Then the pebbly slope, no problem, and then a little sand, and then the sea, saucy and inviting, rippling its lacy edges and twinkling its eyes at him.

Come on ahead, boyo, it said. Let's do it.

Standing up and brushing off his jeans, he grasped the rope loop at the prow and dragged it to the light where all good craft should be. He imagined it blinking and rubbing its invisible eyes after an age spent hoarded and hidden in the darkness.

At the door he set it down and gave it a quick pat, and then went to the house at a jog for his phone, to check what the tide was doing; what the weather was to be like. There was a little smile on his face, an unfamiliar sensation of glee, as he pushed the back door open and stepped inside out of the light. He glanced back once more to see the kayak there, peeping its long nose past the door of the shed, the paddle tucked nicely into the frayed bungee on its back, waiting for him like a dog with its leash in its mouth.

For an aggravating moment he couldn't find his phone in the clutter on the table, pushing through the pile built up over a few days in someone else's house, where nothing belonged anywhere, and no one cared, but at last found it tucked under a scatter of t-shirts in the corner, waiting to be washed.

A notification lit up the screen. A proper email this time, from Lorna.

He opened it quickly, the new jaunty happiness replaced by the tight anxiety her messages always brought. As he skimmed down, he felt all the joy of the kayak run down his spine and out through his heels onto the cold tiled floor. He had to lean against the table for a moment and read the damn thing again.

I've thirty missed calls from you Evan. Thirty. I counted them. That's precisely the sort of thing I'm talking about. I'm sorry. I'd prefer it if you wouldn't call me. I can't be with you atm. I can't talk to you, and you shouldn't make me. You've been good at saying nothing for a long time now. Why change it? I'm OK and Luca's OK and we are looking after each other the way we've always done. Stay where you are and we'll catch up and sort something out when this is all over. And stop calling me. There's nothing we need that you can give us atm, except space. L.

Evan dropped the phone on the table and walked to the door, where he leaned for a while and watched a beetle navigate the long green spikes of grass, fall off, disappear under a stone. Then he pushed himself upright and headed back to the shed. Still in his jeans and t-shirt and trainers he dragged the old kayak right out and bumped it unceremoniously across the grass. The half-door to the kitchen creaked and swung in a rising breeze behind him as he scraped the boat around the corner and onto the lane, but he didn't go back to close it.

Ahead of him, the sand was ribbed and lumpy and dotted with little scraps of seaweed, green and pink and purple and white, all intermingled. The squelch and ooze of each little patch mashed to nothing under his weight and that of the boat hauled behind him, and he dragged it onwards relentlessly, checking now and again that the white blades of the paddle were still to be seen on its long broad back.

The little lacy waves were gone by the time he reached the water's edge and stopped to catch his breath, but the sun still shone. The water had swollen a bit, to make waves that crashed and foamed at calf height, pawing at the sand, but he paid them no heed as he stooped to release the paddle and push the boat that last sticky length into the water.

He didn't stop to remove his trainers, and noted idly the purplish colour of wet denim as the waves broke under his knees, and the feeling of the boat like a live thing on the curl of his fingers, bucking and pulling and eager to be free. He pushed on, wading through the deepening water, little things skittering out from underneath his feet, until the water almost reached his thighs and the crash of the shore-waves was behind him, and the boat lay calm and ready.

Chapter 8

——

FROM HER POSITION AT THE TOP of the grassy slope, her hand on the dog's head, Grace watched the man settle himself and adjust his grip on the paddle so that the blades pointed the right way. She watched him dip first one, then the other into the rising water, and move smoothly away from the beach.

Seemed to know what he was doing. She'd give him ten minutes, then.

The dog nudged her hand. She'd stopped stroking its coarse head, its ugly, twisted back. There were lumps under the skin as big as potatoes, and it moaned quietly as she moved her fingers over them. A badger had done it, and no wonder. When she'd found the dog in the grass it had been almost dead, no match for a cornered wild thing in its lair. She'd pulled the battery pack from the harness on its back and ground it into the earth with the heel of her boot, before lifting the animal, blood squirting everywhere, and taking it to the old jeep.

They sent them into the setts to drive the badgers out for fighting, but this one was no size for the job, she'd thought, as she trudged up the hill with its dead weight in her arms. A squat little thing, it was, every kind of terrier mixed together and none of them good-looking. She'd expected it to be dead when she drew up at Mike the Vet's that day, but there you are. The blood had pooled and clotted on the car floor, was all down her front, as if the animal had no more left in it.

Mike looked like he'd have pulled the shutters down when he spotted her coming, but she'd been too quick, was through the doors with the dripping burden before that nice wee lassie with the buck-teeth could get out from behind the counter. It had taken a while, and a shitload of grumbling, but he'd done the job. Always did. A decent spud, all told, was Mick, with more time for animals than the human population, which was the way it should be, and she couldn't blame him.

The dog jumped up eagerly now as she grunted herself onto her feet, and looked brightly at her face to see which way she was going. One ear went one way, one went the other. This was the thing she liked best about it.

But she didn't go anywhere for a moment, just tucked her head to one side to watch the skinny tourist come out on the kayak from the shelter of the bay and encounter the local currents. Almost immediately his smooth paddling began to falter, as the vicious old boat fought him, its stern swinging out with the swirling movement of the water, the mini whirlpools caused by the submerged reefs underneath, and by the receding waters of the ebb tide. It never was an easy ride, that thing, like a bad horse that wouldn't take direction, and it belonged in the darkness of the shed or in a skip somewhere. What was he doing, taking it out like that?

Damn fool.

She watched him set the flashing paddle gently on his lap as the old boat twisted and turned and slapped the water insolently. She saw his shoulders slump down and his gaze settle on his wet knees, his feet, anything but the deep and dangerous water all around him, which lipped over the sides now and then as if testing him to see what he'd do. She saw the boat heading of its own volition further out into the current, this way and that way, sharply up and sharply down, its rider almost unseated at every twist, but still there, still there, bending and straightening, riding the waves in the treacherous craft. She saw him shove his glasses back up to the bridge of his nose with his wrist once, as the kayak slewed right around in the water as if it would tip. She saw that he didn't cling to the sides, didn't lift his head. She sighed, loudly, and pushed a straggle of hair back behind her ear. He was fucked, for sure, but she had to admit, he had great balance. He was still aboard, wasn't he, even if that wasn't his intention.

She clicked at the dog who was already tight on her heels and began down the slippery slope towards the little boat in the bay.

As they reached the place where earth met sand, the dog jumped down and ran ahead, afraid of being left behind. It leapt into the boat and settled itself at the prow, watching her approach more slowly, stumping in her loose boots through the soft drifts of sand, and pulling her Tilly-hat down tight on her head.

The dog's claws scraped and slipped as she shoved the boat into the water in three short bursts, but it didn't lose its seat. Hitching her poncho up out of the water she reached in for the rope with a practised hand and looked around to take a last measure of the sea, before she climbed aboard. She couldn't see the kayak at the moment, because of the curl of the cliff, but it'd come into view very shortly, she knew, hooked on the harsh line of the tide.

With one last shove from her boot, the boat took to the water. She was in her seat and the oars in her hands in one smooth movement, and rowing strong and easy over the lumps of the swell that was building in the water. The boat sailed easy over the worst of these, and she knew exactly when to pause and when to work, to move it neatly forwards. The dog hunkered down for grip, but it kept its snaggle-mouth hanging over the bulwark and its bright eyes ahead. Now and again a little spray of salt water would pop up and over the sides, but neither of them paid this the slightest attention.

After about two hundred strokes they left the shelter of the cliffs and were out in the open sea. She hauled on an oar to bring the boat broadside to land, and looked around, letting it bob and drift as it wanted. To the right was the humpbacked shadow of the Isle of Man, several hours away, and to the left were the slick, dark cliffs, her own little house picked out red and white in the distance. All around in the water were small pink and orange buoys marking crab-pots and keep-boxes, but Grace was looking for something larger.

She was surprised to see, when she spotted it a little way away, that the thin dark figure still drooped on its back like a tired cowboy at the tail end of a rodeo. She'd expected him to be in the water by now, those glasses long gone. Fair play to him, she thought, fair play.

He'd lost the paddle, of course, and as she came closer, she saw his face was very pale. His t-shirt was a slick dark green and his jeans full of water and, of course, he wore no lifejacket.

'Fuckin' townies,' she hissed at the dog, which flattened its ears and blinked at her.

The man hadn't seen them yet. He was still sitting motionless on the bucking kayak. Grace slowed her rowing and let her boat rest a little way off, to see what would happen next.

She nodded as a run of water slewed the kayak around, hard, and the man fell with a subdued plop into the icy rush of the sea. The dog barked as he came to the surface, gasping and spitting as they always did, horrified at the incredible cold, the terrible depth of the water around and beneath him, shocked and spinning and swallowing water, flapping and slapping and choking.

She let him settle. He looked like he knew how to swim.

Suddenly he caught sight of her and howled.

'Help me! Help!'

She looked at him for a moment, shouting and splashing there. Then, with a few deft strokes, she came alongside him and twisted around on the bench to kick the little ladder over the stern with a lazy boot. She leaned down beside her to grab the paddle out of the water as it drifted slowly by. When she looked up, the townie was still clawing at the slippery green sides of her boat as if he could swim himself in, and thanking Christ and all of that, and she realised that without the glasses he probably couldn't see a thing.

'Go to the end,' she barked. 'There's a ladder.'

When he failed to move, she said it again, and the dog barked for good measure. Nodding quickly, still coughing seawater, he began to inch his way down to the end, until he found the thing dangling into the sea, its metal strands clacking quietly as they all moved up and down, up and down. Grace settled the paddle where it wouldn't interfere and watched the kayak floating away on the pointed swell. She got the oars ready in her hands and sat waiting, until she felt the sharp downward lurch of the man's weight on the ladder, getting a hold. Then there was the groan of effort as he pulled himself up out of the water and became heavy, heavy, heavy again, but she didn't turn around to help. The dog whined as the boat listed hard to one side. He'd got one leg over, probably, she thought, and was doubtless lying over the stern like a drying sheet. Yep, she could hear him gasping for breath.

Better watch his balls as he swings himself in, she thought, but didn't say.

Another lurch and a thump and a *Christ almighty*, and the man was in the bottom of the boat. The little craft sat low in the water now, but it was fit for this. It would be a hard old pull to catch up with the kayak under this double weight though, so she bent to the task without delay. As she rowed, she heard him scuffle around and swear quietly, and finally right himself.

'Thank god you came along when you did,' he said loudly, to her straining back.

God had nothing at all to do with it, she thought, but didn't say.

'I dunno what I'd have done if you hadn't come along.'

I do, she thought, but didn't say.

Instead, she jerked her head towards the neat coil of rope on the seat beside her.

'We'll be alongside the kayak in a minute. Get that rope through the loop at the end of it so we can tow it in.'

'Right. Right you are,' he said, more quietly, and she smiled to herself.

His hand reached out and took the rope from beside her, and the boat lurched and swayed as he got clumsily into position. There was a clunk as she brought the boat up alongside the kayak and she sat still and quiet, letting the man fumble for the loop by touch, muttering to himself, calling himself all the names he deserved, panicking when he couldn't find the loop of rope at the prow because he was a blind stupid bastard, a thick fucker, a dopey specky cunt.

Nice language, she thought appreciatively, but didn't say.

Instead, she shipped the oars and twisted around, lifting her legs up and over the bench in a smooth movement.

'Here,' she said peremptorily, and took the rope from him. He gave it up, blinking, and sat back a little on the bottom of the boat to give her space. Quickly she reached for the loop and threaded the tow-rope through. Tying a rapid square-knot she gave a tug to secure it and handed the remaining coil to the man.

'Let it out a couple of foot and then hold tight.'

He nodded wordlessly, and she saw he was beginning to shake with cold and shock. She tutted.

'Here.'

She took off her hat so that she could yank off her poncho, and held it out to him. It was time she was back at the oars. The current was taking them away from shore.

'No. No, I'm all right, really.'

55

'Put it fucking on.'

He took it from her then all right, and she didn't wait to see him put it on. She clamped the hat back on her head where it belonged, and was already rowing, rowing, rowing, pulling back the advantage from the sea, angling across the run of the current and making the boat go straight, even with the bumping, splashing encumbrance of the kayak tied on behind.

It was forty, maybe forty-five minutes before they reached the sands and she was sweating hard as she let the boat bump and swing around in the surf. The dog didn't wait. It leapt out into the water, pelted up onto the sand and ran around and around in circles, barking, delighted to be back.

'Your turn,' she said, over her shoulder.

She felt the man stand and smelled her own scent strongly as he stepped cautiously over the low side of the boat into the water. She hoped he was holding the poncho well up out of it. It was a bollocks to dry, altogether. That was the thing about wool.

She lifted the oars and tugged out the rowlocks, and by the time she stepped out of the boat herself, big Frank and Eamon Logan were there beside her and had their hands to it, ready to pull it up the beach for her, flip it over like a huge turtle in the crisping seagrass and litter at the edge of the lane, where it lived. The littlest O'Hagan was there too, in the water up to his waist, hauling at the kayak and fussing with the knot tying it to the boat. She paused and watched as he got it loose with small cold fingers.

Good lad, she thought, but didn't say.

'Go easy with that, you!' she called to him instead and he nodded and lifted the paddle from the boat to go with it, started dragging them in to shore. She pushed her legs through the last of the water and stood on the sand for a moment, letting her breath settle. Then she headed for home.

'Interfering again, Gracie?'

Frank's voice was low and amused as she passed him.

'Wouldn't know to let a thing alone, would you?' he asked. 'Sure, one less townie'd be no hardship, would it?'

She said nothing. Walked on.

Mrs Hitler, Frank's wife, was marching the townie away already, Social Distancing forgotten in the heat of a drama. Grace could see her hand in the small of his back, her sharp wee face turned up to his, chattering about hot milk and brandy, and god isn't it desperate the cold of the sea, and all that balls. They were on the lane now, heading back to the rental cottage, although if the poor unfortunate man made it inside alone, he'd be lucky. Mrs Hitler'd have his feet in a mustard bath and hot rocks up his arse in a matter of minutes, given any encouragement.

'We'll get the kayak put away out of the road, don't be worrying!' Eamon called after her and the bouncing dog, but she didn't turn round. She was suddenly very tired, and all of her fifty years lined up on her shoulders to be carried.

Behind her the men counted three and pushed the little boat over so its belly faced the sky.

'Christ that was a pull and a half,' Eamon said to Frank, watching her go. 'I don't think I'd have been fit for it meself.'

They shook their heads and watched the tall shape of her disappear over the brow of the hill, the broad hat flapping gently in the rising breeze.

'Some woman for one woman, that Grace,' Frank said, and then a thought occurred to him. 'My Maggie's away looking after yer man, the townie,' he said, and winked at his friend. 'She'll be a while, I'd say, the mother-hen she is. You want to share a dram or two in the back shed?'

There was no need for an answer, and the two men left the shore, hands deep in pockets and their talk soft and easy, as the water hissed behind them and shadows crept over the hump of the little boat, hunkered down in the grass as if resting.

Chapter 9

———

EVAN ROSE SLOWLY FROM HIS SEAT by the fire and went to the window to look out. It was becoming an addiction in this dark little house. He stood for a long time, staring through the single-paned glass at the sea, even though without his glasses he could see only moving bright shadows, the play of wind on grass, the shift of the last of the sunlight on the water.

Maggie had lit the fire before she left and although he'd protested, he was glad of it now. He'd never known cold like it, deep in his core, worse than anything he'd felt in any of those adventures he'd enjoyed when he was younger – white-water rafting, climbing, coasteering, mountain biking in the ice of winter. He'd done them all, but this had been so much worse. This cold had been as much to do with despair as with anything physical.

He'd thought he wanted to die out there, beyond the bay. He'd set out to do so, he knew that now. He remembered paddling fast out past the hulk of the cliff, in a hurry to get there, to do it, another challenge to take on and, this time, to succeed at. But the cold shock of the water had jolted him awake as soon as it hit his body as surely as if it had been a defibrillator. There'd been a nightmare period of thrashing and gulping in the horrible dark water when he realised what a fool he'd been, what a mistake he'd made, and all too late, all too late.

And then the sight of that blurred figure in the little boat, the thought that after all, he might be able to change his mind and try again had surged through him with such intense hope and joy that it had been physically painful. He recalled the agonisingly heavy pull of himself up the impossibly bendy ladder, out of the black grasp of the sea to the deliciously firm footing of the boat, and the memory of that gladness and relief made him shiver and return to the hot little heat of the fire in the grate, rubbing his arms through the thick wool in which he was wrapped.

Even after he'd changed, he'd drawn this huge all-engulf-ing poncho-thing back over his clothes and snuggled in it, to coax back the heat and the memory of what he had just escaped. He rubbed his chin on the rough wool, over and over, as he thanked his lucky stars, counted his blessings, rel-ished his heartbeats, and each and every breath.

He wouldn't think about Lorna. He was alive, that was all. Worry about the rest, later.

Hugging the huge poncho tighter around him he smelled woodsmoke, and something earthy underneath.

So Hat-man had turned out to be a woman, and she'd saved his life.

'Don't be saying that sort of thing, sure it was only a dip you took,' Maggie had tutted at him, earlier. She'd poked the fire energetically when she spoke so that it flared up and snapped at the wood stacked around it and the first heat of it reached his feet, his shins, his knees.

'A dip?' He'd laughed, then stopped suddenly as her back remained turned to him, her shoulders set. 'I'd have drowned out there, if she hadn't come along.'

He'd nursed the mug of thick sweet tea she'd made him, and savoured the heat on the flat of his fingers.

Maggie had sat back on her narrow haunches then, and

regarded him for a long cool moment, the poker dangling. He could feel her stare through the mist of his myopia, and it had made him blink and sit low in his chair as if he were a bad child in trouble.

'Now listen to me,' she'd said, in a clipped and quiet voice, 'that woman's not right. She's as mad as a box of frogs. Don't go bothering her and talking this nonsense about drowning and the like. Round here, people know about the water, that's all. She was just able to help, so she did. That's what we're like, nothing to make a song and dance about, at all.'

'What's her name?'

'Whose name?'

Sharp again. She didn't like Hat-woman. Evan waited.

'Oh. You mean Grace. That's Grace Kielty. Lives all on her own around the corner behind the house, away from the village. Doesn't like people, like I say. Wears the strangest clothes, looks like a bag-lady, although there's plenty of money about her, and that's a fact. Does it for the attention, I'd say.'

She sniffed again, and glanced down to check her own shirt was still pristine after all the poking, all the wiping and tidying she'd done in the short time she'd been in the house, oblivious to government guidelines. It was.

'Well, thank you. Thank you very much for all your help, Maggie,' he'd said quickly to appease her. 'It was very kind of you. Really. I appreciate it.'

She'd warmed a little then, and smiled at him. He could see how she loved her children, bullied and coddled them and managed all their lives for them. The smile was sweet and warm, as far as he could tell, squinting at her.

'Didn't you used to wear glasses?' she'd asked then, suspiciously.

'Oh. Yes. They fell off. Lost them, I'm afraid. When I – went for my little dip . . .'

She'd refused to be teased, and headed for the front door.

'Well, I hope you have spares, because you'll get no appointment in the town now. Everything's closed, you know. Signs on all the doors. Dentist and all, would you believe it. Poor Frank was crucified yesterday with that old tooth of his but no, they wouldn't see him.'

She was talking to herself now, shrugging on her cardigan from the hook on the door.

'—Anyway, keep the fire in, young man, that's the best thing for a soaking – a real fire,' she'd said, 'and I'll throw a wee drop of something round to you later for the tea, when I get the chance.'

'Oh no, please don't bother—' Evan called after the bright colour of her shirt.

But it was too late. She'd gone, the door rattled and slammed in her wake, and the house sat quiet and shocked in the silence again.

Well. He was warm now. And dry. He'd go and dig the spare specs out of his holdall, and then get this woollen thing back to its owner, the hero, mad as a frog or not.

Grace, indeed. The midnight swimmer. The mighty oarswoman. Madwoman who lived round the bend. Well, he was mad too, a bit. He'd go and visit her.

Chapter 10

—

A SHADOW STUMPED ACROSS THE LANE in front of him, startling him in the half-light. The sun, setting behind the drumlins in the west, cast the shape in sharp relief and he saw a thin stick in her hand – a fishing rod – carried low, a bucket swinging in the other, and that hat, an unmistakeable shape, on her head. She was moving away from him, towards the silver stripe of the sea in the east, over the rocks that poked sharp and black into the gathering darkness.

'Grace?' he called quietly, afraid to startle her.

The figure stumped on without hesitating, but a shadow at its ankles growled, a dirty, phlegm-filled noise. Evan stopped where he was. The bag was heavy in his hand.

'Sorry—' he called, louder this time '—Grace? It's me – Evan – the man from the kayak? I have your – I have your—'

He held out the bag in explanation.

She didn't turn her head, didn't acknowledge him in any way. The dog barked once, sharply, and then followed its owner into the blackness of the rocks, which swallowed them up.

He stood for a second in the lane, in the dusk, feeling his face hot with embarrassment, although he couldn't think why. He'd been warned, hadn't he? Mad, she was. He laughed quickly and looked around to see where she'd come from. There was a house a few metres along, even smaller than his, it seemed, from its shadow against the bank. He took a step forwards in the gathering darkness and stopped again.

From where he stood he could make out a little window or two at the front of the cottage, just glinting, and a tiny porch jutting out directly onto the lane. He clicked the torch on, and the place came alive with detail. A high stone wall ran along both sides, almost to the roof of the house itself, protecting the rear of the place from prying eyes. There were little clouds of bright pink flowers nodding in stone jars to each side of the doorway, pretty. A long rope like a clothes-line ran down the wall with brown rags hanging dry and shrivelled all along the length of it. He went to the closest of these and fingered it cautiously. Crispy. A strong tang of brine from it, and it cracked and snapped under his fingers. Seaweed?

He shone a light to his left. The door in the porch had been left ajar. He stared at the gap between door and indoors, for a moment. Anyone could just walk on in. Didn't she care? He found himself right there, now, at the gap and putting his head inside, casting the light around. The little space was scrupulously neat and tidy. A dog-basket sat heaped and cosy in one corner, and the walls were rough and bare and white. Another door led inside the house, red and solid, but it was closed tight. A basket against the wall held twisted snaggles of driftwood, and the floor was the same stone of his own place, grey and rough and swept spotlessly clean.

The place held him for some reason he couldn't explain. He wanted to stand inside the little porch out of the vastness of the dark, and close the door and rest. Instead, he closed his eyes and stood where he was for a short time, breathing that scent of woodsmoke again, and earthiness, and wet dog, and timelessness.

Suddenly he felt his neck and shoulders hot with the

sensation of being watched. His face flared and, with a quick movement, he dropped the bag in his hand into the porch and turned around, trying to appear casual.

'Did you get it wet?' she asked.

He swung the torchlight around, yellowing the lane, the grass, the banks, until it flashed across a face, still and watchful like a ghoul. There she sat on a big rock. She'd waited to see what he'd do, he realised with acute mortification. The torch was lighting up her face, the hat upturned. She didn't flinch from the glare. The eyes of the dog flared green behind her, but it didn't move either. The fishing rod lay on the rocks at her side, all the little feathers flashing in the light, the hooks invisible.

'Oh, hi!' he said, dropping the beam of his torch to the ground, where the earth was alive with scurrying things. 'I thought you'd gone.'

She looked at him steadily, saying nothing.

He waved behind him at the house, at the bag in the porch in the darkness.

'—You didn't stop when I – so I just . . .'

The hat was tipped back on her head, and the peripheral light of the torch lit up the lines on her face, the bags under her eyes, like a Halloween trick. Her elbows rested easily on her knees, and her hands clasped loosely as she regarded him. Her feet were long and bare, in flat, plain sandals. She sat perfectly still.

'—The cape thing. It's in the bag, thanks so much. I wanted to return it – no, it's perfectly dry, thank you. So I left it . . .'

Once again, he gestured behind him to the house, but she didn't take her eyes from his face. He stopped floundering and looked down at his feet, where a swarm of small, winged things were now milling across the toes of his trainers in the yellow light, snaggling one another with their unfamiliar wings.

'Nuptial flight,' she said.

'What?'

She nodded at the little bugs. 'Winged ants. They leave the nest to start a new one. Mate.'

'Oh. Do – do they bite?'

He held very still, resisting the urge to stamp his feet, shake the tiny things off, squash them underfoot. The hairs on his neck lifted, but he held still.

'Not that you'd notice.'

She got to her feet in one smooth movement, gathering her rod.

'—I wanted to say thank you,' Evan said urgently to her broad shoulders, as she began to step up and over the rocks and away, finding footholds with unerring accuracy, moving into the dark. She stopped climbing, but kept her back to him, waiting. The dog was already gone. 'God, you came just in time. I'd have drowned if you hadn't—'

'Thought you wanted to,' she said.

'What?'

'Looked like you wanted to. Drown.'

She turned slowly, and the hat shadowed her face entirely, but somehow this made the gaze more piercing, the sensation of being under observation more acute. Once more he looked at his feet, and the procession of nuptial ants was gone. When he raised his head again, so was she.

Chapter 11

——

ANOTHER BEAUTIFUL SPRING DAY, the sky full of birds and the air warm on her skin. All was as it should be, and yet things seemed strange, discombobulating. She pondered the feeling for a moment and was surprised at what it was she missed.

No tourists.

No townies, except the one in the cottage.

Without the foolish annoying bastards the place was eerily quiet. The sea rolled up onto the beach as if looking for an audience, and she felt strangely disconnected herself, untethered. She was glad to hear a sudden scuffle and a clicking of nails behind her, and when the dog appeared at her heels, panting, she bent to touch its head.

'What have you been torturing, you evil thing?' she asked it, noting a clabber of soil on the paws and smears of cow-shit or similar on its lumpy flanks. It wriggled its arse at her and trotted ahead, sniffing and pissing at every tenth step.

'We'll just have a wee check on the townie,' she told it, 'Since you're not in any hurry.'

The little cottage was dark and still as they approached, and the door closed. When she'd lived there the door lay open from March until October, her mother trying like mad to let out the damp and the smoke of the place. It was a little better now, but could still do with an airing now that spring was here. She'd say that to the townie, if she saw him about the place.

Now that she had something ready to talk to him about she marched on with more energy in her step, but there was no sign of him as she reached the little house. Going up to the big front window, she pushed her hat back from her face and cupped her hands against the light of the day to peer inside. She saw him straight away. He was there but he wasn't moving. She held her breath so as not to steam up the glass and looked for bottles of pills or pools of blood or random nooses, but could see nothing untoward.

He lay on the sofa, all tangled in the bright woollen throw from the back of it, his glasses on the floor beside him, his eyes closed and an arm trailing down. As she watched he shifted slightly, pulling the coverlet tighter around him so that his feet stuck out the bottom. His socks were grubby, with a hole in the toe of one. She tutted quietly.

She turned to check the height of the sun and shook her head. It was at least ten o'clock, and the day half gone. She turned back to the window again. Place was a mess, but you'd expect that. Table piled high with clothes and papers and dishes. Stuff on the floor. And him in the centre, looking younger without the specs, without any expression, comfortable in his sleeping skin, relaxed. As she watched, he stirred and pulled the trailing arm back under the blanket and rolled over onto his back. He was long, she thought, when he wasn't all stooped over and bent down under the weight of whatever burdened him. His skin was so pale, so white, that it was almost translucent and only a light grey shadow crept across his jaw and around that full, sensual mouth.

She stepped back smartly from the window and, pulling the hat lower against the glare of the sun, headed on towards the shop and her waiting parcels.

When she got there, the door was locked. She could see Becky behind the till, and old Tilly Magee talking to her, *natter-natter* like she did, without sense or stopping. She took a firm hold of the door knob and gave the door a good rattle so that it made a clacking sound as if the glass was loose. Becky looked up and saw her, smiled and waved, then made a little push-push motion with her hand as if to say, wait. Grace stared at her but she had gone back to the conversation with the woman and was slotting tins of cat food into a bag.

She waited, sighing loudly although there was no one to hear her. There was a small sign she hadn't noticed, on the window to the right of the door, all in those yellows and greys of the pandemic.

Let's shop safely. Three at a time in the shop please.

Grace bristled. She at least could count.

There was the O'Hagan woman, inside, browsing the shelves for something cheap and filling, a couple of kids trailing behind, picking things off the shelves and being told sharply to put them back again. And a couple of the old farmer brothers at the back, she could just see, rummaging among the hardware items, holes in the elbows of their jumpers, their soft old trousers tucked into welly-boots. And Tilly, that made six, if you weren't counting Becky, which she presumed you weren't. But unless she was very much mistaken that was a human backside waving about in the corner, too, and a familiar one at that. She'd seen it many a time straining over kegs out the back of the pub.

'What is this, a club or something?' she asked the door loudly, but didn't dare rattle it again.

As she glared impatiently through the glass, Becky picked something up from the counter and slotted it over her face, ear to ear. A mask, like a doctor would wear.

'You look like you're about to perform a lobotomy,' Grace

told her grumpily, as Becky unlocked the door and pulled it wide. 'Hope it's on Mickey Flanders – he's long overdue.'

'Embrace the change, Grace,' Becky told her, ushering Old Tilly out in front of her like a VIP. 'It's the only way to get through it.'

'Embrace my arse,' said Grace in return, acknowledging Tilly's cheery greeting with a nod and pushing on inside. 'But you're going to kill yourself on the step with your glasses all steamed up like that.'

'Ah Gracie,' said Paddy the Barman, sitting back on his heels with relief at the sight of her. 'Just the woman.'

He was kneeling in front of a tiny sink in the corner as if at an altar, and his face was red and sweaty and annoyed. Grace grunted and went on towards the little red and white desk at the far side, with the big POST OFFICE sticker on the front of it and the dinky little scales Becky was so proud of.

'No, seriously, Grace,' he called to her receding back. 'Come and give us a hand, won't you? I've been at it for an hour or more, and I can't get the vent to work right.'

'Last I heard, you were the Master's brainiac,' she retorted, banging hard on the little counter with her knuckles and yelling, 'Shop!'

When she looked over her shoulder, Becky was still outside, petting a tatter-eared cat through the window of Tilly's car and beaming as if it were the loveliest thing. The farmers were looking at her tapping foot, their faces identical, smiling. She tutted and took her hat off, putting it on the counter, and went back to the little sink in the corner. Paddy the Barman smiled his mole-smile and blinked at her through his glasses, sweetly.

'Budge over, then,' she said, dropping to her knees and taking the torch from his grateful hand.

She stuck her head into the dark shadows and peered around at his handiwork. Not a bad job for a barman, she thought, but didn't say.

70

'You've the vent pipe pointing the wrong direction,' she called back, and set to work untwisting the connection and reversing the fixture. It fought back a little as they always did but she took no nonsense and soon had it lined up and operational. She heard Becky return as she twisted the seal hand-tight and eased herself back with a grunt into the light.

'Thanks, Gracie,' Becky said, removing the mask at the door and flapping it around a little in the air outside.

'—It's to get rid of the droplets,' she explained, when she saw Grace staring. Grace lifted her chin as if to say, oh, right, but in a doubtful way, and pushed herself back onto her feet, brushing herself down as Becky saw to the little queue that had built up.

'Give it a go,' Grace told Paddy, nodding at the sink, and watched as he turned the tap. Bright water ran into the bowl and they smiled. They both listened for a minute or so, heads cocked to the side, to see if there were any gurgles or misfires in the pipes but it ran clear as a bell. He turned the tap off and patted the sink like a little dog.

'Nice one, thanks, Gracie,' he said.

The shop was empty now. 'Is there any chance I can get served,' Grace called to the girl, who was squirting some kind of gel into her hands and sliding them over and over each other, 'before he starts putting in a toilet as well?'

'It's for the pandemic,' Becky said mildly, going to the post office counter and clicking a switch underneath so that a little sign above her head glowed brightly. She beckoned Grace over, smiling.

'You can serve me without the sign on, you know,' Grace said, retrieving her hat and putting it on. 'I know what you are.'

'Ah but it's great craic, so it is,' Becky told her. 'Like putting on a costume or something. Changing roles. I've applied to get the parcels outward contract too, you know, so you won't have to go all the way to the town to send your stuff off for much longer. It'll all be here, under the one convenient roof. Who says progress is a bad thing?'

Grace rolled her eyes.

'Now. There's three here for you, I think.'

'What's this I hear about your new tenant?' Paddy asked, still playing with the running water, turning the tap on and off and on again like a child.

'What about him?' Grace checked the parcels. Fabric, good. Printer labels, late. The last one was dog food, a heavy sack of it in a plastic wrapper. She stopped Becky from hoisting it up onto the counter. 'I'll leave that one here. Too heavy. Get it when I'm up on the quad next time.'

Paddy had gone into the little kitchen and she heard the skirr of the kettle filling and the click of the switch.

'Nutjob, is he?' he called out. 'Your tenant? Tried to kill himself in that old boat of yours?'

She felt herself bristling, and didn't know why. 'Now where'd you hear a thing like that?' She glared at Becky, who shrugged and shook her head. 'That bloody pub, sure you're like the Women's bloody Institute in there. Nothing to do but bad-mouth helpless strangers on their last legs. Just as well the government shut you down.'

'Is he?' asked Paddy with interest, coming to the doorway and wiping his hands on a towel. 'On his last legs?'

'I'm sure it's none of our business whether he is or whether he isn't,' Grace retorted. 'I'm just taking his money off him.'

'Well, Ballybrady's the last place I'd want to be if I was at the end of my rope, if you'll pardon the turn of phrase,' said Paddy. 'That's all. You could die of loneliness here.'

'You could die of loneliness anywhere,' Grace said sharply and lifted her parcels and marched out, leaving them looking at one another in the empty shop.

Chapter 12

———

HE DECIDED TO TAKE THE CAMERA outside to explore. The morning was steamy, the windows moist and the grass on the lane outside gleaming with tiny silver drops. Throwing an old sweater over the t-shirt he slept in, and dragging on soft jeans and boots, he lifted his camera and a shining red apple and stepped out.

The waves were coy this morning, curling pretty around his boots, seeking his attention. It was difficult to reconcile this silvery expanse with the dense, dark muscle and threat of Tuesday's sea. His apple was done, nibbled down to the core and the taste still sweet in his mouth as he drew his arm back and cast it out onto the smooth water, where it smashed the surface for an instant, and was swooped on by a black-backed gull.

Quickly he raised his camera and flashed off a series of images, hoping to catch the feral sideways gleam of the creature as it saw him, and dived for the apple anyway. Next, the sparkles on the surface of the water caught his attention, and the difference in texture between the wet smooth rocks and the waves, so he spent a while snapping until his arms got tired with the weight of the camera and he let it drop on its strap again and hang heavy against his belly.

The sun was warm again today, no sign of rain yet, and he tasted the thick salt of the morning air on his lips as he licked them. Feeling it swirl into his lungs, cool and fresh, he thought of those people he'd seen on the news, grey and drained and strapped to ventilators, sedated beyond communication, concentrating their total effort on pulling in the next breath, and the next, and the next, until they could do it no longer, until the body failed.

And there she was.

The hat's peak pointing sharp towards the rising sun, she sat on the slope of the rocks at the edge of the sea, the hat low over her eyes as before, against the morning sun. She was fishing. From where he stood he could barely make out where the thread of her line made a sharp angle to the water, but something in the way she sat, so tense, so still, reminded him of the heron, watching the glinting surface with its full attention, oblivious to anything else, to feelings or sensations or doubts or sorrows.

He would like to feel how that would be, he thought.

Lifting his camera slowly to his eye, he zoomed in and took rapid shots of her, catching the thick bunch of light hair running out from under the hat at the back, the sharp points of the face – nose and chin, the firm base of the lap where she rested her elbows, her knuckled hands loaded with the fishing rod and the promise of fish. As he pressed the shutter again and again, the mechanism silent, his actions smooth and slow and unobtrusive, she turned her head slowly and looked straight at him, into the eye of the lens. They regarded one another for a moment, until he lowered the camera, turned it off, and dropped it once again on his belly, his face hot.

She looked back out to sea.

He walked over to where the rocks ran onto the sand, and sparkling little pools reflected the morning sun like a multitude of mirrors. Putting his hands to the chill of the wet stone, he began to climb carefully across the promontory, towards her. He watched himself as if from a great height, and let himself go. He used his hands wherever he could, forgetting dignity or skill and regretting the camera which swung and bumped around his neck and struck the rocks if he didn't take care. They were slippery and even more so where they were covered with long green strands of weed. Here and there a rockpool appeared like a trap, blocking his way, and he was forced to retreat, renegotiate, and take a different route. His progress was slow, childish, laborious, but he went doggedly on, and always he kept the woman in the corner of his eye, watching all the time to make sure she hadn't got up and gone, that she was waiting there still, at the edge of the sea.

Each time he straightened to look at her, he wobbled on the points of the rocks. Her back was turned to him. All her attention was on the water again, and just as he came over the top of the last formation, her line jerked and marked a slice across the surface. He hunkered down to see the catch, the camera to his eye again. He saw the rod make an arc and the woman lean back, smooth and quick, winding. He pressed, click-click-click. There was no run, no fight at all, and in just a few seconds the flapping curve of a fish came flying up out of the sea, flipping and twisting for just a short moment between water and earth. He pressed the shutter again and again.

Then she reached out and took hold of the thing, brought it wriggling into her lap. One hand held it firmly while the other loosed the line and secured it, then lowered the rod to lie at her side. He saw her take something from her pocket. Her fist flashed, and the dead fish was dropped into a bucket cooling in a pool alongside. The dog, a horrible thing, rose from where it had been watching him a little distance away and came to the woman to lick her palms clean.

She lifted the rod and cast again, and the silence settled back. He felt with his hand for a grip on the slime and sat down quietly, heedless of his clothes, one foot in a pool, and watched her, the camera ready.

All the time, she kept her eyes on the water, never acknowledging his presence, and all the time he was certain she knew he was there. Up came the rod again and with a flick the line was cast back. He settled himself as best he could on the lumps and bumps beneath him, and watched the water slide lower and lower on the rocks, until a thin grey line of sand separated land from sea, and she had to cast further and further out. He worked the camera now and then but for the most part he sat, as she did, watching and breathing and waiting.

Time passed and the sun slid across the sky.

Once or twice the rod had twitched, but only once more had she caught a fish, and now she breathed out, a long exhale, rolled her shoulders a couple of times, got her legs under her and stood up, taking her own good time, bucket in one hand, rod in the other. He felt as though they were waking from a shared dream, and he smiled at her as if he knew her. As if they were friends.

She stood square, and looked at him, where he perched a few strides away on the rock like an overgrown child. 'What d'you want?'

This time, it was he who didn't answer. He shrugged. Then he stood carefully and held out his hand. 'Can I help you with that?'

She snatched the bucket back against her body as though he were trying to steal it.

'I'll carry it for you, if you like, that's all.'

'I can carry it very well myself.'

The dog barked at her tone. She spoke clearly, her words well-formed and confident, and she had no discernible accent.

'You helped me, the other day.' Suddenly it was important to him. '—Now I'd like to help you, if I can.'

She laughed, an unfriendly sound. 'Right you are, then.'

Her hand rummaged in a huge pocket in the front of the jacket she wore, some faded black thing all streaked with flickering silver scales and muck, and came out with a little knife, a deadly looking thing, already out of its sheath. She held it out until he, hesitantly, took it. Only then did she yield up the bucket, which stank of the sea.

'You can clean these for me, then, if you're so keen.'

She laughed again, and clicked for the dog.

Evan looked down at the layers of fish, bent like scythes in the bucket. There must have been twenty in there, silky black above and shining beneath.

'I don't know how,' he said, quietly, as the fish gazed up at him with their dead eyes. 'But if you show me, I'd be happy to.'

'Humph,' she said, pushing past him, the dog a part of her, but she didn't take the knife back, or the bucket, and he followed hesitantly, camera bumping, bucket clanking as he slid and slipped, the sharp knife held carefully, pointing outwards, away from his heart.

She was waiting for him on the sand, and without a word led him around the back of the rock formation and along a stretch of wrack-slippery foreshore, to where the tide still lurked, slower on the ebb. She waded in until her feet were submerged and indicated a large concrete block beside her, for the bucket. He hefted it there, avoiding a thick curl of metal which had once held a boat like a kite on a chain. Silently, she requested the knife, and he passed it to her, stepped in a little, to see what was to be done. The air filled with silent gulls overhead, thin shadows passing over the bright water below them.

He was unprepared for the shock of the first cut.

The wicked little blade took head from body and the quick-clotted blood oozed out. There was a thick dark sensation in his head, both sight and smell repulsed at once. He took a step back, but she didn't look up from her work. Next, a neat slice took the tail. He winced and squinted away as she fitted the point into the anus and sliced the creature's belly, letting the purple and cream intricacies of its innards into the light. The knife was flashing now, in practised flicks, fast, dislodging the guts, finding the skeleton, slicing, scraping. Then swooping down, she rinsed the neat fillet in the water at her feet, set it to one side, and swiped the leftovers into the sea, sending the gulls into a frenzy of impatience as they waited for the ebbtide to feed them.

He felt his belly squeeze and release, and stayed a little way back.

She looked at him, and her teeth flashed white. In daylight, skin browned and eyes bright, she was not so old after all.

She took the knife by the pointed blade and offered it to him. He saw her hands were streaked with black slimy stuff and speckled with fish scales that the sea had failed to wash away. The stink of blood and brine was strong. The sea glittered, the gulls screamed, the knife gleamed, and he took it.

Stepping up to the block through the shifting water, he was full of the pungent air and a surreal sense of groundlessness. He pushed the camera around on its strap until it dropped down his back, out of the way. The woman stepped to one side, keeping her distance, and the dog wandered off, giving up the chance of offal. He took a breath and looked out over the sea, and then down into the bucket. There were the fish, cold and dead, looking back. He dipped his hand in and chose one, his skin crawling. A chill soft spiky thing, all wrong in his hand, he gripped it tight as he lifted it out, and tried not to look in its eye. As he placed it on the bloody block, it gave a quick jerk under his hand, and a sound of horror jumped out of his mouth before he could stop it.

She laughed, a deep, rich sound this time, came close and placed her hand over his to hold it steady, the fish flat beneath. The hand, warm, and the fish, stone cold, and his skin between was numb.

'Nerves,' she said, taking his knife-hand instead and guiding it to the head, under the gills which were pink slices notched in the satin flesh. 'It's dead, just nerves, that's all. Like a chicken.'

She smelled like biscuits and fish and her hair, wiry, tickled his face as the sea breeze blew it across. She pushed his knife-hand down firmly. There was a sickening crunch under his fingers and the wicked little blade moved through the fish to meet the block beneath. He allowed himself to breathe, and forced himself to look at the stuff that oozed out. She didn't give him time to think but guided him to sweep the head out of the way with the knife and move down to the tail.

He pulled his hand away. 'OK. OK. I can do it,' he said, through gritted teeth, feeling his treacherous stomach lurch.

He knew she raised her eyebrows as she stepped back, but she said nothing and he kept his eyes on the knife, on the fish. He liked that she didn't laugh again. She stood quietly in the thinning water with her fishy hands shoved in pockets, and watched, quietly, letting him concentrate. This time the sinewy sensation was not such a surprise and he cut off the tail and slid it to one side with no difficulty. She didn't interfere as he made a ragged incision up the belly, and he all but forgot her presence there beside him as he wrestled with the knife and the resistant flesh, nothing as smooth or as easy as she'd shown him.

When he was done, he laughed softly to himself and shook his head as he lifted the ragged flesh and dipped it in the water to rinse it, placing it like a bedraggled offering beside the first pristine fillet. He looked up, but she didn't laugh at him. She took a penknife from the depths of her jacket instead, clicked it open and came back to the block without speaking. She dipped her own hand in the bucket, found a fish, and got to work. He chose his second and got on with it beside her.

Neither of them spoke, but Evan watched her deft movements surreptitiously and tried to match his own to them. She

79

cleaned four fish to every one of his, but he worked doggedly on, nicking his finger only once on the knife, joining his own blood to that on the stone. He forgot about the smells. He forgot about the fish being dead. He forgot about Lorna and about Belfast and about Luca and about coronavirus. There was just the sound of the waves and the hungry birds and the companionable silence, his feet in the water, his mind intent.

Together they worked their way through, until there was nothing but a pool of shit and blood in the bucket, and the tide was almost gone. Without being asked, he waded out a little into the last of the water, letting it lick over the top of his expensive boots, and swished the bucket several times through the water, cleaning it out. When he straightened, he saw that she had wrapped his three scrappy fillets in a broad brown kelp leaf. She held it out to him with a nod and the hint of a smile.

'Your dinner,' she said. 'Blocken, they are. Coalfish. Grill them, bit of butter and salt, but mind the bones.'

Clicking at the dog, she took her bucket and her rod and strode off up the sand.

'Thank you,' he called to her retreating back, but knew by now not to expect an answer. As he turned for home the bright sea beside him was alive with huge bright wings, as the gulls celebrated the departure of the ugly dog with swoops and shrieks and squabbles.

Chapter 13

———

THE NEXT MORNING FRANK was sitting on a thick grass cushion on the bank beside the lane, pretending to look at the sea.

He held something on his lap, but Evan couldn't make out what it was from his doorway. As he closed the door gently behind him it scraped on the tiles, and the big man rose slowly and came towards him. Evan put a smile on his face and waited. Frank was bearing something wrapped in tinfoil. He didn't stop when he reached Evan but strode right past him and up to the doorstep.

'Maggie says I'm to put this on your step, not give it to you,' he said. 'Fucked if I know what all this palaver is about. Fucking ridiculous carry-on altogether, isn't it?'

'That's really kind of her, Frank. Please do thank her for me. There's really no need, though, because—'

'I'm seventy-three, like.'

Frank came heavily back down the short path and out onto the lane as if he were leaving. He stopped a few metres away. Hands on his hips, he surveyed the expanse of sea with a proprietorial air.

'Seventy-three,' he repeated, shaking his head. 'Do you

fucking think I'm worried about a bit of flu?' He looked at Evan straight, 'Do you?'

Evan laughed, a nervous sound, and shook his head.

'Fucking stroke'll carry me off. Or heart attack. Something with a bit of wallop,' Frank said. He resumed his staring out to sea.

'Well, the news says—'

'The news,' Frank spat the word out as if it was dirty. 'Sure what the fuck do them English cunts know about over here? What, am I not allowed to go near me own kin? The son of my own, and the grandkids up the hill, there? Treating me like a fuckin' leopard, for fuck's sake?'

This was obviously a sore point, so Evan said nothing, adjusted the camera strap around his neck and waited.

The movement caught Frank's attention. 'What d'you do with that thing then?'

Evan almost replied, take pictures? But the sound of this was rude, even in his head.

'You a journalist or something?' Frank's eyes were suddenly narrowed, as if paparazzi had been discovered lurking in his garden hedge, on the lookout for scandal.

'God no!' Evan held the camera up and looked at it as if he'd never seen it before. 'I'm, well, I'm in finance?'

Frank looked at him blankly.

'Wealth management, that sort of thing.'

Pause. Frank was still looking pointedly at the camera.

'Well, this is, well, it's sort of a hobby. Well, I'm trying to get the hang of it but it's quite—'

'What d'you do with the pictures, then?'

Evan looked at him, puzzled. 'Nothing! I mean, they're digital, you know? So I can, well upload them, choose the ones that turn out right. Ones I like, you know? Haven't had many of those, so far . . .' He laughed bashfully.

'Like, on the computer? Upload them on the computer?'

'Eh, yes. On the computer. You can edit them—'

'Did you put Grace Kielty on the computer yesterday?'

Evan went blank, then blanched as he connected the name to the still figure on the rocks the day before.

'Oh! No! God no! It's not like that! You mean, social media! No! You can't – I wouldn't—'

The man was staring out to sea again, but there was something in the set of his jaw which told Evan that the subject wasn't dead yet.

'Look, Frank. Honest, I don't put any photos on social media. It's just, like my own personal files, that's all. Like you'd keep photos in, I don't know, like a shoebox or something?'

The man looked at him and jerked his chin up sharply, to say keep going.

'I just choose subjects – things – to photograph, that take my fancy—'

Frank looked square at him again and Evan heard the echo of his own words.

'Jesus! No! I don't mean Grace took my fancy – I mean, she's a lovely—'

'She's had it rough. The folks round here, we look out for Gracie, you know what I mean?'

Evan nodded madly, and shook his head at the same time. 'Absolutely! Yes, of course, I understand, but listen, I just thought, well.' He paused, to try to clarify what he had thought. 'The whole scene was so calm . . .' He saw it again in his mind now. 'She was just a part of the – of the rocks and the sea, you know? The stillness. The absolute, unbelievable stillness. It was quiet, the sun – after the sea the other day, when I nearly . . .'

He remembered the urge he'd had on the beach, to raise the camera and catch something, elusive, from the air, that fleeting moment of peace, content, serenity – something magical that had touched him anyway, even if he didn't know what it was called. The woman had just been part of it, that's all. The human part connecting it all together, earthing it.

'Well, like I say, she's had it rough. Gracie.'

'What – how did she . . .?'

'Ah now.' Frank shook his head. 'That'd be telling, like.'

Evan nodded quickly, looked at the ground, *of course.*

'Went off, didn't she?' Frank said. 'Always a bit . . .' He circled a finger at his temple. 'Spacey, you know? Sitting in fields, staring at stuff, walking around with bunches of grass and flowers and shit. Like a hippy. Drove the Ma distracted, Elsie Kielty as was. Couldn't get a drop of work out of her at school or in the shop either. It's Becky has the shop now, round girl with glasses? Well. Went off to England, our Gracie, dunno where, exactly, wanted to be an artist or something. Left the family, her sister, and old Elsie worried sick. Sure – she couldn't mind herself here, among her own. How would she do over there?'

Evan shook his head.

'Dunno what happened. Nothing said about it, but Elsie had to go over and fetch her. Fetch her back. She was away for a week, maybe two, Elsie was, and then they came home together. Ah, there was nothing to her when she got home, poor Gracie. Thin as a rake. That was about thirty years ago, maybe. Not right in the head after that, at all. My Maggie says drugs, seeing as it was the eighties and all, but I dunno. She never came out of the house for a while, anyway. When she did. Well.'

Frank shrugged and turned to go. He shook his head as he made his way back across the crunching stones. The day was still and calm around his retreating shape.

The scent of something rich and delicious wafted up from the dish on the step behind him.

'Tell Maggie I appreciate it!' Evan called.

Frank didn't turn around, but raised a big hand and walked on.

*

In the house his phone rang.

It took a moment for Evan to recognise the sound. He rested his behind on the sunny little wall and watched Frank disappear round the corner.

The ringing stopped.

Once again, the silence came down like a tangible thing, enhanced by the shushing of the sea far out, the foreshore slimy with brown weed in a tangle, the seabirds quietly grumbling as they floated like sugar on the surface.

Turning away, he went to the door and took in Maggie's offering from the step. No wonder Frank carried that belly around. The woman could cook. He peeled back the tinfoil and peered inside. Toad in the hole, today. He stuck his finger into the pastry just because he could, and extracted a small, juicy sausage, still warm, still fragrant. The casserole dish in one hand, the sausage in another, he walked thoughtfully around the small dark room, munching.

He took the dish to the stuffed armchair he'd shoved beside the window and sat down with it on his knee, finding a fingerful of crispy pastry. Savouring it, he looked out and enjoyed the peace and quiet and the view framed by thick walls, thin window.

The phone rang again.

'Evan?'

'Hi Lorna.'

He waited, drawing in the dust on the tabletop with a greasy finger. There were grass stains on his jeans, he noticed for the first time, from a tussle with the ancient scythe yesterday, and his trainers were crusted with sand.

'I need you to take Luca.'

There was a sharp move into focus, as if she'd wiped a mirror clean of mist. 'What?'

'I can't manage, that's all. He is your son, too, you know.'

He waited.

'I'm flat out, trying to resource everyone, working all the

hours god sends. You've no idea, there's no PPE available anywhere and I've to find a supply for my whole fucking division. And of course Julie's cracking up with all the extra hours I need her – you know how difficult Luca can be. It's impossible.'

She never, ever swore. Her voice was high, stressed, on the verge of tears. He stopped doodling on the table, feeling his old life flooding back.

'Are you there?' she said, into the silence.

'Yes.' He didn't like that she was upset.

'She says she can't handle him. You know he can't go to just anyone, there's no provision – and I'm absolutely stuck. So. I need you to have him for a while. I'm an essential worker, they say . . .' she huffed a laugh and he could hear her small pride. 'I need to be in the office, and there's no one else.'

'How?' he asked instead. 'We're not allowed to travel, go to different houses.'

'I'll say we're just going for exercise, drop him off.'

Trust Lorna. She had it all thought out already, knowing he'd agree.

'Monday, OK?'

She sounded tired when she said it, and he knew what that felt like. A fly buzzed on the window, drawing his attention to the beach, to the sea, to the long stretch of sky outside as if the world had taken its lid off.

'Yes, that's fine, let's do that,' he said, as if he were arranging a dinner or a casual appointment.

'Oh thank god,' she said. 'That's such a relief, you've no idea. Look, thanks for – for not being difficult about things. We can keep in touch, you can call me, and will you get Luca to text me, let me know how he's getting on – I'm not sure how he'll be, you know he's used to me being there, he's not good with change—'

'What time?'

'What?'

'What time on Monday?'

As if he had anything pressing to do, somewhere else to be. He had to concentrate to remember what day this was. Saturday?

'Oh. Where are you?' she laughed, embarrassed. 'I don't even know where you are!'

He told her the address and heard her write it down. 'I have absolutely no idea where that is,' she said. 'Is it OK?'

'What d'you mean?'

'Is it a nice place? You doing all right, there?'

He let a pause hang in the air between them. 'Sure, it's fine. Right by the beach.'

'Oh, he'll love that.'

Evan said nothing.

'Evan—'

'Yes?'

'OK, nothing. That's fine. OK. Monday it is, thanks so much for being—'

'Like you say. He's my son, too.'

'Yes.'

'Right, then.'

'Bye.'

'Bye.'

The air hissed with silence as he hung up, but he was no longer alone. The half-eaten food sat precariously on the edge of the armchair, but he was no longer hungry. The hollow eyes of the little bird skull looked inquisitively at him where he stood, thinking about Luca. Thinking about his son.

Part Two

—

Part Two

Chapter 14

———

A LITTLE BELL JINGLED as Evan entered the shop.

Tucked into the corner was a tiny new sink, with soap dispenser and towels above it, the plaster on the walls around it still pink as new skin.

'Twenty seconds at least,' came a voice from behind the counter.

'Sorry?' Evan was still looking at the sign.

'You gotta wash your hands for twenty seconds at least. In between your fingers, like. Not just a quick wet. Or you can hum "Happy Birthday to You", twice. Same as the counting.'

Evan looked at her. 'Really?'

'Yep. Really,' she said, and her voice brooked no dissension. 'It's better than the sanitiser. That gives you dermatitis.'

At the sink he asked, 'Do I need to sanitise the tap then, before I touch it?'

'What?'

'Well, other people have been in, haven't they? Washing their hands?'

There was a pause while she looked at him, thinking. 'You can if you like,' she allowed, eventually, and then brightened. 'But if you wash your hands carefully, sure, you'll kill any virus you've picked up from the tap.'

Evan shrugged and smiled, and turned the tap.

It felt inappropriate, the soaping and rubbing and rinsing under her watchful eye. Even more inappropriate, he realised, as he dropped his limp towel into a bin under the sink, took her nod of approval, and lifted a clattering basket, were the strains of Handel coming over the sound system, as incongruous as an exotic bird in a thorn bush. *The Pastoral.* He shook his head, and headed down the aisle.

He chose things a boy might like. Pot Noodle. Coconut snowballs. Tomato soup and white bread. Coco Pops. When the basket was heaped he brought it to the till and, as directed, stood back onto a new red circle on the floor.

'Oh my god,' Becky said, blinking at his load.

'Excuse me?'

'You're going to give yourself Type-2 with all this.'

He looked at her blankly, as the music layered up and gathered energy and volume overhead. 'Eh. It's not for me, actually.'

She folded her arms and looked at him. He noticed the smudge was back, in exactly the same place on her glasses. Couldn't she see it? Couldn't she wipe it?

'It's for my son,' he said loudly, across the space between them. 'He's coming to stay.'

Her eyes, already enlarged behind the glasses, opened alarmingly. 'Stay? Sure, it's *Stay-Safe-Stay-Home.* He can't come to stay.' She pointed to a rainbow poster overhead, as if this explained the difficulty.

Evan looked at the basket. She should start to slide things through, any minute. She didn't.

'His mum's an essential worker. Getting PPE for the NHS. No one to mind him but me.'

She narrowed her eyes, computing the issue of separate homes for mum and dad, the import of the magic initials NHS and PPE, and then she nodded. 'Right then.'

He nodded at the basket. 'So. Becky. Can you—'

She put her hand on the wire and stopped. 'You really

want to feed him this stuff? You really need to cut down on the sugar, here. Balance it out, a few complex carbs, like, your pasta or your rice on Aisle Three. Doesn't have to be whole-meal if he's picky, you know? And definitely more green stuff, more coloured fruits, like.'

He nodded slowly. 'OK . . .'

She brightened instantly. 'Right, well, like I say, go to Aisle Three for your carbs, soup and all is in Aisle Six, and the fresh fruit and veg is there behind you, you walked right past it on the way in, I couldn't believe it. And you know, there's nothing wrong with fish fingers – the freezers are down at the back. You can leave this basket with me, take another one, sure, and I'll put all this muck back on the shelves.'

She dismissed him with a nod and another smile, and like a chastened schoolboy he fetched a new basket and retreated into the relative privacy of Aisle Three. Lorna and this woman would get on like a house on fire, he thought. Or destroy one another on sight.

The bell tinkled again, and a loud voice could be heard through the shop. 'Oh hi, Becky! Oskar, don't do that. How nice to see you!'

He heard Becky say something in a quiet voice, not at all the one she'd used for him, and the new arrival laughed, a jingly sound that had taken practice.

'Oh god, what next? We washed our hands before we left home, didn't we, Lexy? We don't need to use that funny little sink, do we? Anyway, we've got squirt, haven't we, if we need it? Such a funny idea, Becky, you're so funny! Now. Come on, kids, we've only a second to choose something nice before we head to Dad's. We're sneaking in, Becky, so we are, being a bit sneaky and going to see Dad – a bit of cabin fever, driving me nuts – don't tell anyone! Now, go on then, quick – you can have anything you like as long as it's not chocolate.'

There was a pause, some small feet running, and Evan heard the new arrival sigh.

'Well!' the voice said. 'It's been an absolute age, hasn't it? I'm never here at all, any more, flat out, honest to god, it's no joke.'

Becky said something, low.

'Och yes, yes. Oskar's six now, and Lexy'll be four in a few weeks, would you believe it? Seems like no time since we were sitting in Mrs McGee's class, throwing rubbers at the boys, doesn't it?'

A murmured response.

'Oh no I'm a mess, an absolute wreck – I know it! It's all go, you've no idea, home schooling now – it's a nightmare – and working from home – no escape!'

Again the laugh, and a pause. Evan picked up a box of Frosties and put it back again quickly.

'But hey – what about you, Becky? You haven't changed a bit! What are you up to, these days?'

He heard Becky brace a little, and say, 'This is me, Caitlin. What you see is what you get.'

'Aww, sure you've your mum to look after, haven't you?' The new voice was consoling. '—I always thought you were so good, staying here like you did, while the rest of us . . . sure, you've a heart of gold, haven't you?'

There was a long silence in which Evan imagined Becky's stare.

'Anyway, how is your mum? You'll have to tell her I was asking for her.'

He came out of Aisle Three duly laden, to hear Becky say, 'I will if you want, but she's completely gaga. Bonkers, Caitlin. She hasn't a clue who I am, never mind you. Thinks the cat's the parish priest and eats the houseplants if I don't keep them out of reach. Now. Is that all for you, then? That's two thirty-four please.'

Two shine-haired children had put their sweets up on the counter, and Evan could see their mother pinken, and push around in her handbag for her purse. He noticed that she hadn't been directed to the big red circle two metres from the till, like everybody else. Becky indicated the card reader on the counter wordlessly.

'Oh good, you take cards here now?' the woman tried, brightly. 'Well, isn't that great? Moving with the times. Good for you, good for you.'

She bleeped her card.

Becky smiled tightly and tore off the receipt, scrumpled it up in her fist. 'No receipts, sorry,' she said, not sounding it. 'It's the guidelines.'

'OK, well, fair enough. Aren't they strange old times, though?' said the woman, still smiling, as she shepherded her children to the door. Clanging it open she paused, tossed her hair back over her shoulder and said, 'It was nice to see you, Becky, really it was. Take care of yourself! Byeee!'

'Byeee!' echoed Becky, twinkling her fingers and baring her teeth.

As the door sprang shut again Evan dumped his basket on the counter and saw her shoulders sag. 'Old friend?' he asked sympathetically, stepping back without being told.

Becky took off her glasses and rubbed them on the hem of her sweater. When she put them back on the smudge was gone and she looked straight at him. 'Every day,' she said.

He looked at her.

'Every bloody day I put my thumb right here—' she pointed to the spot on her glasses that she had just cleaned '—and d'you know why?'

Evan shook his head quickly. 'No. Why?'

'Because then I can choose who I want to see and who I want to be just a *blur*.'

He looked at her.

'That,' she said dully, beginning to take items from his basket and bleep them through, 'was a Blur.'

Chapter 15

———

SHE RUBBED HER BARE FOOT against its belly and the dog moaned with pleasure, that crazy ear flopping back against the soft rug. Smiling despite herself, she sighed as she turned back to the sewing machine, determined to start again, to keep at it. All around her were coloured scraps, her favourite of the moment a bright blue dotted with little daisies. The quilt was taking shape now, a challenging Liberty print, but it was coming along nicely. She should make the deadline easily at this rate, but today for some reason she was dithering and distracted.

'Go on, then, you stupid bugger,' she said, getting up and opening the back door so that the scents and the sounds of the day spilled in. 'Out you go – clear off and annoy the chickens and leave me in peace to do some work.'

The dog drooped its head at her tone and slunk out onto the grass. It'd rub itself silly there, she knew, easing the pain of the old wounds and luxuriating in the spring sunshine. She listened. The croon of her hens told her it was sniffing around the coop, a bad sign – there must be foxes again. Her mind wandered from the colours in her hand and followed the dog around the lush garden, as it checked the corner of the big wall where the old stone was crumbling to let the fox in;

pissed against the greenhouse to mark its territory; scratched the scent from the flowerbed, snapped at a drowsy bee.

The bay would be a-sparkle over the wall, she knew, resting her chin on her fist – the tide right out and perfect for harvest, the ground underfoot nice and firm for the donkey's neat hooves. They could go to the beach, the first trip of the year for seaweed, and no tourists around to point and take pictures on their phones, to ask could they pet the dear little creature, to say *ewww* at the seaweed spilling over the panniers. They were all locked safely away in their horrid little houses in the city, where they belonged, and the place was her own.

'Kelp, then,' she said suddenly, pushing the blocks away from her, muddling the blues and the yellows and the reds carelessly. 'It's still work, isn't it.'

She got to her feet and stretched, glorying in the movement after stillness, the silence, the length of the morning left, the gleam of the light through the window. Pulling an elastic from her wrist she fought with her unruly hair to tie it back. Still thick, it was now the consistency of straw; salt and pepper through and through, with a mind of its own. Better out of the way. Patting it down she went quickly into the little cloakroom and the dog came lolloping inside at the squeak of the door. She stamped her feet into one boot, then the other, ignoring the gritty little lumps inside against her bare feet, and opened the front door to test the weather.

'Poncho or cardi?' she asked the dog as she pulled it wide.

The townie stood there looking at her, his hand raised stupidly as if he'd been just about to knock.

'Oh!' he blushed, and smiled.

The dog pushed past her, barking and curling its lip.

The townie stopped smiling and stepped back, waiting for her to call it, to quiet it.

She said nothing, and watched him eye the dog as it snarled and snapped, watched it stiffen its legs and increase the volume.

'Will it bite?' he called.

She put her head to one side and looked at him through the noise. 'That depends.'

To her surprise he laughed, a looser sound than she'd expected from him. She liked it. The dog quietened suddenly and went to sniff his legs instead. He looked down at it warily, rubbed his fingers at it in a tentative greeting.

'What's his name?'

He didn't bend to pat it, of course. No one ever did.

'What?' She pretended deafness.

'The dog. What's his name?'

She shrugged. 'Dog.'

He laughed again. His face went wide and open when he did it, as if it took him by surprise too.

'Aren't you meant to be staying safe and staying home?' she said, pointedly.

Once again, his smile disappeared, as if she could switch the lights on and off at will. 'Oh yes, sorry,' he said. 'I'm not – I'm just – I wondered about bedding.'

She looked at him.

'It's my son. Sorry. He's coming to stay. There's no one to – I wondered – could I maybe hire another set from you? Just, there's only the one set of blankets, and—'

'There's only the one bed.'

He looked crestfallen, and nodded, as if an argument had been lost. She wondered who had made him this way, so damn craven, all the bounce sucked out. There was no amusement in baiting him at all – it was like slapping a baby.

'What age is your boy?'

He creased his forehead. 'He's eight?'

She nodded, decisively. 'I'll be down to you in a while.'

She clicked at the dog and closed the door as it trotted back inside. She could imagine the man still standing there, scratching his head, wondering what had been decided. She smiled again at herself, and the dog wagged what was left of its tail.

'Let's go get old Dolly,' she told it, lifting her cardigan, and they went out the back door into the wonderful sun. She took her time going down the rows of growing things in the shelter of the big wall, forgetting the townie, forgetting everything, in the joy of being outdoors in spring.

There was old Dolly peeking over the fence, the immense ears like radar following her approach, a wide brown eye tracking her progress. Behind the donkey the grumpy old goat which kept it company and cleared the nettles and the ragwort from the pasture. Its name, she thought with amusement, was Goat.

'Sorry, Doll, gotta get something first,' she said with a handful of grass, and the donkey snaffled it up and tossed its head as if it were young. She stroked its nose, deliciously soft and hard at once, and the donkey chomped contentedly.

After a minute she turned away and went to the big shed at the side of the fence. Slipping back the bolt she hauled the doors wide to let some light in. The place smelled of dust and quiet as she looked about, breathing it in. There were the donkey-panniers just inside the door, dried and clean and waiting since last autumn, and they slid and prickled under her hands as she began to shift them, to drag them outside. The dog ran out into the light and lay on the grass, panting. She dragged the panniers onto the grass and then went back inside, looking for something else.

The donkey scraped the ground with a dainty hoof as things banged and clanged inside and then she emerged, dusty, with a striped and faded thing that she dumped beside the panniers.

'Phew!' she brushed a net of web from her hair and dusted her hands. The dog sniffed at the thing and looked at her.

'Hammock,' she told him, as if he was stupid, and bent to spread it out.

*

As they approached the rented house, she saw a small thin figure standing a little way off on the lane, just in front of the rental, staring out to sea. A boy. The dog growled at his stillness and edged closer to her legs, and the donkey tossed its head. She yanked the rope to make it come on. There was a holdall at the boy's feet she saw, as she came nearer, and a pair of wellies propped up against it. The son. Townie junior. He didn't turn at their approach, but stood on, looking quietly at the sea as it fussed away down the beach, dotted with seabirds like pearls along its pretty edge.

She'd thought he'd have one of those tight haircuts and wear those stupid white trainers; be racing around shouting, throwing things at the seagulls, freaking out at all the space, the way the other ones did, the noisy bastards, the little thugs. Instead there he stood, a thin line against the green of the bank, his arms bare and white and motionless, his hands empty.

There was something so unusual about the boy's stillness, so unlikely, that the donkey took it as a threat and didn't want to go on.

'Hi!' Grace shouted to it. 'Hup!' and pulled it and smacked its rump with the end of the rope until it moved on again reluctantly, the panniers swinging slightly as they all went down the incline towards the little house, their feet kicking the odd little stone out of its hollow, making it trundle, clacking, down the hill.

Still the boy didn't move. Behind him she saw the thick door of the house open, and the townie come out quickly, drying his hands on a tea towel, his glasses wonky as if he'd been caught off-guard. She waited to hear him call the boy's name, to see the kid turn, but instead the father went right up to him without speaking, and all the way around in front of him, and then he smiled and creased up his eyes and rubbed the boy's shoulders, and then he began twisting his hands and dancing his fingers about.

The boy watched for a moment and then his own hands rose and danced in response, telling, pointing back up the lane to the last turning point of the road, where maybe his mother had left him off, shooing him to go on, to knock on the door, to find his dad, she had to go back.

Out of the corner of his eye, the father saw her watching. She felt as if she'd intruded on something private, intimate, and yanked the donkey forwards savagely.

'Hup, Dolly, will you!' she said, and the dog slunk out of the way, off to sniff something behind the house.

The pair turned to look as she came the last of the way towards them, the burden sticking out like great big warts from the donkey's back. She stopped when she reached them and the donkey lipped her shoulder as she looked from one to the other. They were very alike.

'What have you got there?' the townie asked, glancing behind her.

'Bedding,' she said, and looked at the boy.

He dropped his eyes and watched the ground at his feet.

'Humph,' she said, and reached out her hand. She took his small fingers, and they were warm bones in her palm. He looked up, alarmed, but didn't pull them away. She put the end of her rope into the hand and closed the fingers around it. She nodded at him and turned to the little donkey. The boy looked down at the rope and up again with huge eyes at the animal and tightened his grip until his knuckles were white.

'Stand, Dolly,' she said unnecessarily, going down its back to the panniers.

The townie came up beside her. 'He's deaf,' he said quietly, as if the boy could hear him, as if she couldn't work it out, but she said nothing. She was busy heaving the duvet and pillows out, where a hem had got stuck on a pointed wicker shoot.

'Here,' he said quickly, and leaned across her to unhook it. He smelled like biscuits and stale coffee. The load came loose suddenly, and she took a quick step back to balance under the weight.

'Take these on in,' she said, puffing, dumping everything into his arms so that he could barely see over it all.

'Will – will the donkey be OK with him?' he asked, looking round at the boy.

'He looks harmless enough,' she retorted, and went round the back to the second pannier, which now listed like a sinking ship under the weight of its load. From the corner of her eye she saw that the man had gone inside, and that the boy was staring at the animal on the end of his rope as if it were a dragon. She lifted the long roll of the hammock and slung it over her shoulder.

'Now, Dolly,' she said. She clicked her tongue and reached out and took back the rope with her free hand. It was warm where the boy had gripped it. She walked towards the door of the house and the donkey came without hesitation. The boy followed them, stumbling over his own feet and staring. Grace stopped and looked at him and frowned, and then glanced behind him, lifting her eyebrows. His face brightened with understanding. He turned and scuttled back, lifted the holdall, the boots, and came running back towards her, his hungry eyes on the donkey again.

Looping the rope over the boot scraper, she nodded to the boy to go past her, to go inside, and patted the donkey to say sorry for her roughness earlier, and followed him in. The boy kept looking back over her shoulder to the bright doorway where the animal waited, its ears rotating and its eyes bright. The townie was standing inside, his load dumped higgledy-piggledy on the sofa and his smile tense and pointed at his son.

Grace turned away and carried her burden to the opposite end of the house, where the kitchenette ran on into a deep little alcove with a bookshelf at the back. She flumped the hammock down on the floor. The noise made the man turn sharply. He's as tense as a guitar string, she thought, ready to snap.

'Where's the wee steps?' she said.

He hurried to get the little stepladder from the bedroom and brought it, opening it on the way with a rattle, and clicking the lock into place.

He set it ready at her feet and looked at her quizzically.

She liked that he waited. That he didn't ask.

Taking one end of the hammock in her hand, she clicked open the carabiner and climbed the steps with her knees creaking, holding tight to the top as she went. She reached up, holding her breath, found the loop of metal on the ceiling and, click, it was on.

The man was nodding below her, smiling, his hands on his hips, looking up.

'Ah!' he laughed, and turned to the boy. His fingers danced but the boy didn't understand and stood warily against the jamb of the bedroom door. Grace climbed slowly down, ignoring the pain in her hip, shifted the steps and climbed again, found the second hook, clicked the carabiner in place. Right.

The hammock hung and swayed gently now, a giant pastel banana, as she climbed down and put the steps aside. She looked at the others.

She was used to the quiet. Liked it. But with so many people in the one room, and one of them a little boy, this particular silence was oppressive and strange. Some dynamic she was missing, some underground rumble she'd failed to register. She felt heat build in her face as they stared at her, the father tense and anxious, fluttering fingers, reassuring. The boy frightened, foreign, the donkey-treat forgotten, everything new and dark and overwhelming. He looked as if he might cry, might run for the door, and away.

'Here,' she said, and took up a pillow, put it inside so the hammock swallowed it up. The duvet next, and it filled out the belly like a pelican's beak. She pushed it down a little flatter and nodded at the boy. Patted the outside of the hammock like a donkey. He took a step forwards, beginning to understand.

She raised a finger, *now watch*, and kicked off her boots one after the other until she stood on the floor in her bare feet. Taking the outer edge of the hammock firmly in one hand, she leaned back against it and flipped up her feet neatly and lay back. The hammock sucked her in, and a laugh popped out unexpectedly like a burp. For a moment she relaxed and felt herself sway, a child again, and the musky half-darkness of the hammock's interior held her firm as she swung and remembered, the taut fabric holding her firm and strong. She breathed, just for a second, loose and free.

When she listened again there was nothing but stillness outside. They were just standing there, were they, looking at the swinging hammock with the crazy old lady inside.

She'd forgotten again, that she looked out of fifty-year-old eyes.

She stuck her head up over the edge. Aware of her dishevelled hair, her warm cheeks, she saw the boy's face shine as he came towards her. The father was grinning too, shaking his head, his eyes appreciative, so it wasn't so bad.

Grunting, she swung herself out, landing with a clump on the floor, and held the hammock still for the boy to try. He was right beside her now, like a bird tempted by crumbs in her palm. She held still. His hand reached out, but didn't take hold of the rough fabric as she'd expected. Instead he touched her arm, once, gently, and he looked at her for a moment as if reading her face.

She tutted, shaking him off, and jerked her chin towards the hammock.

'Just mind he doesn't fall out on his head,' she said, passing the man who stepped aside to give her space '—he's daft enough looking as it is.'

Then she was outside, the sun bright in her eyes and the donkey already turning, the rope swinging, heading for the wide empty beach and the cool wavelets and the long salty fronds of kelp in the shallows.

Chapter 16

———

EVAN LOOKED AT THE BULGING HAMMOCK; the faded stripes of pink and blue and yellow the colours of an old stick of rock, a forgotten deckchair, swinging gently in the dark room.

He nudged the thing gently. There were solid bones in there, a breathing thing, a whole bag of feelings and needs and thoughts that he couldn't see, couldn't reach. He nudged it again, a little more sharply, and Luca's head appeared, hair sticking up like hers in the mornings.

They looked at each other.

What would you like for tea?

Not hungry. Had sandwiches on the way.

The head disappeared. Sharp pointy bits grew and shifted about in the sling and then a tell-tale light glowed.

'That's that then,' he said to the empty room. 'Right.'

He turned to the bag dumped on the floor, just for something to do. He could clear a shelf or two of the bookshelf in the alcove, put the boy's stuff there. He felt the need to keep busy now that he had company, although for weeks he had luxuriated in laziness, had spent whole afternoons sitting on the wall outside watching the sea, or curled on the sofa here, drifting in and out of a fuzzy kind of sleep.

He shifted a damp and dog-eared selection of summer fiction from the bookshelf to the floor alongside and fetched soapy water, gave the shelves a wipe. Then in went pyjamas, underwear, changes of jeans and t-shirts, the nice fluffy blue hoodie Luca preferred. As he stacked the things tidily, the scent of home wafted out and filled the room. For so long, her clothes, his clothes, the house, the bedding and curtains, the baby's sleepsuits and vests, everything in the house had smelled of this clean linen scent, fresh, sharp and totally Lorna's. It brought the feel of her skin sharply back, the electric crack of her laughter when truly amused and not just pretending.

He buried his face in a clean t-shirt and breathed her in. She could have come down the hill with the lad, surely. Seen where he was, had a word. Not even a call from behind the wheel as the big 4x4 circled round and left just the boy, skinny and hesitant standing there, taunting him with his vulnerability, with the distance between them.

He put the t-shirt on the shelf with the others, and stroked it gently. Then he went to the hammock again and pushed it so that it swung wide and his son's head popped up like a jack in the box.

Hey!

Come on, that's for sleeping in, and it's not bedtime!

The tousled head disappeared again. At home, it was Lorna who called the shots, but she wasn't here to drive the boy's itinerary, that manic round of learning and visiting and healthcare, to push Evan away and say he didn't know, didn't understand.

He pulled the lip of the hammock back and peered in. Luca scowled up.

Seriously. Come on. I mean it, Luca. And leave that phone here too.

It was really difficult to sign and hold the fabric open. He stuck an elbow in, to help.

Now.

He put on his sternest face.

Where are we going?

Out.

Luca sighed. Where to? There's nothing here.

Outside, they paused to look at the sea. The tide was fully in, and there was only a matter of a few feet between the waves and the little bank on which the lane ran, and on which they stood.

What was it like, in the city? Evan asked.

The boy watched his hands moving and let the water roll in and out for a moment.

Boring, really. I miss school.

They stood in silence again and the place looked like an empty bowl.

Mum OK?

Yeah, suppose so. Bit busy.

Evan looked at the side of the boy's face, trying to read it. Luca walked away instead, and stepped down awkwardly onto the shingle of the beach, looking around at his feet, lifting a stone and throwing it, hard, into the water. Evan sighed. Now was the time to start a friendly rivalry, he knew. He should go down alongside his son, pick up a stone and throw it further, make a game of it. Maybe teach him to skim the stone, flat against the skin of the water so that it hopped and skipped before sinking.

He sat instead, easing himself onto the knobbly grass at the bank's edge. The sky was cloudy, and a purple tinge lay on the water. Luca didn't look round for him, but bent and threw, bent and threw for another while. The wind was cool on their faces, and for the first time in days it felt like rain. Evan was comfortable on the grass. He enjoyed the sensation of the prickling grass-tips under his leaning palms, the ease of his legs stretching down to the shore and the tick-tock of his mind checking that, no – once again he was free of all deadlines and schedules – and yes – once again he could relax and do absolutely nothing. It was delicious. He hoped the boy wouldn't spoil it for him.

Luca flumped down beside him.

Will we go to the shop now? Evan asked him. Meet my friend? You'll like her.

Is she your girlfriend? Luca asked, looking away.

Evan laughed, a short harsh sound. He turned the boy back around to look at him. Course not, course she's not! Your mum's— he stopped.

They looked at each other.

What has your mum said to you, about – things?

Luca shrugged and kicked the toe of his trainer against the grit and sand, looked away. The seabirds squabbled on the rocks as the silence grew between them, as it always did.

Luca.

He tried to turn the boy again, but the thin shoulders resisted under his hands. He turned him, anyway, and signed under his bent head.

Look, it'll be OK, you'll see. Your mum. She just wants a bit of time, that's all, to get her head around things.

Luca shrugged again, and they sat quietly for a long moment. Can we go and see your other friend instead?

Evan was blank for a second. Who?

The donkey lady.

Another short laugh. Friend? She was terrifying. After a quick hesitation, he flashed his fingers, saying, Friend? She's terrifying!

To his delight Luca laughed, that strange nasal sound of the profoundly deaf, and then nodded in agreement. But she's nice too. Except for the dog.

Agreed. But maybe another day, OK? I don't feel like getting bitten today.

This time it was the boy who pushed up off the grassy bank and held his hand out, and his father who took it, and allowed himself to be hauled to his feet.

As they left the beach and rounded the corner out of sight, Grace got up slowly from her seat on the grass high above and lifted the donkey's trailing rope. She clicked at Dolly, who was grazing neatly beside her, and the beast lifted its head and moved slowly on, the panniers spilling drips of slick kelp at every nodding step, the dog padding silently alongside.

Chapter 17

SHE TOOK THE LOWER PATH one afternoon, with nothing in mind and no particular reason, just getting out from under books and quilts and seaweed and orders for a while, doing an errand or two and letting the breeze blow the cobwebs away. She carried nothing but a sharp pointed stick as she expected to return closer to the evening when the rabbits might be a bit more active. She and the dog could corner one with a little skill and a lot of luck and in that state it'd go into torpor and she'd get it for stew.

She'd done a full morning's quilting, and the thing was lovely now, even she'd have to say so. The buyer was French, the recipient English, and so she'd worked a rich royal blue and that delightful cherry red through the pattern, picking out the geometric shapes. Her mind was full of the pattern and colour of it as she walked, and the buzz of the old Singer machine in her hands, and it pleased her still, even when she was away from it. She was humming as she went along, and poking the stick into the crust of the lane with every step, making a satisfying little crunch.

As she rounded the corner to the rental she saw that for once the door was open to the fresh air. She could imagine the fingers of sun poking in around the door and feeling their way across the dark tiled floor, picking out the lines and marks in the surface and making themselves at home.

'Good,' she said.

Small wellies lay tumbled outside the door, on the grass of the lane, with a sweater in a soft heap beside them.

The boy lay on the beach, on his belly, looking intently at something, the socks on his feet waving up behind and his bare legs white as milk.

There was sand in this bay, solid and grey, from the ancient greywacke rock which made up the sheer short cliffs at its edges. This beach was much better for walking on than her own pebbly bay, so she swam here when she could, in preference. It was easier on the feet.

Easier on the belly, too, by the looks of it. She watched the boy but he didn't shift, apart from the thick dark hair blowing in the gentle breeze. Whatever he saw was taking up his full attention and he was as still as a stone.

At first she tried to walk a little more lightly, so as not to disturb him, and to make sure she got by, undetected. Then she remembered he was deaf and couldn't hear her anyway – she could march past in a bloody brass band and he wouldn't even know it. She growled at the dog beside her, just in case, and pointed away behind the house so that it bristled and ran there, thinking there were rats. It was the stuff of nightmare, that animal, when you weren't expecting it. She watched its ugly brown arse disappear around the side of the house and headed on. It'd catch her up somewhere on the lane.

She was glad it was gone when the boy suddenly twisted around, and saw her. She stopped still, as if caught stealing. He'd felt her footsteps perhaps, or smelled her. His hair was sticking up. He had narrow features, a pointy nose, like a mouse, she thought, and she could see his father in his wide eyes and the worried crease between them. She looked at him and pushed her hat back. He was a pale thing, as if the light could shine through him, almost. One of those kids they pushed around in the playground, probably. One of those kids who kept to himself, played his own games or watched from the periphery. He'd take fright now, at the sight of her, and run indoors. She waited as he pushed himself quickly up onto his feet, ignoring the grey wet of the sand on his t-shirt, on his legs, everywhere, and looking at her with wide eyes.

Then he was running towards her, not away. She took a tiny step back as he pelted up to her, scattering sand and smiling. The socks, grey and red, flapped loose from his toes, sopping and ridiculous.

He stopped in front of her, puffing, and grabbed her hand. She felt her own big fingers in his, hanging slack and surprised like sausages. He was tugging now, bringing her fingers alive inside his own, looking earnestly up into her eyes, trying to tell her something, smiling and eager. She felt her own eyes smiling back, crinkling at him without her say-so, and was surprised at herself. He kept tugging. He was trying to drag her towards something, she realised.

Come this way! Come here! his tug said.

A laugh popped out of her and she allowed herself to be pulled forwards. Her feet in their boots felt massive and heavy.

'Wait!' she said, without thinking, and then tugged back gently. He looked at her. His bare knees were grey with caked sand and the legs beneath them impossibly skinny. He watched her kick off her boots and they fell loosely on the beach – one, two.

'Ah!' she said and set each foot on the cool sand as if it were delightful, and in fact it was. The boy looked down at her feet, long and brown, striped from her sandals, and then dropped her hand quickly and sat on the sand to tug off his own wet socks and drop them anywhere. Then with a flash of a smile he was standing again and running forwards without her, confident now that she'd follow, so she did, looking past him to see where he was going. He dropped to his knees and beckoned to her to come, quick, quick.

There was a small rock, all tumbled with seaweed, half buried in the coarse sand, and the receding tide had carved a pool around it on one side. The boy was on his knees here, poking in. Shucking her poncho out of the way she joined him, feeling the cold wet of the sand on her legs, and a good stretch in the tops of her feet as she sat down on them. His finger was hoking around in the pool like a terrible worm, pulling up weed, pushing in behind, looking for something, and he'd forgotten her completely. She was happy with that. She took off her hat to let the sun onto the water and sat still beside him and waited. Her leg was up against his, they were so close, and she could feel him as a tight string of energy beside her, a wire of intent.

Suddenly he made a noise in his throat which might have been a laugh or a shout, and snatched his hand up out of the water and sat back against her in alarm, and a tiny spotted fish darted out from the seaweed fringe on the rock and began to wiggle a place to hide itself in the soft sand of the pool, under his goggling eyes.

She sat very still. The boy was leaning all his meagre weight back against her and his wet hand clasped her arm, the coarse fabric of the poncho all scrumpled up, staring at the little thing in the water which was almost gone from sight already. She held still. As the flatfish, with a last squirm of its whole body, whisked a final covering of sand over itself and disappeared, the boy let a whoosh of air out of his mouth in a slow, delighted stream and looked up at her with huge eyes. She nodded back, yes, she'd seen it, yes, it was amazing altogether and she felt her mouth curve in a smile at his astonishment.

They looked in stillness at the water, flat and empty now, until she felt the boy relax. He loosened his grip on her arm and bent forwards, trying to see the place where the little creature hid. He tapped her arm for help, without looking back. She leaned over to the pool and peered at the tiny place where the gills fluttered, two minuscule lines of movement betraying its position. She felt the boy's breath on her face, warm. She glanced at him, his face so close, and widened her eyes in a question, dipping her fingers just a little into the water. Giving them a waggle.

'Will I?' she asked.

He nodded, hard, a little afraid, and pressed himself into her again, just in case. She felt his hand again on her forearm, holding tight, and laughed softly, and went in search of the fish.

Pushing her fingers carefully into the sand she winkled out the little thing before it could escape and lifted it gently from the water. Keeping it away from the boy and moving it slowly, letting the grains stream from its pretty back until it sat, exposed, on the pale circle of her palm, she watched him. The boy leaned back a little, but his eyes were fixed on her hand, and his fingers still clasped her arm. The fish was juddering now, trying to flip itself over the edge, trying to find the sea, so she had to curl her hand round it to keep it from escaping, and she made a big show of its speed and her difficulty containing it, and the little tickly wiggles it made on her skin, until she felt him make that funny sound again and was sure, this time, that he was laughing.

Chapter 18

———

EVAN AND LUCA CLIMBED the steep little hill slowly, leaning on their thighs, breathing hard, to the scattering of sheds and outbuildings which marked the village centre. A bus stop sign stood like a lonely flag at the shuttered post office, and a group of old men took advantage of the adjoining bench to hide from the wind and their wives, huddling and smoking. Evan saw them pause in their talking. They watched him approach with the boy, saying nothing. Frank was there, holding court in the centre of the group, and he nodded at them both as they came near. 'Well,' he said.

The other old faces continued to stare, expressionless, so that Evan became conscious of his gait, of his clothes, of his hair. He felt Luca move closer beside him, head down and careful, and felt a hot flare of discomfort for him under their gathered gaze.

'Hi, Frank,' he said, walking briskly by, and hoping the kid would keep up.

'That your boy?'

Nothing for it but to stop. He smiled tightly and put his hand on Luca's shoulder to claim him. 'Yes. Yes indeed. This is Luca.'

The men looked at Luca. Luca looked at his shoes.

Always the same awkward moment, Evan thought, opening his mouth to speak.

'He simple?' asked a fat man with a drinker's nose. His expression was one of casual interest.

'What?'

'Handicapped, like? He looks a bit simple, is all.'

'No, he's not simple!' Evan was alarmed at the volume of his own voice. 'He's *deaf*.'

'Ah.' The men nodded sagely as one.

The boy's head was low. Evan's face flamed at the sight of his bent shoulders, his white neck. He took hold of the boy's arm, to move him along, keeping his smile tight on his face, wishing it wasn't always so.

'Hiya, hun!'

They stopped because Becky was there, crouched down right under Luca's nose, smiling up into his face so that they both took a quick step backwards, surprised. They hadn't seen her standing out of sight in the deep doorway of the little shop, taking the afternoon sun on her face and coming forwards quickly when she heard what was said.

'Don't you mind these old crocks.' She smiled up at Evan, but stayed low, near Luca. '—I dunno who ever elected Frank the Lord Mayor, the nosey oul gobshite.'

The last words were louder, and tossed back over her shoulder at the aged council behind her, who cackled as one, appreciative of her cheek and the view of her ample behind, nudging one another happily.

Becky straightened up and looked at them, arms akimbo. 'And whatever happened to social fuckin' distancing?' she asked in that tone of voice Evan recognised. 'Eamon Logan, you're practically on his bloody knee, and the poor NHS risking their lives to keep us all safe!'

Frank raised a finger to tell her something, but she shoved her face forwards at him and said, 'Don't be at it, Frank! You know the rules – it's only round the corner to your house from here, and I can get you grounded if you don't behave yourself!'

There was a huff of supportive laughter from the bench around him, a couple of quiet catcalls, and Frank himself grinned, delighted at the banter. He dropped the finger and called her an awful one, just like her mother before her, and Becky softened, as if at a compliment. She waited to see the men shuffle and mutter and space themselves out a little, and then with a sudden swing back around she was facing Luca again, hauling smartly at her jeans to get them up around her waist and comfy.

'Wait a minute!' she said, her finger in the air, and they all waited, quiet.

She bit her lip and squinted up her eyes behind the glasses, smiling. Evan noticed that today, the smear was gone. She bent down to Luca and finger-spelled, 'I'm Backy.'

Then she straightened, smiled and nodded vigorously, as if sheer enthusiasm would make her intelligible.

Luca glanced up at Evan, who quickly showed him, 'Becky' back, and smiled.

Luca blushed and said, 'Luca' with slow, careful fingers.

There was a short pause, and Becky squinted her eyes to think. '... Lucy? Luca?' she asked Evan at last, and grinned when he nodded.

'Well, who knew? Got something useful outta that Tech at last. Did a bit at Enrichment, in Health and Social Care, you know? But it was yonks ago.'

She turned back to the boy and made the sign for sweeties, twirling her index finger at the corner of her chin, and now he grinned, and nodded, and followed her back into the shop without waiting for his father. The men on the bench watched them go, taking long, slow drags on their cigarettes.

'Some arse on that girl, and that's a fact,' Evan heard one say, as she went out of sight into the shop, but his voice was very low, and no one answered.

Inside the shop *Madame Butterfly* was playing softly. Evan led Luca to the little sink and told him to wash his hands. Becky got busy squirting something on the counter and wiping it down, humming a little as she worked.

'D'you own the shop?' Evan asked, more out of gratitude than interest.

'Naw, it's my uncle's,' she said without looking round, her voice jiggling with the vigorous movement of her elbow. 'Lives in the South now, doesn't really bother with it.' She paused, and regarded the rack of chewing gum beside her. 'Probably keeps it going just for me, when I think about it. It's all right. Keeps a roof over our heads, in the summer months, outta buckets and spades and that kinda thing anyway. Doesn't make a fortune from the locals, and that's for sure!'

She shook her head and started polishing again.

Luca had dried his hands and was making his way slowly along the shelf of chocolate bars, looking intently at each row, although he would always take a Crunchie, in the end.

'Well, you do a very good job, I think,' Evan said, and meant it. She didn't respond, but he saw her smile a little as she scrubbed her way around to the till and started on its keyboard.

'What's the story with the woman in the little house down beside mine?' He leaned on the counter and watched his son deliberate between the shiny wrappers.

Becky put away the spray, and tucked a strand of hair behind her ear, looking at him speculatively. 'Who? Grace, d'you mean?'

'Yeah,' he said.

'What about her?'

'—Just that Frank said, well, something about her not being, well, right?'

Becky huffed contemptuously and looked him in the eye. 'There's none of us right, in the world,' she said. 'Grace is just fine, believe me. Different isn't wrong, is it?'

She looked pointedly at Luca as she said it.

Evan shook his head under her stern gaze and was glad when the boy tugged his sleeve and held up a Crunchie and a Milky Way in one hand, made as if to put them both on the counter.

He hesitated, but Becky did not.

Stop! Just one, she signed and smiled to take the sting out of it.

Luca made a face and then stuck his tongue out at her, and she laughed and did the same. They watched him return the Milky Way and tidy up the shelf, lining the bars up straight.

'Oh dear, now you'll have to spray them all,' Evan said, only half joking, but she nodded in agreement, and hunkered her elbows on the counter comfortably, to wait.

'How long's he here for?' she asked.

'Who, Luca?' Evan sighed. 'How long's any of us here for?' He watched his son. 'Well, until this lockdown thing's over, anyway, I suppose. At least he's out in the country now. A bit of fresh air. He was stuck with his mum in a cul-de-sac for the last three weeks, and they couldn't go out the door.'

'God.'

'I know – bored out of his mind. But she's a key worker or whatever they call it, so he's here with me for the duration now, I should think.'

'Och, he must miss her, poor thing,' Becky said softly, and smiled at the boy as he came over.

'I don't know,' Evan heard himself say. 'He's a funny wee lad. Doesn't do feelings much, I don't think. Does his own thing. Disconnected, sometimes. On the spectrum a bit, maybe, actually?'

He trailed off, unsure why he'd said this aloud, or how long he'd thought it.

She raised her eyebrows, and then looked at the boy beside him, who was gazing around at the shelves and the lights of the shop, his hand on the counter.

'S'pose I'd get disconnected too, sometimes, if I couldn't hear anything,' she said softly.

The orchestra was getting worked up overhead. Madame Butterfly was singing her broken heart, getting ready to die. The boy looked up at Becky and signed slowly, his hand sliding backwards and forwards over his raised palm.

'Music,' Evan said.

She blinked and laughed delightedly, 'How does he know?'

Evan laughed too, and shrugged. How do you know? he asked.

Luca took his hand and placed it on the counter, holding it there. The beautiful voice was arching overhead, painting its sorrow in sound, and the orchestra thrummed beneath it, a deep rumble. He waited; the boy's eyes fixed on his face. There was a tiny buzz in his fingertips. Astonished, he looked down at his son,

'Wow,' he said quietly. 'He can feel it.'

Becky smiled and nodded as if she'd proved a point. 'Ask him if he'd like a job,' she said.

Chapter 19

———

THE FUCKING QUAD WOULDN'T START.

There she was, all loaded up and ready to go, looking forward to blamming along on its thick tyres across the pebbles and sand towards the village and the nine o'clock bus. She was heading to town and the post office, where she'd offload her parcels, full of orders, and her work would be done for the week. But when she turned the key, the old clanker of a machine just groaned once or twice and died with a last sick burp. She cursed the thing where it sat, squat and useless like a huge frog, and plumped herself crossly down on the damp morning grass outside the shed to think about what to do next.

One, she told herself, she could either trudge to the farm for Carmichael, who'd come and fix it in his own good time, as slow and bleary as the dairy cows he trailed across the road twice daily for milking; or two, she could throw off her years and shoulder the two bags herself, old-style, and hike them up to the bus on her own two feet. They weren't that heavy.

She began unloading the bags from the quad's carrier, glad that she was ahead of herself for once, and had some time to spare before the bus left. The dog howled from the kitchen door and she growled at it to be quiet. 'Would you go and lie down?' she barked as it slunk away, and slammed the door harder than she needed to. She stumped back up the little path to the quad again. The two bags sat like boulders beside it, the top of one sagging into a curve, as if grinning. Her little phone was in her pocket, an alien thing, with the QR codes Abbie had set up by magic from her bedsit for the post office. Propping her hands on her hips she looked at the bags, which seemed to have grown larger since she'd set them down, and they looked back at her. The old goat stared out from the bars of the gate with its clever slotted eyes and whisked an ear in the warmth of the new sun.

She bent and hoisted the heaviest – the one with the double quilt for England – onto her good shoulder. With a groan that was not altogether temper she bent, heavily laden, to hoist up the second, the *Gracie's Kitchen* seaweed parcels, onto the left side, the left shoulder, the one that ached.

'Right you bastards, let's go,' she said and set off down the lane. The day was already hot.

'Plenty of time, Gracie, plenty of time,' she said, as the strap on the heavy bag cut into her right shoulder. She felt a prickle of sweat in the small of her back.

'Jesus,' she said. She hadn't even reached the corner. She wished she'd thought to bring a bottle of water, the way the townies always did, attached to them no matter where they went. One hand for the water bottle, one for their bloody phone. She heard herself make a little grumbling sound, felt it pass through her teeth and out into the air and checked herself sharply. Mad old women talked to themselves out loud. She hoisted the seaweed bag further up on her shoulder, away from the ache, and pressed her lips together firmly.

The morning sun cooked her slowly as she stumped along, panting slightly like the dog.

It was no good.

It was no good.

At the corner, she dumped the biggest bag down and

rubbed her shoulder. It was worth a small fortune, this quilt, but if she had to carry it all the way to the fucking bus she'd end up having a cardiac. As she cogitated, hands on hips and body steaming, the door of the rental banged open a little way down the little hill, and the boy, the deaf one, came charging out.

Straight away the father ran out after him, caught him by the shoulder and swung him around and shook him. The boy's head waggled back to front.

'Didn't need to do it that hard,' she said to herself and stood very still to watch.

The father's fingers danced under the boy's bent head and of course it made no sense to her at all what he was saying, but the way they both stood told its own story. The kid's shoulders were up around his ears and he wouldn't look at his father's hands. His own were shoved deep down into his pockets as if under arrest, as if he wouldn't let them say what they wanted to say. The father's face was dark, and he poked it forwards, scowling. He waggled his fingers some more and the boy looked up and stared right at him and spat a thick sound that carried all the way to her where she stood.

'Nuuuuh!'

She saw him shove his father, hard, and run away.

'Little shit,' she said, quietly.

The man held up both his hands and lifted his twisted face to the sky. 'Fuck's sake!' he bellowed, and a seagull veered overhead.

The boy used one hand to spring down onto the loose shingle of the beach and run on, scattering pebbles and making that same loud guttural sound as he went. There was nowhere to go, of course, there was only the salt sea ahead and the high rocky promontories to either side which held the little bay calm and still on even the wildest days, but he ran anyway. She remembered the feeling, that need to get away anywhere, anyhow, and she felt for him as he slipped and skidded, his feet and legs clumsy like a new foal. When he came close to the high dark rock wall he slowed and then stopped and then turned, and just stared at the sea, trapped and fuming and groaning loudly like the donkey did when it was looking for Polo mints.

She remembered that feeling, too.

Adrenaline buzzed at the memory, and she hoisted the bags again and headed down the lane, her head lowered as if she'd seen nothing. When she lifted it again, the townie was standing in the doorway, running his hands through his hair in distraction and watching the boy. 'Christ!' he said aloud.

She grunted a greeting and went to walk past.

'Look at him!' he told her, in a high voice.

She looked, and then lifted her chin to say yes, she saw, so what?

He shook his head.

She walked on. She had her own troubles and one of them was cutting into her shoulder.

'Look at him!' he called after her, in a strangled voice. '—You'd think I was trying to fucking torture him or something, not get him out into the fresh fucking air, the little bastard! Jesus!'

She turned slowly, and looked back at the man. She really did appreciate the way his language blossomed forth when he wasn't aware of it. His glasses were pushed wonky in his distress and his hair tufted up at the top like a crested grebe. But she wasn't getting involved. She lifted her chin to register that she'd heard, made a small smile shape with her mouth and walked on, leaving him standing there cursing quietly to himself, justifying his anger, his unjustifiable force.

As she trudged along, she watched the boy, who stood with his head on one side regarding the rock wall in front of him, at least five times his height. She saw him stretch a tentative hand up and take hold where the rock folded just at his shoulder, getting a grip. She knew how it would feel under his fingers, that rock, cold and slimy, still dewed from the receding tide, and treacherous. She saw him lift one leg up, sharply angled, his whole body leaning, the toe pushing to get into a crack or a fold almost at waist height, too small to see from here. He didn't look back at his father. It wasn't a bluff. He pulled himself up until he was off the shingle, and kept going.

'Christ the night,' she said under her breath. 'Wee bugger's going to try and climb that.'

She kept walking and watching him get higher and higher, expecting him to slip and skid into a bruised and angry heap on the sand at any minute, but he climbed on. Spider-like, his arm extended to find a higher hold.

She stopped. She let the bags drop, rubbing her arms absently.

The other skinny leg was groping now, the toe poking here and there in search of a slot in the rock as the fingers held all of his meagre weight, and then he was spreadeagled, stretched out wide across the high, high plane and hanging by his fingertips and the very points of his trainers.

The townie was behind her, she could tell, running across the beach – the crashing, scraping noise she heard was caused by his feet, as clumsy as his son's, strappling and floundering to get underneath the child in time, to catch him as he fell, or to be a landing pad, at least. The boy was looking up, up towards the summit of the rock, the end of his climb, and he didn't look back or down. A hand moved, found a grip, a leg moved, pushed him upwards, and all his attention was on the task in hand, all his concern was for the next place on the rock for him to reach. His little pointed buttocks strained against the shorts he wore, and his knees would be rubbed raw.

'Well,' she marvelled, and shook her head.

Any other dad would be shouting and hollering now, of course, but the townie knew there was no point. He was putting all his effort into getting to the rock before his son fell.

'Fuck!' she heard him breathe as he scattered past her, and that was all.

The boy was moving more quickly now – reach, pull, toe-grope, pull, stretch. She could almost believe he'd make it.

'Oh!' she said involuntarily as his toe slipped and he looked as if he'd go. She found her hand was at her mouth like an old lady, and snatched it away at once.

The boy recovered, took a little break, and then was climbing again, almost there, almost at the grassy plumes and safety, but the spell was broken, and she had things to accomplish today, lockdown or no lockdown.

She looked at her watch to check the time. Damn, late.

When she looked back up, the child had actually made it, and was moving on out of sight, on hands and feet like an ape, still angry, and his father stood speechless below, his hands on his hips, his neck craned back.

She shook her head and laughed softly. He'd have a long journey round by the lane to catch his son. He didn't look as if he were inclined. He was still squinting up at the high rock as though expecting the boy to reappear. His head was on one side, as if assessing the climb. Maybe he was wondering about trying it himself, kill himself another way. Bloody specky lunatic. She wouldn't put it past him.

Meanwhile, she'd missed the nine o'clock and would have to see if she could get the express to stop for her instead on its hectic way through at nine thirty – the one that took the nurses and domestics to the hospital in the town. She nodded, lifted the bags once more and set off, trudging. From the corner of her eye she saw the man look over.

'If I see him in the village I'll send him home,' she called back over her shoulder, and he raised his hand tiredly.

But the kid hadn't gone to the village. As she turned the corner, he was there on the top of the rocks high above her, perched like one of those sacred monkeys you saw on the television. She stopped and craned her neck back to see him, his shape dark against the morning sun. He scowled down at her, still angry.

She cocked her head to one side and regarded him. Small, but he'd do.

Lifting her hand, she beckoned him to come down. He looked at her and didn't move. She beckoned again, more sharply, as she'd call the dog, or smack the donkey to move over, that kind of sharpness to it. Slowly he began to slither down the rocks, using the little ledges and lips as steps this time. This side was much more accessible, a gentle gradient down off the green top of the promontory, not an almost flat plate like where he'd climbed. He jumped the last bit and landed well, and then looked at her expectantly. She liked the way he did that. He wasn't simple at all.

She slid the bag full of quilt from her shoulder to the ground with a plump, and some relief. Lifting one soft, woven handle of it she held it out to him with raised eyebrows. He stepped forwards and took it, and she smiled at him, suddenly genuinely grateful. They turned to face the village and up the bag came, between them. It was easy now, with a handle each, and the lighter bag switched over to her strong shoulder. His arm was thin, but it seemed strong enough. At any rate, he made no complaint, and set his face towards the village and started to walk. It was good not to have to make conversation. They puffed up the hill into the village in a companionable silence; the burden shared.

At the bus stop they set the bag down, and she felt in her pockets for loose change, thinking she'd send him to buy sweets as a reward. But he sat himself up on the plastic seat instead, and swung his legs, his face closing over again with unhappiness as he looked around the empty space. His knees were filthy and skinned. Dark red and dark black.

She shrugged elaborately at him, what's wrong? But of

course, he couldn't answer, and looked down at his feet, his face almost old with misery.

Taking the little dark phone from her pocket she pressed the button until the light came on and it began to waken. Glancing up, she saw he was smiling a little at the sight of it, small and plastic and thick, so she waggled it in front of him until he smiled properly and made a derisive face. She watched as he reached into his own pocket and brought out a device twice the size, smooth and grey and slim like a slate, and waggled it back at her, saying that's not a phone – THIS is a phone.

She cocked her head and looked at him. His smile faded. She could see the beginnings of freckles on the bridge of his nose. The dreadful blue-whiteness of his skin was fading.

She tapped the little green speech bubble on her own device the way Abbie had showed her and typed,

Are you ok

She turned the device so that he could read the message.

He grinned suddenly and his thumbs moved quickly on his own device to show her,

U don't say you

She pretended to be perplexed, and tried holding her phone the way he held his, so that the thumbs could do the typing instead of one poking finger. She hammed it up a little, put her tongue between her teeth, and he was delighted.

Smart arse, she showed him, and he made that thick sound in his throat that she liked. She moved into the bus shelter herself, and sat down beside him on the bench, sticking her elbow gently into his side to make him budge up a bit. Her phone showed her there was still five minutes before the express flew through.

Whats your name. ur name i mean

Luca wots urs?

Grace. if ur going to cut out half the letters ill never be able to undrstand u

U txt vry slow

It ws a long sntnce

They smiled at one another, and thought about what next to say.

Grace went first.

U staying here long

Too long

Y 2 long

He shrugged. Don't u lke it here

😖Dads an arse

Amazing how do u do the wee face

The boy reached over and took her phone, and showed her how to make the little faces come. They sent each other cats and flags and cars and cakes for a contented moment, until she noticed the time. She looked at him.

Going to town. thanku for help with bag

😊 Ur welcm

'Here.'

She fetched some coins out of her pocket, leaning back and grunting to get her hand deep into her pocket. She held the money out, and nodded to say take it, but he shook his head and smiled. He reached out his hand for her phone instead. Behind them the growl of an engine back at Marty Clancy's announced the imminent arrival of the bus.

She hesitated, then handed it over.

He smiled and his thumbs moved over it at great speed. The bus was almost here. She flapped her hands at him – quick quick give it back – and he handed it to her with a smile. Glancing quickly down she saw he'd put his name on it, and his number too, just under Abbie's, the only other one there. She could send him messages now, she realised, the way she did with Abbie.

Quickly she wrote, Dont evr do what im about to do, and pressed send.

Then she got to her feet, heaved the bags up and without

even looking round, stepped straight out into the middle of the road, her hat and flapping bright-coloured smock and the big bags making her look gigantic, impressive, as wide as she was high. The great bus was just hurtling around the corner from Glassford, ignoring the speed limit as it always did, and it screeched to a halt, the horn blaring, the hazard lights coming on automatically, the people all looking quickly up. She stood her ground calmly, watching the driver's eyes open wide over the top of his mask, and his whole body move sharply forwards, then sharply back as the bus came to a halt just a short distance away from the toes of her boots, hissing.

She nodded decisively as if to say about time and waggled her bus pass up at him through the window high above. He shook his head incredulously, then reached out his hand slowly to press the button. The doors slid open. She tramped around and up the steps, grunting with the weight of the bags, ignoring completely his scolding, and the other passengers' glaring.

She took her time to wedge herself and all her belongings into the very front seat and then nodded to him regally – you can go now. With a shake of his head, the driver put the bus in gear, and they moved off, just as a faint ting came from her coat pocket. Patting around, she found the little phone and took it out, to see the screen bright and a message ready—

☺ Ur a cool old lady

She tucked the device away again safely and settled back in her seat, watching the fields and fences flicker past, the thin reflection of her face in the window gently smiling.

Chapter 20

———

'BECKY! HELP! I NEED WI-FI!' Evan called.

She was away down the aisle on her knees in front of the spaghetti hoops, with Luca beside her. He could see the thick white loops of a facemask over her ears. She was showing the boy how to spray and wipe each can and set it back again, nice and orderly. Some little-known choral work groaned and wallowed over the sound system at an unnecessary volume, like a great pelagic in agony, sucking all the air out of the place and preventing the travel of sound. She didn't hear the ting of the doorbell or his enquiry, and if Luca saw him from the corner of his eye he chose not to say so.

Evan saw his son turn a spaghetti can around slowly so that its label matched exactly with its neighbour, and Becky patted his hand and gave him a thumbs-up in praise. He'd been working here for over three weeks now, and got up every morning without complaint, running up the hill in the bright sunlight as soon as breakfast was over. He seemed to get a solid satisfaction from being useful here, although he wouldn't wash a dish back in the cottage, of course.

'Five o'clock,' said a man loudly, setting his basket on the counter beside him.

'Sorry?'

'Five o'clock, you'll get Wi-Fi then, till about eight. If you're the guy down the hill in Grace's rental?'

He wore several shirts and muddy wellies, but had friendly eyes at the top of a black mask.

'Christ, that's no good,' Evan said, and he could hear the high-pitched note in his own voice, feel the flex of the laptop charger bumping against his ankle as he leaned further in, 'I've someone Zooming me in twenty minutes and it's not even loading down there!'

The man tapped his ear apologetically and raised his eyes to the ceiling, where the bass section boomed. Then he left the basket on the counter and nodded to Evan, outside. Evan stepped back gratefully to let him out.

'Jesus, that woman's a public health nuisance,' the man said, as the door swung closed behind them, the dreadful shrieking muted at last.

As he spoke, he unhooked the mask and breathed a sigh of relief. His cheeks were the ruddy brown of an outdoor man and his smile was easy.

'Wife's pregnant,' he said, by way of explanation. 'Or I wouldn't.'

Evan smiled at him blankly and lifted the laptop slightly towards him, gathering up the trailing flex as he did so.

'Anywhere there's a booster or anything?' he asked. 'For Wi-Fi?'

The man looked at him with creased eyebrows.

'It's really important, or I wouldn't be running around here with this like a looper—'

He'd had an email from John when he woke up, and brusque – that new tone – requesting an urgent Zoom call in half an hour, no buddy-buddy or please or thank you added.

The man nodded slowly, and then raised an elbow to point at him. 'Simon Carmichael,' he said. His voice was calm and slow. They were about the same age.

Evan made himself breathe, and tamped down the fire

133

that flared in his belly. He raised his own free elbow with a wry smile, and they bumped them together awkwardly.

'Evan Moore. Sorry to interrupt your shopping—'

'Ah, you wouldn't need to be in a hurry in Becky's place, sure you wouldn't,' Simon said.

Evan looked at his new acquaintance, who was looking back at him, and held his breath. At last the man nodded. He'd made his mind up about something, because he jerked his head towards the dark and shuttered face of the village pub which stood in splendid isolation across the narrow street, all its hanging baskets dry and dead, the sign creaking gently in the breeze from the sea.

'Come on, let's talk to Paddy.'

Evan trotted behind him as the big man went on steady boots around the side of the building and stopped at a small, battered door at the back. Raising his hand he knocked, a definite rhythm, waited a moment, and then did it again. He put his hands into his pockets and looked at Evan, who smiled uncertainly. There was a clunk and a scrape, and the reinforced door opened a small crack, darkness and the odour of stale beer leaking into the sunshine.

'Paddy. Here's our new neighbour looking a favour.'

A short silence, and a voice said, 'Sure there's nothing we can be doing for him, Sy. Pub's closed, don't you know.'

Big Simon rocked on his feet, the very epitome of a friendly man. 'Ah, he's all right, Paddy, let him in. He'll throw you a coin or two, tide you over the hard times, won't you, Ev? Just wants to use the Wi-Fi, that's all. Will cause no bother to anyone, I'm sure.'

Evan hated being called Ev, like a hiccup. He nodded hard, and said quickly, 'Yes, happy to pay, if you've Wi-Fi – won't take long, just a quick meeting, you know?'

He hated that his voice was still that high, anxious noise, but he needed to speak to John. There was another of those pauses that allowed for thinking time around here. He still couldn't see anyone inside, so concentrated on making a friendly face. He imagined a troll guarding the gates of some hideous chamber, but when the face appeared it was ordinary enough, a pair of brass-wired spectacles low down on the nose, and the whole face poked forwards like a mole.

'Wi-Fi, is it?'

The spectacles looked at his big companion for a second and then stood back, grating the door open a little further, allowing more of the sulphur-coloured air to billow out.

'Take it easy, Ev,' said Simon, and nodded his head, go on in. 'And for god's sake don't ask for coffee or a glass of water in there, will you?'

'Thanks – thanks a lot, Simon,' but the man was already walking away slowly, each foot taking the ground a bit at a time, first heel, then instep, then a slow lowering of toes, heading back to the shop for his groceries.

It was a small space, full of old wood. Rafters sloped away from the bar, behind which a yellow strip-light glowed, illuminating a bright row of optics and the faces of at least eight men, dark-clad, big-shouldered people, who didn't turn around as he came in, but stared quietly down into glasses of amber liquid cradled in their hands. Smoke curled from forbidden ashtrays everywhere and prickled his eyes. He blinked.

'You'll want to plug that yoke in,' said the mole, turning to look at him.

'Er, yes. Yes please, that'd be great. Thanks.'

The mole indicated a dark booth behind him. 'Socket's in there. Phone charger too, if you need.'

'Great! Thanks so much.'

'What'll you have?'

'Sorry?'

The mole indicated the bar and the optics with a jerk of his head.

'No, I'm all right ...'

The man remained, staring. Evan mentally reviewed the contents of his pocket. 'D'you take debit cards?'

The mole nodded.

'OK.' It was eleven o'clock in the morning. 'Do you have . . . Stella?'

'No deliveries. We're using the old stock.'

Time was ticking on.

'Oh. OK, sure. What do you have, then?'

'Carlsberg, Irish or Scotch.'

Christ. He couldn't possibly drink Carlsberg. 'A wee Irish'd be lovely, then, thanks.' He paused, then ventured, 'I'm Evan, by the way. Evan Moore.'

The mole just nodded and turned away, lifting the flap of the bar and going behind. Evan glanced quickly at the others in the bar, but they were all stolidly staring down into their glasses. He sat down, and found the socket, booted up. They'd all hear every word, he realised as he stared at the circling wheel on the screen, fiddled in his case for a notebook and pen.

A tumbler had arrived at his elbow with an oily golden liquid in the bottom, no ice. When he raised his head to ask for a drop of water to put in it, there was no one there and his debit card was gone from the table. Someone muttered something up at the bar, and someone else muttered something in return. For the first time, one of the men raised his glass to his lips and took a sip. Another tapped his cigarette on the ashtray and took a drag. Behind him, he heard the muted tones of a racing commentator, saw bright images flash on the mole's glasses as he pointed the remote at the TV high on the wall. He kept the volume low.

Evan clicked on the link for the meeting, and pushed the whiskey out of sight behind the device. He could feel the old familiar heat prickling its way from his core to his neck, and John hadn't even joined yet. He reached up to loosen his collar and tie to let some air in, and found only the soft seam of a t-shirt. He was sweating suddenly, and his stomach burned. His own face appeared in the corner of the screen, the eyes wide and startled.

Waiting Room, the screen said.

Quickly he reached for the whiskey and took a burning sip, swished it around in his mouth and felt it rasp his gums, melt in, lovely. He shoved the glass out of sight again, just in time.

'Evan!'

'Well, John.'

His university roommate. His expedition pal. His best friend. Now, his business partner and a stranger.

'Sorry for butting into your furlough, mate,' John said. His face was pale, his eyes with exaggerated black shadows underneath from the camera angle. He was in their gleaming kitchen, sunlight sparking off everything, the sound echoing and bouncing everywhere. The light wasn't flattering. 'Christ, is that racing in the background? Where the fuck are you?'

Evan saw the mole raise the remote again and the TV clicked off. The muttering ceased in the background. Sweat ran down his back.

'Sorry, there's not much Wi-Fi around here,' he said, wanting another swig of the whiskey. He made his hands relax on the sticky surface of the table.

'Where did you end up, anyway? Lorna said it was somewhere on the coast. Hope you're getting nice weather.'

The sarcasm was thinly veiled.

His face flared hot. Of course he'd have talked to Lorna. Of course she'd have answered *his* calls.

'Yes. Ballybrady it's called – nice spot but, like I say, not much in the way of modern amenities.' He laughed a little, acutely conscious of the listeners all around.

'Right, well, listen, I know we agreed you needed a break and all, get over things. I understand that, right?'

He didn't look understanding. Evan smiled his thanks, again, and said nothing.

'—And it fitted in well with the furlough thing, too, this shitty COVID thing, no doubt about it, OK, OK.'

John had put his hand up as if Evan was arguing. He looked like a New York traffic cop.

'—But the thing is, Ev, time's marching on, isn't it? We need to get our heads together, get a game plan going, you know? I need you back here, on your game. There's decisions to be made.'

His voice was rising.

'Clients are getting antsy, to tell you the truth. Seems they don't want to wait until this is all over, and why should they? I can't fob them off for you much longer, mate.'

When John called someone mate, they weren't.

Evan realised he was shaking his head and made himself stop.

'Like – I need you in Belfast on this, doing your thing, not hiding away in fucking Ballygobackwards there.'

John was rattled. John was the people person. If he was rattled, if he couldn't handle their clients, those stupidly rich, alarmingly loud, imperious people, then Evan certainly couldn't. That was always John's domain, and Evan just did the forecasts in the background, the numbers work – the real work, he'd always thought – smiled at meetings, raised a hand like a geek when introduced, that sort of thing.

'I'm the numbers guy, John – you know I'm no good to you on the people end,' he tried, and his voice was that thin and reedy thing it became around his partner nowadays. It almost squeaked on the last syllable, and he coughed to hide it.

John's exhale was a sigh of practised exasperation.

'Fuck's sake, Evan,' he said quietly. He ran a hand over his thinning hair. Evan saw him cast a quick glance up at someone in the room, behind the camera, exchange a silent message. Eloise, no doubt, wife of the beautiful arse and guilty midnight fantasy.

'Can't you email me the portfolios, John, or something?' he

tried. 'I can work through them here, maybe, and send them back—'

'It's not about that, Evan!' John's voice was loud.

The silence in the bar was deafening.

They used to bellow out each other's names, check the route was clear, before dropping downhill on the bike, into dark trees and the unknown, their buddy already down there in the distance, looking back. Then there'd be a screech, a whoop, into the forest with a breathless skid-stop, heart in the mouth – *Yeeeeoh! Fucking minter, man!* Then claps on the back, adjust where needed and ready to go again, together.

John's face took up almost all of the screen.

'We've got people to do that now, Evan, for Christ's sake. We've got people to do the numbers stuff, if you recall. I need you to work the shareholders with me, man – they're not happy. They keep asking about you, how long it's going to be, like, how long it's going to take before you come around, get over all this, sign off on stuff.'

Evan's face burned hot in the darkness and the air around him was electric. He could see the mole polishing the same glass over and over again. 'Right, yes. Sorry,' he said.

'Look—'

John was sitting back in his chair now, his new boardroom posture, adopted since they got the new offices, the share-holders, all the chrome. He didn't look into the camera, but down at his clasped hands. His voice was trying to be patient. Evan reached for the glass behind the laptop and downed its contents quickly. It burned, but in a good way, and he ran his tongue over his teeth to get the last of it.

'Like. Fuck, Ev. I'm carrying this thing alone, aren't I? Have been for a while now.'

If he wasn't careful, he'd start to sound like a whinger, Evan thought, but didn't say. He nodded slowly instead, but he didn't try to speak.

John sighed elaborately. 'Shit, man, I know things've been tough for you – no one better than me, right?'

Evan nodded slowly.

'But, hell, even Lorna says you're – well, you're fucking wallowing in it, for fuck's sake, mate!' Now the accusation was out, he was gaining confidence. His voice was louder, and he looked directly into the camera. Evan could imagine Eloise nodding encouragingly at that lovely sunny window they had, into the garden. His ears burned with whiskey and shame. He imagined the conversations over coffee leading up to this – Lorna at their breakfast bar, letting it all out, the blame, the disgust, the anger. Eloise shaking her head, that Gallic tang to her words as she comforted her friend, denigrated him, who was once a friend too.

'Like, fuck's sake, Evan. What happened, happened – you know?'

John looked at him as if expecting him to agree.

People always said that. What the hell did it mean? Evan felt a huge unaccustomed heat build in his core, move up his spine, evaporate all the drying sweat and flood his cheeks with flame. He'd say she was dead, now, the cunt. Can't change that, yadda-yadda, can't bring her back. Don't you dare, John, you bastard, he thought, don't say it, he prayed, mashing his lips together between his teeth.

'Like, you've got to face it, Ev. She's dead – and that's that. Doesn't matter how, does it, really? You can't bring her back, god knows we'd love to. But – got to stop beating yourself up and get back in the saddle.'

Evan let the words fall into a dark pool of silence. He saw his friend's eyes flick to the corner of his screen, checking his own image. Making sure he looked cool, collected, assured. Had good fucking business hair, what was left of it. He didn't know this man. He watched him take a breath, turn his face slightly to the left, and continue.

'Like, we've a business to run.'

Evan nodded.

'—and these times are mental for the industry, confidence at an all-time low – and I can't make all the decisions myself. They won't let me, or believe me, Evan – I would.'

Evan looked at his hands, long and brown on the tabletop from weeks of sun, and said nothing.

'Like, hello? You there, even? Come on, for fuck's sake! Talk to me, man!'

He heard John scrape his chair back from the table, stand up and walk away. He'd pace and rub his head, swear under his breath. It's what he did. Lorna used to joke in the dark of their bed that he rubbed all his hair off in these rages, and they'd giggle together like naughty schoolkids. He remembered the slow scrape of her toenails on his leg, that secret signal of invitation, and felt something click out of place inside, that had just been hanging on, before.

'Buy me out,' he said.

The mole put down the glass with a click and it gleamed yellow in the dim light.

John hadn't heard, so he waited until the big body flumped itself back down in the chair.

'Buy me out, John,' he said again, louder.

There was a silence as they looked at each other. Evan saw the scar from the rock that had flung up off his wheel that time and almost taken John's eye out. It was raised and white against his heated face.

'What?' John said slowly. 'You've got to be kidding . . .'

His voice lacked conviction, and there was a rustle as Eloise came up behind her husband and put a hand on his shoulder. Her glossy hair swung across the screen as she leaned in to the camera.

'Think about this, Evan,' she said, a deep crease between the heavy brows. It sounded, as always, like Yvonne, almost her pet name for him, and he remembered how much he liked her. He realised how much he would miss them both, if he did this. He smiled at her warmly, and waited until she shook her head and moved away, and his partner's face appeared again. The drinkers were forgotten, the wives and families, the shareholders and clients, and there were only the two of them left in the small bright frame.

'Make me an offer. Something reasonable. I don't need much,' he heard himself say quietly. 'Will that sort things for you?'

'Aw, don't be like that,' John said.

'No, I mean it,' Evan told him, and realised two things.

One, he did mean it. A whole wash of lightness ran through him at the thought that he could be free of it, of all the responsibility, the uncertainty, the dependence on the whims and demands of unreasonable others – the lot. Could it be possible?

And two, that another glass of whiskey had materialised at his elbow.

His belly glowed.

He found himself smiling.

'You've always wanted to be your own boss, make your own decisions, John – be honest. You don't need me any more, you said it yourself, you've got people to do the numbers. I'm just hanging on. Well. Now's your chance. I want out,' he said.

There was another long silence, where he lifted the glass and drank, relishing the hot rasp of it, and meeting his friend's eyes over the rim.

'You back on it?' John asked, eyeing the glass with the concern of a friend. '—That what this is about?'

'No. Not really. Not like that.'

He held his friend's eye until John blinked and nodded. There was a long thinking pause. Someone scraped something on the floor, a soft sound like a boot or a stool-leg, like a horse shifting in the stable at night.

'What'll you do?'

John spoke slowly now, but the creases round his mouth were

a smile hiding. There was excitement there. Evan could see it dancing in little sparks across his face, as he let this new idea in.

'Don't know.' It was the truth. 'Doesn't matter.'

He thought about what did matter.

'I've lost Jessie. Lost Lorna, John. My own fault, and I need to get a handle on what's going on. These are the things that matter to me, mate. I'm no use to you like this.'

For the first time in a long time, they were really looking at each other.

John nodded slowly. 'Right, then,' he said. 'OK. Let me start things at this end – if you're sure?'

Evan smiled. 'I'm sure.'

'OK then. OK. OK!' His grin was as broad as it used to be, the old life gleaming in his eyes. '—I'll sign off, then. Get on it. Be in touch.'

'Yeah,' Evan agreed, '—but make sure it's between five and eight, for the Wi-Fi, will you?' and they actually laughed together for a second.

He clicked the red button and the screen turned black.

His shoulders dropped to where they should be.

He rolled his head on his neck, conscious of its new looseness, and then rolled the remains of his whiskey in his hand. He looked for a while at his screensaver, the wondrous Lupra Pass in Nepal, the last adventure they'd had together, John and himself and the mountain-bike gang. Maybe ten years ago, now, but still magic. The bikes now greased and packed away in the sheds at home, all that time. The hours and minutes and seconds of parenthood eating up the years like a hungry caterpillar until it was nearly all gone.

With a sigh he closed the laptop and looked around as if just wakened.

'Fair play to yeh,' said one of the drinkers, and lifted his glass in salute.

'Sorted him out, nice one,' said another, and patted the barstool next to him.

'Yeh, another alco layabout for the club, come on, you can buy us a drink,' said the first. 'Sure you've nothing else to be doing, any more, hev ya?'

The mole nodded as he slid another whiskey onto the bar, Evan's debit card beside it.

Evan left his things just where they were and approached – the circle of bright faces, the amber glass.

Chapter 21

HER SHOULDERS ACHED FROM A DAY dragging kelp around and hanging it out piece by piece to dry on the wall. It tended to snaggle on itself, and all the little hopping things, *Eurydice* and *Coelopidae* and all the various pretty hydroids required careful removal before the algae was processed for sale. Nobody appreciated little protein extras in their health-food, she'd found.

The donkey had developed a disturbing appetite for the stuff recently too. Perhaps her regular diet was low in minerals, but it meant that Grace couldn't let her out of the field while she worked, or half the haul would be snaffled when her back was turned. So the afternoon had been spent stretching and straightening and cleaning and listening to the donkey's loud and mournful lamentations from behind the fence, instead of enjoying her neat-footed company as she wandered around on the lane, keeping the grass down, and every so often coming up behind her to snuff at her hair.

So she was tired and ready for a sit-down and a quiet drink as she knocked on the door of the pub that afternoon, a quiet rat-tat-a-rat-tat-tat. She checked in the pockets of her smock for coins in the warmth of the sun. When a crack appeared between door and frame, she pushed her head forwards and Paddy opened wide for her without hesitation.

'Now, Grace, you know you're not wearing that hat in here, give it to me now,' he said as she tried to sidle past him.

'It's not a fuckin' fashion parade, Paddy, is it?' she fired back, but stopped to remove the hat, nonetheless. 'Sure you've the ugliest collection of bastards assembled here that the world has ever seen.'

It was an old complaint, made without heat as she put the wide-brimmed thing into his waiting hand.

'We're not having you sitting glowering in the corner under it like a fucking bandolero, that's all. We can watch Clint Eastwood on Netflix anytime we take a mind. You know where it is when you want it,' and he hung it on the peg beside the toilets.

Grace muttered under her breath as she went on in to the dark and fuggy interior. The drinkers had heard the interaction and were ready to greet her as she came in under the lintel. A quiet series of 'All right, Grace,' 'Well, Grace,' 'Hiya Grace,' greeted her, but she replied to none, and went straight to her own stool in the corner and eased herself up onto it with a hiss. Her elbow was sore. She'd overdone it.

'Now we've all said Grace can you give me a fuckin' drink?' she asked Paddy, who had a glass of whiskey ready anyway, and slid it to her with a smile.

'An old 'un but a good 'un,' he told her, and held out his hand for payment. 'Don't know why you don't get a wee card like everyone else. Soon enough they won't take cash anywhere, you know, with this virus about, and then what'll you do?'

'Don't tell me you'll ever refuse good hard cash, Patrick Murphy,' she retorted, counting carefully and filling his cupped hand with clinking coins. 'That I'll never believe.'

'Aye, sure she's loaded with coin, anyway, isn't she?' said a skinny man a few stools along, peeking at her with sly eyes over the top of a pint glass. 'Betcha can't sleep at night for the money sticking into yer arse through the mattress, isn't that right, Gracie?' and he laughed at his own humour.

'Come you down any night you like, Mickey Flanders, and see what sticks into your own arse,' she fired back without hesitation. 'It'll have two barrels, and *that* I can promise you.'

There was a general ripple of laughter at this, and then the bar fell quiet again, and Grace took a sip from her glass and felt it warm her. In a minute it would start to loosen her, too. Good stuff. She propped her elbows on the drip-mat in front of her, looked at the oily swirls in the glass in the yellow light, and scanned the faces to see who was in, today.

The usual alcos, who'd have been standing at the door waiting for Paddy first thing in the morning, not a smile on their faces, their bodies racked with the need for a drink, hurry, hurry, Paddy, open the door. Now of course, all was well – they were relaxed and comfortable and they'd be away homewards for the tea soon, walking the long way down the road with a clinking bag in their hands, from ditch to ditch to ditch.

Then there were the afternoon sippers, both of them together. Lonely old men with dead wives and time to fill, tired of the hiss of the silence in their own houses, quiet and slow of speech, watching the others like a TV show.

Then near the TV, the racers, the speculators, putting their money on a nag with a pretty name or a dog with a good rep, even now that the races were American repeats. She was surprised to see them at this time of the day. It was time they were away home now the meet was over and the TV off, surely. They got paid today, maybe, or had a wee win to celebrate. Their heads were together now, four of them muttering, and there wasn't much left in their glasses.

And who was that behind them, quiet, nursing a drink and watching the wood of the bar? She leaned forwards surreptitiously and saw the gleam of light on a pair of glasses and the ruffled hair of her townie tenant, his face slack and empty. Raising her eyebrows, she asked Paddy a silent question, and he shrugged in reply.

'Quit his job,' said one of the old men sympathetically, reading the signals, and put a hand on the townie's shoulder in a brotherly way. The townie didn't raise his head. He was well gone.

'Came in for the Wi-Fi and got the Spanish Archer,' said the other.

'Didn't get the elbow, you thick cunt, he quit, like I said.'

'Seriously,' Grace said sternly. 'You're like the two oul gits off *The Muppet Show*. Would you ever listen to yourselves?'

She looked again at the townie. 'Christ. How many has he had?'

'Cheap date,' said Paddy. 'That's his fourth.'

'Sure he's nowhere to put it,' boomed big Alfie. 'Thin as a rake he is. Hit him like a lump-hammer. He'll regret it in the morning.'

He raised his empty pint glass to the barman as a signal.

'That's the keg empty,' Paddy replied with satisfaction, 'I'll have to go and change it. We'll be on the last one, then,' and he ducked down under the flap to go out to the back where the kegs lay.

'Thank fuck,' said big Alfie. 'That stuff's dreadful muck altogether. I'll have to hit the spirits then, like this wee fucker here,' and he laughed and leaned around behind the old men to give Evan a little shove. The townie keeled over and limply tried to grip the bar, but it was well polished, and only a hand on his shoulder from the old man beside him kept him on the stool. He looked around with bleary eyes, and recognition filled his face when he saw Grace at the far end of the bar.

'Grace!' he said, and smiled wetly.

'Christ!' she said, under her breath.

Behind the bar, a phone lit up and played 'Bat out of Hell'. Paddy's voice came through the yard door, muffled, as he wrestled with the couplings on the new keg.

'Someone get that for me, will you?'

Mickey Flanders slipped off his stool and under the bar-flap with practised ease, and grinned when he saw the name on the bright screen.

'It's your girlfriend, Paddy!' he called with glee. 'Oooh! You sure you want me to answer?'

There was no reply from outside, only the clang of a hammer on a stiff nut, so he pressed the green button and said, 'Well Becky, you looking for a good man or a good time?'

The assembled drinkers heard something loud and forceful through the phone, and Mickey held it away from his ear for a second, smirking. When he put it back to his ear he laughed and said,

'He's hiding from yeh under the table, Becky,' and then, quickly, 'No, I'm only kidding, I'm kidding – he's out changing a keg. What can I do you for?'

The voice chattered on in his ear and the drinkers held their peace, sipped their drinks and waited to hear what she wanted.

'Oh aye,' said Mickey, looking over at the townie. 'You miss nothing even with those dirty specs of yours, young lady. He's here awright, been here a while.'

The voice asked him something in an urgent voice. 'Nah, he's pissed as a fart.' Mickey covered the phone with his hand and addressed Evan directly, 'You're pissed as a fart, young townie, ain't ya?'

Evan smiled sheepishly and nodded his head. He tried to take another drink from his glass, but found it empty and looked at it sadly.

'Right. Oh, shit, OK. I'll tell him but he isn't prob'ly in any state to take care of a youngster. Paddy's just poured him another.'

With his free hand he lifted the whiskey bottle from the bar shelf and tipped a generous amount into Evan's glass.

'For fuck's sake, Mickey!' Grace said, but everyone else was laughing.

The townie nodded and raised the glass in salute before taking a long drink.

'Aye, and that kid's simple, and all,' said big Alfie. 'Fuck knows what'd happen if ye let this one here take care of him tonight. Tell 'er to take him home to hers. Best place. Women's work anyway, looking after youngsters, in't that right, Gracie?'

'Go fuck yourself, you big lug,' Grace said without heat, and took the last lovely drink of her own whiskey, let it work its way down her throat and settle warm in her belly. She looked at the skinny, nodding townie and sighed.

'Tell Becky I'm coming now, Mickey,' she heard herself say. 'I'll take him to mine for a while.'

She twisted around on her stool and eased herself to the floor as Mickey relayed the message. The others were nudging and nodding at this unexpected train of events but knew better than to say anything aloud.

As she passed the townie, whose head was nodding low, she turned to the others and said,

'Make sure and tell him where the lad is, now, you pile of gits, don't let him have a heart attack when he comes round. And – anyone gives him another drink'll have me to answer to, you hear?'

Mickey Flanders ducked his head as she passed him, but she slapped him round the back of the head anyway. Paddy came back into the bar, wiping his hands and humming, and raised his eyebrows at the sight of the bright smock swinging back out under the lintel.

'Where's she away to?' he asked the assembled company, who all raised shoulders and twisted mouths. 'She hasn't had Number Two yet. She always has Number Two.'

'Somebody musta offended her,' Mickey Flanders tried, as Paddy went after her, to shoot back the bolts and let her out into the early evening. 'She's awful touchy these days,' he called, '—such a sensitive wee thing,' and the bar dissolved into laughter.

'Everything all right, Gracie?' Paddy asked in the back room, as she put the big hat on her head and pulled it down over that bright cloud of hair.

'Must be losing my mind, Paddy,' she said, going past him. 'Must be losing my fucking mind—'

She turned back just before he pushed the door to, and said,

'—again.'

Across the street, the girl Becky was locking up, wearing her surgical mask like a chin-sling, still hooked over both ears. She was yanking down the rattling shutters and clicking padlocks shut. The boy was standing in the bus stop looking at his phone and shifting from foot to foot.

Grace patted her pockets but of course she didn't have her own phone with her. She took it only to the town with her parcels for the QR codes, the way Abbie had taught her.

The boy was looking uncertainly between Becky and her own big shape in the dusk. She was conscious of the hat, and how it must make her face totally dark, so she pulled it off and hung it on the strap over her arm.

'Got a phone, Becky?' she asked.

'Sure.'

The girl looked surprised but took it from her bag, made the lights come on, and handed it over. It was larger than her own, but Grace managed to type a short message and showed it to the boy, the screen bright between them.

Come 4 tea

He didn't smile, but showed her his response on his own device.

Wot is it

What is what, she wondered. She made a confused face and he frowned and typed,

For t

Little shit, she thought, and then paused. She wasn't much into food herself and actually there wasn't very much in the cupboards. Beans? Bread?

Beans on toast? she tried, while Becky stood, arms akimbo, watching.

He made a disgusted face, his tongue small and very pink.

'What's up?' Becky asked.

'He doesn't like beans on toast.'

The girl huffed a laugh and gave the boy a long-suffering look. 'Wait one,' she said, and the keys came out again, the mask went back up. With a grunt she slid the door-shutter halfway up and gestured to the boy, come on. He grinned and followed her, ducking back in under the metal and leaving Grace alone in the darkening street.

'Christ,' she said to the empty air, and stuck her hat back on, her mind strangely held by the thin sad man drooping against the bar in the pub behind her. She'd seen sorrow like that before, had felt sorrow like that before, and the danger was that it might swamp her too, if she didn't avoid it, so what was she doing here?

She looked away from the shop, down the dusky lane towards home where the dog waited for her. She should go – she should head on without him, and they could blame her madness for it. They always did. She got away with anything nowadays.

Then they were back and it was too late, the girl Becky and the kid. He was holding a bottle of something that shone a vivid green even in the failing light, and a plastic packet.

'Burger. Nuke it in the microwave, about three minutes,' Becky told her. '—But take it out of the plastic first, yeah?'

'How much do I owe you?'

Grace handed the phone back, and fiddled in her pocket for coins she knew weren't enough.

'That's OK, I'll take it out of his wages,' smiled the girl, and she looked pretty for once, relaxed and content.

'You're a good girl, Becky Breen,' she said approvingly.

'I'm twenty-bloody-nine, Grace!' the girl fired back, still smiling. 'Haven't been a girl for ten years.' She stuck her face out to say, 'And there's nothing wrong with the word woman, you know. We need to use it, Grace, to get it back into common parlance, don't we, instead of girl? For too long it's been allowed to have negative connotations, the word woman – we let the men use it to put us down, like, sit down woman, shut up woman—'

'You're right there – shut up, woman, will you?' Grace held up her hand. 'You're on your bandwagon again, missus. We talked about this. I'm not bloody interested. Neither that or your hippy Buddha nonsense either.'

Becky smiled and turned back to lock up the shop once more.

Grace jerked her head at the boy, let's go, and they set off down the road as the last of the light left the sky and the shutter rattled down again behind them and Becky called goodnight after them into the darkness. The boy showed her his phone screen.

Wil the donkey be there

She took it from him and replied,

No dont let her in the house poops everywr

She gave him back the phone and he laughed, that lovely noise, and stuck it in his pocket. As they rounded the corner into the very dark, she felt him take her hand, and his fingers were warm and dry.

Chapter 22

———

IT WAS AFTER NINE WHEN she brought the boy back to the old rented house, and the place was dark.

'Hello!' she called and walked on in, the door sticking halfway as it always did, her shoulder ready to shove it the rest of the way. The boy came trotting behind her, carrying the book she'd lent him, the marine invertebrates one. He'd spent the last hour turning its pages over, his eyes growing huge at the photos of the antennaed and alien creatures which lived, as she told him, just under his feet when he went on the sand, and all around him if he ever went into the water. He'd shuddered and made a *no-way* face, but had been clearly delighted to take the book home with him for a day or two.

The man was sitting on the edge of the sofa, in the dark.

She clicked the light on and took her hat off to see better, and then marched forwards, right up to him. She looked down into his face. 'You in a fit state to look after this one?' she asked loudly.

His breath was sour. 'Ah, Grace, Grace,' he said, stupidly, and smiled up at her.

'Christ,' she said aloud. 'Coffee.'

The boy had already kicked off his trainers and swung himself up expertly into the hammock, and she saw the glow of his phone as he shifted gently and settled, the pointed corners of the big book sticking out sharply. He hadn't even acknowledged his father where he sat, and she wondered how often this happened – the pub, the stupid blank drunk face.

'Do this often?' she asked rudely from the sink, skirring the kettle full of water. 'Get pissed, I mean?'

The man smiled amiably from his perch. 'No,' he said. 'Not really. Not any more. Did for a while. Oh yeah. Did for a while, Gracie, all right. But not any more. Or . . .'

When the kettle clicked off she turned away to make him a cup of instant coffee, two spoons.

When she returned his hand was draped clumsily over his eyes. He lifted his feet from the ground as if about to lie back.

'Oh no you don't!' she said, and pressed the coffee into his hand, holding his shoulder tight to steady him and feeling his warmth through the t-shirt. 'Drink this. Careful!' she warned as he tilted. 'Don't drop it!'

He smiled again and held it in two hands, to sip obediently.

'God almighty – what happened to you when I left?' she said, to herself. 'I told that bastard not to serve you any more drink.'

'Aha!' laughed the man foolishly, and pulled a half-empty quarter bottle from under his hip, holding it out to her like a gift.

She shook her head.

'Well, clearly you're not fit to handle it,' she muttered, taking it sharply. She stuck it into the voluminous pocket of her smock for later, and perched on the arm of the matching chair. She watched him take little tastes of the coffee to please her. 'So what the fuck was this all about, today?'

He moved his face, trying to assemble his thoughts. She waited. 'Quit my job,' he said at last, speaking very slowly and carefully.

'I know, that's what I mean. What the fuck made you up and quit your job? Are you mental? At a time like this?'

'Hated it.'

'Oh. Well, that's a reason, I suppose.'

'Hate lotsa things.'

He was speaking to himself now, slurring. She didn't move.

'Hate my job, hate my life, hate that my wife fucking kicked me out, hate that my kid's weird, hate that—' His eyes grew huge behind his glasses and he put a hand over his mouth as if he was going to be sick.

'Wait now!' she said urgently, and fetched the basin from under the sink, put it by his leg.

'Thank you, Grace,' he said quietly, his eyes red and weepy. 'You're so strange but you're so kind. It's a – what d'you call it again?' He creased his brow, trying to remember, 'A amolany. No. A monolony. No, a—'

'Anomaly, you drivelling moron,' she said, without heat.

It didn't look as if he was going to use the basin after all.

'Yes. That.'

She shook her head, pushed herself up and went to the hammock, pulled it open and mimed teeth-brushing. The boy inside made a groaning sound – *no* – and pointed at the book illuminated by the torch on his phone, at the close-up of a shore crab, all waving antennae and mouthparts. She reached in without further ado and snatched the book up. He made a yowling sound – *hey* – looking outraged, but not surprised. She mimed teeth-brushing again and watched the emotions move across his face like weather. After a moment, he broke eye contact and shrugged. He began to pull himself out of the hammock and she stepped back, putting the book down pointedly on the little table for when he was done. He trailed past her, exaggeratedly slowly, heading for the bathroom. She stopped him on the way past, and tugged at her shirt – get changed too. He rolled his eyes and trailed on.

'You're a good mum,' said the man thickly from behind her. 'Got kids?'

'No,' she said shortly. It was time she was gone.

'My daughter died, you know.'

She turned right around and stared at him. His chin was propped in his hand, and he wasn't even looking at her. He was telling himself. 'Yep,' he said, still not looking at her. 'An' I killed her. OK. Oh yeah, say it loud, get it out. I did.'

She sat down again on the arm of the chair. The breath was tight in her throat.

He shook his head for a solemn moment before continuing. 'I fuckin' killed me own little girl.' He shook his head, big fat greasy tears starting to come. 'I hate that most of all. I hate that more than anything. Wee Jessie, wee Jessie, wee Jessie.'

He was crying now, big wet drunken sobs, pushing the back of his hand roughly under his nose, smearing the snot and tears.

So that was the sorrow she saw in him.

From the bathroom came noises of toilet flushing, and then an electric toothbrush buzzing. She went to the sink and fetched a handful of kitchen roll and crossed the room and gave it to the townie silently, and then stood looking down at him as he mopped at his face, and she fought with herself in her head.

She was eavesdropping. He'd never tell her these things, sober. But she was afraid to leave him alone, with those dreadful words he'd just said rolling around in the lonely house, and the kayak incident not so long ago, and no one to balance it all out with listening.

She sat slowly back down on the arm of the chair and watched him, and waited. After a moment he stopped mopping and coughed wetly, and twisted the soggy paper round and around in his hands.

'What happened?' she asked gruffly, trying to sound gentle, not used to softness any more. 'D'you want to tell me?'

He shrugged like a schoolboy and shook his head, looking into the empty fireplace.

The boy came out of the bathroom with shining cheeks and pulled her sleeve. He pointed at the book, asking. She smiled a little and nodded, and he scampered to it, and carried it back to his hideaway, without even a glance at his father, without even registering his tears.

The man, Evan, watched him go. 'Poor wee guy,' he said. 'Poor spud. Never had a look-in, did he?'

She wished she had the dog at her leg to stroke while the man stared at the floor, to take away the bleakness that had welled up between them.

'Fucking retarded, that's what I thought. What Lorna thought, too, but she wouldn't say. Wouldn't say.' He huffed a bitter laugh. '—Turns out he's just deaf. Just deaf, like. Fucking doctors, specialists, hospitals, therapy, fucking playdates. Playdates, like? Other fucking weird kids, all groaning at one another like spastics in our back garden. Shit.'

'That's not nice,' she said firmly.

'I know!' he raised his voice. 'I fucking know! I know, Grace! But it's in my head! And it's driving me mad!' He was growling now, and he poked himself viciously in the temple as she got up to leave. 'Why can't I fucking ever – fucking – just – say – what's in my head?'

Poke, poke, poke.

She watched him, fascinated, just as she'd watched the dog tearing at its stitches that time, ripping itself open until she'd intervened.

'Jesus,' she said, sticking her hands deep into her pockets to ground herself, making her voice calm and solid. 'You just did, you lunatic, so leave it now, will you? You'll fucking hurt yourself poking away like that, and what good will that do? And you'll scare the boy, if he looks out. Calm down.'

She stood watching, holding him with her quiet eyes until his hand dropped to his side and he swayed where he sat, exhausted. She went to the sink and filled a big glass of water and put it in his hand. 'Time you were in bed, townie. Get that down you and off you go, now. You're going to know all about it in the morning, you stupid sod.'

He smiled at her and drank the glass down, and handed it back to her without meeting her eyes. Then he rubbed his face and nodded, and sat down to start pulling at a shoe, then a sock. His foot was pearly white and bony, even after all this time, the toes long and elegant like his fingers. 'I killed my Jessie,' he said weakly.

'I know,' she told him sadly, picking up her hat from the counter and putting her hand on the latch, 'I know, honey.'

Chapter 23

———

EVAN AWOKE TO A STRONG and briny smell. Lying still, he checked to make sure it wasn't emanating from himself. It wasn't. Raising his head gingerly, he saw his son at the little kitchen table with a bucket, dipping his hand in and out, slowly. He let himself sink back into the pillows gently and pulled the duvet over his head.

When he awoke again the boy was gone, but the bucket was still on the table. The stink was still there too, pungent and rotten, but it didn't matter. He had to get water. With care, he put his feet to the floor and noticed they were bare. That was something, at least. He sat up nice and slowly, and stayed very still for a very long time, until the room did the same. When the thirst got too great, he carefully stood and went inch by inch to the sink, which gleamed painfully white in the sun through the kitchen window. He turned the tap and the water rattled loudly into a collection of unwashed dishes, cutlery and pans. Feeling around in the mess and gloop he found a cup and let it fill to the brim, then drank every delicious drop.

He was leaning there, the warmth gentle on his back, sipping carefully and feeling the water run down cool into his burning belly, when Luca came back inside. It struck him straight away how brown the boy was already. How healthy he looked, flesh on his bones and a smile on his face, and this morning he seemed particularly cheerful.

Hi Dad, are you up?

Evan set the glass carefully down on the counter.

Yes at last. What are you doing? Having fun?

Come and see.

Luca went to the bucket and shook it a little, looking inside with a smile and then looking back up at his father, waiting for him.

Oh, god, Evan thought, not the bucket.

The stench rising from it was almost visible, a noxious swirl filling the room, but he went anyway, slowly. He wasn't invited to come and see very often. Holding the edge of the table in both hands he leaned carefully over, breathing shallow through his mouth, and looked in from the corner of his eye. The contents seemed to be rotten seaweed with a little water – not as bad as he'd feared, as long as he didn't breathe through his nose. He looked a question at his son, who eagerly pushed him out of the way and stuck his hand right in through the muck. When he pulled it back there were several little creatures on the palm, curled and transparent like toenail cuttings. As he watched, they dried out a little and began to move more vigorously. Suddenly one sprang like a flea, right off the hand that held it and onto the kitchen floor.

'*Arrghh!*'

He jumped away from the table.

Luca! What IS that?

Bemused, he saw the boy laugh and shake the remaining creatures back into the bucket, then run to fetch a large book and open it on the table for him to see, right in a puddle of salty water where strings of seaweed soaked.

'Careful!' he said aloud, and moved the book to a dry spot.

Luca nodded impatiently and pointed at the photograph

on one side of the page – the same little creature. There was a label below. Evan blinked.

'Eury-dice?' he sounded out. He looked at his son.

You're collecting these?

The boy nodded and smiled, a huge grin.

They're cool, aren't they? And there's lots. But you've got to have lots of old seaweed too or they'll die. This stuffs a bit smelly. They eat it, yuck. Look, it says here.

Evan had rarely seen him so animated, and followed his pointing finger to read the text aloud.

'"A small and distinctive louse-like isopod",' he read slowly, aloud. 'Yep, that's it, right there on my floor, a louse, great. Let's see, "The body is flattened with an oval outline. It has large eyes."'

Then he felt something he had not, for a long time. His son had put his fingers lightly on Evan's cheek and held them there. He'd done this often as a very small boy, when engrossed in something someone was reading for him, as if to try to hear the words as they were made in the mouth, as if he could hurry the message up, or read the information directly from the vibrations coming through the skin of the face. Evan had read to him for comfort, to settle them both, in the early days, and even though the child couldn't hear he would sometimes follow his father's finger along the words on the page like a thread. He felt the heat of the small fingers and paused a moment. Then he resumed, the hand still in place.

'Eh – "It has large eyes positioned laterally and a long second pair of antennae. It may be pale grey to brown in colour, with black spots covering all surfaces of the body."'

The boy nodded and took his hand away, beaming.

See?

Cool, echoed Evan.

And Grace says I'm to draw them until I know all their bits and then I'm going to learn another one, but not crabs yet. They're too scary.

He shuddered and grinned again and then was off through the door and down onto the beach with the bucket, his wellies clumping loudly on the lane and then shushing off onto the shingle. Evan watched him go. He touched the place where the hand had rested, then looked around with bleary eyes to see what had to be done. There were signs of a DIY breakfast scattered here and there – a milky cereal bowl and spoons and a trail of Rice Krispies on the floor where the box leaked, so at least the child had eaten while he lay in his drunken stupor. He shook off the guilt – too often, too harsh – and briskly opened all the windows to let the smell of stale booze and rotten seaweed out. He began to feel a little better. He clicked the kettle on and ran water into the sink.

But the thought of the hand on his face lingered as he worked, mingling with the hazy events of yesterday and the occasional greasy sweat that washed through him and then receded like the tide. He'd quit his job. Luca had smiled and touched his face. He'd quit his job. Luca had touched his face and smiled. The hours between yesterday and this morning were gone as if he hadn't lived them. He'd quit his job. His son had touched his face.

'So you're alive, then.'

He was pouring bleach into the basin and giving it a swirl, the dirty dishes teetering in a pile on the draining board, waiting their turn. Grace was in the house, a huge presence in those voluminous clothes of hers, browns and beiges and greys today, taking up all the light.

She always just walked right in.

'Just about.'

He gave her a weak smile and felt the sweat build again, clammy, and this time his innards cramped as well.

'Oh god, excuse me!' he groaned, dropping the basin into the sink and running for the bathroom.

When he finally emerged, the house was empty. The silence hissed around him as if something was missing. He concentrated on one thing at a time. Taking a piece of bread from the end of the loaf in the cupboard he ate it slowly, standing at the sink, washing it down gently with more cold, clear water, and felt the sugars race through his parched body straight away. Better.

Going slowly to the door he shaded his dry eyes against the sun and looked out to check for Luca. There he was, by the rocks at the edge of the beach, crouching over a large pool like a caveman. Beside him was Grace, the hat discarded on the sand behind her, and her clothes puffed out around her as she knelt beside him. She had shucked back her long loose sleeves and was reaching a brown arm into the water, her face intent, the large nose giving the impression of an eagle or some other raptor on the hunt. Luca was squeaking – he could hear him from where he stood at the door – and his hands were covering his mouth, then his eyes, then his mouth again. He was trying to look at what she was bringing out and also trying not to look. Evan smiled despite himself.

He saw her brown hand come out of the water, dripping. She was nipping something gently between finger and thumb. Maybe a crab. Not all that big, by the looks of it, but Luca covered his eyes and squeaked anyway. Evan heard her laugh, a big man-sound, and he watched as she put the little thing onto her palm and held it still, using her other hand to corral it as it scuttled about. He found himself wanting to see Luca's eyes open and peep at the creature, maybe take it on his hand.

He'd go out to them, welcome or not.

Crunching over the shingle towards them, the sea air was salt in his mouth. It felt good going in. The water was close and still, lying placid at almost full tide with only little licks on the beach to say that it was moving at all. There were no birds. There was only his great big feet making noise across the tiny stones and then muffled on the sand. The strangest lightness in him that he couldn't understand, as if something had opened and let the pressure out.

Grace must have heard him coming up behind them, but she didn't turn around. All her attention was on the little creature on her hand – black, he saw, its claws thin and dainty – and on the peeping boy still squeaking beside her. She was a long, wiry shape in light brown, kneeling on the sand and comfortable, even though it must be wet under her, even though her clothes and skin were surely getting soaked with the seeping under-water from the rising tide. He reached them just as Luca slowly took his hands away from his eyes, reassured that she wouldn't throw the crab at him or let him be frightened by it – that she would stay quite still like before, and let him look at this new one, this bigger fellow.

Evan stood nearby and watched the boy breathing at the crab for a while. The sea rustled beside them quietly and the slight breeze cooled the sweat on his neck. The little creature was still scuttling about from thumb to finger on Grace's hand, trying to find its way home, but she held it steady, watching the boy's eyes, smiling at him as he relaxed, inch by inch, and leaned closer. Finally she had her reward as the boy smiled, tentatively, and showed her his fingers meeting his thumb in a nipping motion, crab, and she nodded, yes.

'Ask him will we put it in his bucket,' she said without turning.

'Christ, yes, at least he'll get rid of the stinking seaweed then,' agreed Evan, coming forwards, and signed quickly to his son who'd looked up at his movement, at the change in the light.

Luca shook his head.

I want to keep the stuff in the bucket. We'll put him in a smaller pool, he decided – one with no seaweed. Then I can look at him better.

He watched Grace's face while Evan relayed the message to ensure she agreed, and when she smiled and nodded, he tugged at her sleeve – *come on then* – trying to make her stand more quickly. Evan could see that she was having difficulty getting back up from her perch on the sand, wet clothing trapping stiff legs, and her hands busy with the crab.

Go and find a pool and tell us when it's ready, he told the boy, and put his hand to her elbow to help her up as he ran excitedly off.

She shook him off immediately and glared at him. 'I'm not a geriatric yet,' she said.

'Well, give me the crab then, while you sort yourself out,' he said, gently. 'Luca'll never forgive us if we let it get away.'

Grace looked at him but said nothing. Instead, she reached up and took his hand and opened it. He felt the strength of her bones through the skin. She tipped the crab delicately into his hand and he clamped the other over it quickly like a roof. He could feel the tiny prickles of its pointed toes against his skin, tiptoeing around. Now that she had both hands free, she pushed herself to standing with a fluid strength and shook out her long skirt, dark patches of wet and sand encrusting it. She lifted it off her shins and knees and brushed the worst of the damp sand from her legs and feet without bashfulness. He saw her legs, strong and pale and bare, and looked away quickly to let her finish. Behind him Luca was scrambling about on the rocks like a monkey, looking for a suitable crab-pool. The boy was a really excellent climber, just like his old man, he thought, and felt a quick and novel pride.

'You're in better form this morning, I must say,' he heard Grace comment. He turned to see her retrieve her crazy hat from the sand, smack it quickly with an open hand and plonk it back on her head. Then she was tucking wild strands of yellow and grey hair back underneath and out of the way, remarking, 'I thought you'd be dead on the sofa when I came down, or at least unconscious, the state you were in last night.'

He dropped his eyes and looked sheepish. 'Yes. Sorry about that. I am. And thanks for—' He gestured towards Luca. 'It was disgraceful, I know—'

She nodded her agreement.

'—but I won't be doing it again, I promise. That's it sorted. Over. The last bit finished.'

She looked at him keenly and nodded. 'Well, some of us have work to do,' she said. 'There's mackerel shoaling off Lignacallah and at least twenty of them are mine.'

She clicked for the dog, which had been lying hidden high on the rocks, its snout on its paws. It scrambled to its feet and hopped up out of sight over the top, heading for home the quick way.

'Make sure he knows that's a velvet crab, now, not a shore crab. Important to get the taxonomy right, especially at the start,' she told him. 'It's all in the book.'

He nodded and smiled as she shook her wet skirt out once more and strode off towards the lane. The mottled fabric swung around her ankles and she looked like something from another time, exotic in her difference and her indifference. He watched her step up onto the lane and swing round the corner out of sight. She didn't look back.

'Nnngh!' Luca was waving excitedly from the rocks on the other side of the bay. He'd found a pool that would do. Evan felt the little crab in his hands poking its tiny pointed feet into the skin of his palm, feeling anything other than velvet, so he jogged across the sand, his cupped hands awkward in front of him, feeling the little creature bounce inside.

Where's Grace going? the boy asked.

Evan lifted his roof-hand and made it move like a fish, and as he did so, the crab made a speedy run for daylight and freedom. It hung from his finger like an acrobat for a second until he got his hand under it once more, catching it quickly and covering it up.

'Shit!' he said.

'*Nnnaagh!*' the boy yelled. Don't drop it! Here! Quick!

Grace was forgotten as Evan climbed the rough rocks, handless, pushing off the face of them with his elbow. Luca's face was stretched with excitement as he approached, and he jigged up and down as he waited for his father to set the little creature into the pool.

Evan crouched down and held his palm under the water. As soon as its toes felt wet, the crab ran from his fingers and into the bright space. Luca was crouching on the rocks beside him, so close to the pool that his nose almost touched the water, his chin on his hands. The sun was high in the sky now, and a lone seagull circled overhead. Time had stopped, it seemed, in the spacey shiftiness of Evan's recovering body, and it seemed that they hung in the liminal space between sleeps, the two of them, alone in this place, together.

They watched the little creature scurry in its strange sideways gait from corner to corner of the pool. There was no way out, at least until the tide came in. He felt a quiet pity for the thing. Its blind captivity disturbed him, so he looked at his son instead. There was a new dusting of freckles on the bridge of his nose, and his arms and legs were brown. His face was calm and open, absorbed in the contents of the pool, without that crease between the brows which had once been habitual, and made him sometimes look like a little old man. Evan realised they hadn't had an argument for days. He reached out and rubbed the boy's shoulder gently. Luca looked up at him in surprise, and then smiled.

It has a lot of legs, Evan said.

The boy nodded.

Ten. But the front ones are sort of arms, and he nodded at his father in friendly way, and fell to watching again.

Evan's stomach rumbled loudly. He touched the boy's shoulder again.

You hungry?

Luca shook his head, wriggling to pull out his little notebook from his pocket, the one used at home for complex messages or requests for new words. He opened it at the next blank page and set it carefully on the rock, its little pencil dangling from the string.

I want to draw its mouth, he told his father. If I can find it. Them, actually. Grace says it's got two!

He shook his head, dazzled by so much complexity, and Evan took the chance to stand up and ease the stiffness out of his limbs, rub the points of the rocks from his skin. He had no appetite, never did after a bender, but he'd put on some bacon, make a butty or something for them, something simple and filling.

Stepping into the dark space of the cottage he saw a girl lying on the sofa, round and fat, her phone in her hand and her shoes kicked off higgledy-piggledy on the floor, her bright floral dress startling even in the dim light, and her big bare white legs shining. She looked around belligerently as he darkened the doorway and demanded, 'Who're you?'

Chapter 24

'CAN I HELP YOU?' was all he could think to say.

'This is lockdown,' the girl retorted, sitting up quickly, her hair huge and thick and yellow all around her head. There was something very familiar in the way she said it which made him look at her closely.

'Yes,' he agreed, and waited.

They looked at one another in silence for another moment, the girl's face suffused with red. 'I always stay here when I come down,' she told him.

He noticed then that there was a rucksack at her feet, the kind they use for school nowadays, and a duffle bag packed to bursting so that all along its sides were bumps and protrusions. They sat quite comfortably alongside all the rest of the stuff strewn on the floor.

'Not at the moment, I'm afraid,' he said gently. 'We're here.'

She knitted her lips together and sat forwards, speaking as though he were stupid, 'But it's lockdown!'

'I know. I came before it started and got stuck.'

'Oh.' She put her head down and fiddled with her phone. Her dress was really quite remarkable, all orange splodges and red splashes on white, like a huge beach towel.

'You're Grace's daughter?'

'Niece,' she said shortly. 'She hasn't got any kids.'

'Oh.'

He stood there and looked at her and she shifted awkwardly under his gaze. 'I suppose I'll go round to hers, then,' she said at last, looking down to find her shoes and dragging them towards her with her toes. Her toenails were an impressive shade of purple. 'See if I can stay there. Fuck's sake.'

She wasn't talking to him, and there was an emptiness in her voice that touched him. She didn't look more than sixteen or seventeen.

'She's not in, I don't think,' he said gently, watching as she shoved her feet into the broad, flat shoes, 'but I'm just making lunch—' he headed for the fridge, letting her gather herself together '—and it's only bacon butties, but there's plenty, and you're welcome.'

There was silence behind him and, when he turned, she was still sitting on the sofa, her feet pointed in at one another and the strap of the duffle bag loose in her hand. She was staring out of the bright doorway onto the beach and her face was tired. She looked older now. Eighteen? Twenty?

'OK then,' she said, in a low voice, and paused. She picked at a short fingernail on a broad hand. 'Thanks.'

He busied himself with food and pans, making a lot of noise to fill the space, and felt her stand up behind him, begin to move around. She picked things up, set them down again, sighed. 'Place is a mess,' she said.

Evan laughed. 'Yeah, we men don't tidy up too well, do we?'

'You gay?' she asked. The little bird's skull was in her hand when he whipped around.

'No!'

'Well, who's the men then?'

She set the skull down carefully again and stroked its head like a friend.

'Oh!' he pointed with the spatula out onto the beach. 'My

son. Me and my son. Luca. He's eight. We're here, sort of hiding, actually.'

She regarded him steadily. 'Yeah. Me too,' she said.

'You want a fried egg on your butty? I can do them hard or soft,' he said.

'Oh yum, yes, hard please. And I can make tea.' She paused. 'Aren't you going to ask me anything?'

'I just did.'

'Oh *ha-ha*. I mean who I am, like, or what I'm doing here.'

'Didn't want to be nosey.' He shot her a grin and gestured to the sink with his chin. 'Better wash your hands, eh? Don't want Becky hearing the squatters aren't keeping to the guidelines.'

'Oh her. She melts me, she really does,' sighed the girl, but washed her hands anyway, before fetching the teapot, fishing out teabags, with a clear knowledge of where everything lived in this little house. As she moved over the tiles barefoot, she began to hum softly and the huge dress swung loose around her, a cacophony of colour in the drab room. The thick yellow hair fluffed around her face and he imagined that this was how her aunt had looked a long time ago, and smiled to himself. It was like sharing a space with a rainbow.

They worked in a companionable silence for a while, until the food was ready, and the table set. Steam wound upwards from the teapot on the table where she'd put it on a folded tea towel, ready. It was nice to have company.

'I'll fetch Luca, if you pour the tea,' he said.

'I'll call him,' she offered quickly, already at the door and taking a breath.

'He won't hear you.' Evan paused. 'He's deaf.'

He put plates down on the table, quite hard.

'You look like you hate having to tell people that,' she observed, over her shoulder. 'Don't worry, I'll go get him.'

With surprising agility she was away out towards the rocks where the boy crouched, and he went to the door after her, to see how Luca would react. The boy wasn't generally good with strangers and his diffidence tended to look like stupidity, sometimes even distress. He watched as the girl picked her way over the shingle, her dimpled shoulders high around her ears, until she reached the sand. Luca's eye had been caught by her swirling colours and he was sitting very still, watching her approach like a bird guarding a secret nest. His face was pale and tense.

'Oh god,' thought Evan, wearily. 'Here we go.'

As the girl reached him, the boy's face crumpled into tears.

'Jesus,' Evan said quietly, shame creeping over him in a hangover sweat. He didn't rush to intervene. He didn't feel like it. Instead, he stayed by the door, the thick smell of fried bacon mixing and twisting in his belly.

But the girl hadn't retreated. Sweeping in on the boy instead, she pulled her dress close around her body and plonked herself down on the rocks beside him, holding out her hand for something with the flash of a white smile. Evan saw the boy look her up and down slowly, awed by the sheer scale of her, his face shining wet, and then slowly hand something over, a dark, flat shape, putting it into her outstretched hand. He was shaking his head as they looked down at it together and getting upset all over again. With a sisterly ease, the girl put the thing in the lap of her skirt and drew him to her, putting her arm around the skinny shoulder and wiping the tears with a corner of her dress. She put her face down low to him and Evan could see her smiling and shaking her head and then, a thumbs-up signal. She pointed at the thing in her lap and then touched her forehead several times, then waggled her finger at him—

I'm clever with this stuff, don't worry.

She lifted the thing and passed her hand over it like a magician transforming it, and again that bright smile flashed down at the boy.

It was his phone, Evan realised with sudden relief. He was

upset because something had happened to his phone. Not the girl coming over. Not crying because of a stranger, like a two-year-old. The phone. The silly kid had dropped it or something, like he was told he would, if he took it on the beach, sticking out of his back pocket like that all the time. It was broken, maybe. Of course he'd be upset.

But the girl hadn't scared him. No, Evan realised, with a soft laugh. She'd cuddled him, instead.

The girl looked up and pointed to the house and jerked her head to the boy, come on. Luca stood up as she did, and took her hand without hesitation, eager to get home, to see to the phone, to see if she could really help. Evan retreated into the house and let them come, waiting until the doorway darkened and they came crashing in together.

Dad. My phone fell but it's OK. This girl says she can fix it. Don't be cross.

Evan kept his face stern and told him, It's your phone, not mine. I *told* you what would happen.

Like the sun going behind a cloud the boy's face darkened, and he trailed to the bathroom to wash his hands. Evan was left looking after him, feeling as if he'd kicked a puppy. He sighed and turned away, brought milk to the table, filled the boy's glass.

The girl had sat herself down in the meantime and helped herself to one of the plates, where soft crusty bread covered Becky's nice thick bacon and the rubbery lips of an egg. He sat down across from her and wished he had her appetite. The sight of the food on the table was making him queasy. He breathed carefully and watched her pour herself a cup of tea right up to the brim and then milk and sugar it generously. She caught his glance and smiled and filled a cup for him too. At his nod she put in some milk and stirred it for him, pushed it over gently. He lifted it with both hands like an invalid and sipped. It was hot and good and comforting. He felt a little better immediately and could almost face his sandwich. Almost. The broken phone lay at the girl's elbow, and to delay having to eat anything he reached across and slid it close to take a look. It wasn't good. The casing had split, and the complicated innards were exposed. He looked at her quizzically.

'It's grand,' she said thickly through a mouthful of bread. 'It's what I do – tech. I'll sort it in a minute.' She licked a blob of ketchup from the corner of her mouth, shook back a fluff of hair and continued eating, her elbows on the table, her eyes scouting the sandwich for the next bite.

Luca came back from the bathroom and slid onto his chair. He kept his eye on the phone under his father's hand and flicked a glance every so often up to his face. Evan watched him pick at his food from the corner of his eye, felt the irritation rise, but said nothing. He wondered if the girl found it strange, this protracted silence. Everything prickled. Everything was scratchy and uncomfortable today, even his own skin. Her presence made it all the more obvious, all the more oppressive. All he could hear was their mutual munching; now and again the clink of a mug against a plate.

When he glanced up the girl had finished already, the mighty butty hoovered up in short order, the smears of ketchup mopped with a crust. He saw her lift the mug and take a long swig of tea and, as she did so, notice the untouched food on the boy's plate. She patted his hand to make him look at her, then indicated the sandwich in front of him. She creased her eyebrows, sternly. Luca shook his head, not hungry, and his face was that dark, closed-down thing that got under Evan's skin and sparked and flickered and made him harsh. But the girl was having none of it.

She put her mug down with a big, significant movement and sat back, folding her arms and drawing her chin in, making it multiple. She had the boy's full attention. His eyes were huge in his face. Deliberately, she pointed at his sandwich. Then she pointed, tap-tap-tap, at the broken phone by her elbow, and then she refolded her broad arms, drew in her chin impressively again, nodded just once, and held the boy's gaze until he dropped his eyes.

Evan watched in awe as Luca picked up his sandwich and took a slow bite. The girl watched him too, nodding in approval when he glanced up, and kept on watching until he had eaten almost half. Then she pointed at his glass of milk. He put the food down carefully, took the glass and drank, holding her gaze over the rim. She nodded again. He returned to the sandwich and ate another two bites, chewing and swallowing with determination. Finally defeated, he shook his head at her – *I'm done* – and the crease between her brows disappeared. The sun came out.

She unfolded her arms and leaned over to pat his hand. *Good lad.*

The phone now? he asked, pointing.

Yes, yes, she laughed, and picked it up, shoved back her chair. The boy slid off his own and went to her, quickly.

'You've got brothers,' Evan said.

'Yeah, three,' she said, laughing, 'but I'm the boss.'

As he washed up, Evan heard her talking to the boy, showing him what she was doing, and telling him things, pointing stuff out. Luca was hanging over her, unable to hear but intrigued nonetheless, following her deft movements, her pointing finger. When she needed a needle, she asked for one through Evan, and the boy darted to fetch it from his father's hand and carried it carefully over. When she needed tape, he had it ready and pulled the end loose to help her.

The sun breasted the roof and sent the first rays of afternoon in through the kitchen window. Evan dried his hands on the towel and leaned against the sink to watch the pair, soothed by the rise and fall of the girl's voice, suddenly dog-tired himself. Her hair fell forwards at one point as she fiddled with some intricate inner part, blocking Luca's view, and the boy lifted the fuzz of it back, tucked it behind her ear for her and leaned further in on her shoulder. She didn't notice.

'There,' she said at last, showing the phone to him as the light came back on and it started up. Apart from the tape holding the break together, it was as good as it had been that morning. She licked the tip of her finger, touched it to her dress and showed it to them. A tiny silver metal thing.

'Dunno why or how, but there's always a bit left over,' she remarked, clapping it off her hands onto the floor with the rest of the mess. 'But it works, anyway, so that's all right.'

The boy took the phone, grinned at her and darted to the hammock, flipped himself in. They watched as he wobbled and wriggled inside like a caterpillar in a chrysalis, and then went still. The girl looked at the faded hammock.

'I loved that thing, when I was his age,' she said softly. 'Fucking rip it outta the ceiling if I tried to get in it now.'

Evan didn't know what to say to that, so asked, 'What's your name, anyway?'

'Oh, right.' She laughed, 'I'm Abbie. Who're you?'

'Evan.' He smiled and raised an elbow. She raised hers in return, but they didn't touch. 'And you know Luca already...'

'Yeah.' She laughed softly. 'Nice kid, shame about the ears. Can you not get them fixed?'

Everyone always asked that.

'Oh, we've tried a few things. Didn't work, because of the kind of hearing impairment he has, unfortunately. There's an implant he can have, but it's sort of radical. Surgery, you know? His mum wants to wait, let him grow up a bit first, says he's managing fine at the minute.'

'Christ,' said Abbie and she sounded just like her aunt. 'I'd want him to have it now. Like, straight away. Shit. Who'd want their kid to grow up deaf if he didn't have to?'

Evan liked her even more suddenly, and grinned, but didn't reply. Lorna had always made him feel like a monster for wanting to have him 'fixed'. When she'd said the word, there'd always been inverted commas around it. Her voice had always been harsh. As if it was monstrous to want his son to be normal. As if he was the perpetrator or the cause, for refusing to accept him as he was.

'Where is Grace, anyway?' Abbie asked, breaking his line of thought.

Evan went to the door and nodded his head out at the sea. 'There's mackerel shoaling somewhere,' he said, and she nodded. 'In fact—' he shaded his eyes, used to the look of the moving water now, able to find discrepancies, small changes sometimes '—I think that's her, there.'

Abbie came to his shoulder and peered out. A little black boat sat still in the distance, a long dark shape at the tiller and a stocky dark shape at the prow. 'Ah, there's Dog, too,' she said, in a delighted voice.

'You like that thing?'

'God, yes.' She pushed past him gently and wriggled herself up to sit on the little garden wall, looking out. Her bottom hung down the near side, and he averted his eyes. 'I'd worry about her, on her own, and she wouldn't have a dog for ages, until she found that one. She had rabbits before, but it's not the same.'

'Rabbits?'

She laughed, 'I know, right? Five of them at one point, hopping round the house. Lovely wee things, like, tame as anything but no company, really.'

'Yeah, not much good against an intruder, either.'

'Nibble you to death!'

They both laughed.

'But tell me,' Evan asked, leaning back against the door-frame. 'The people round here say Grace is, well, a bit—'

'Nuts, you mean?'

She twisted to look at him and he felt a sudden shame, and looked down. 'She's not mad, OK?' Her voice was sharp and loud. 'She's just different, that's all.' She paused, but before he could apologise, she said, 'Nobody can say what's normal, really. The important thing is to do what makes you happy, right?' She turned away, and her voice went soft as she looked out at the little boat on the busy sea. 'I want to be just like her. Live here, do this, the fishing, the quilts, the lot. Graduate from weird to eccentric, do whatever the fuck I like, whatever the fuck way I want.'

Her voice was sad and lost. She propped herself up straighter on her arms and watched the boat again.

'I think you're marvellous,' Evan told her, and she twisted again and smiled a little.

'Really?'

He nodded. 'The way you dealt with Luca. People rarely can, you know. He can be so – difficult.' All the world of pain was in that word, and it wasn't enough.

'I like difficult,' the girl said, turning away again. 'Sure if it was easy, anyone could do it.'

They stood in silence for a while, enjoying the day and the company.

'She was kidnapped, you know, in London,' Abbie offered quietly after a while.

He didn't think he'd heard right, leaned forwards. 'Sorry?'

'She doesn't talk about it much. When she does, she says, kept. She was kept there, but sounds like kidnapping to me. Like, she was always a bit weird before she went, Mum says, but after – well, it took her a long time to get back to her normal weird, if you know what I mean.'

'Right. Shit.'

He looked out at the sea as if the sight of Grace would make this new information more credible. She'd pulled in her rod and was rowing now, heading back. The little boat would hover for a moment as she leaned forwards, and then shoot across the water as she pulled on the oars, then lull again, then shoot, just like Popeye in the old cartoons, scooting across the water at great speed. He could see the dog, going up and down and up and down in the prow, holding its position like a captain following the stars.

'Yeah,' the girl said, as if she hadn't paused at all. 'My gran fetched her back. What a woman. Never was out of the county in her life but went over there to look for her. I'd love to have seen it. All the way to London from Ballybrady – bus, boat and train, in her Sunday best. Stayed till she tracked her down and then brought her back again.'

Her voice was matter of fact; the story well-rehearsed.

'Wow. He just – he just let her leave? The kidnapper?'

Didn't sound like kidnapping to him. Where were the police?

'He let her out all the time, that's the thing. Shopping and stuff, told her what to get. Scared her with stories about what would happen if she didn't come straight back, if she didn't do the right things, so she kept coming back, even after everything. He treated her badly, I think, hurt her, you know? So she did whatever he said.'

The girl had turned fully round now, telling the story properly, trying to work it out herself, in the telling.

'Mum says she was brainwashed. Can you believe it? Auntie Grace, like? Thought she had to stay with him, once they'd – you know. She didn't know any better, you see. He kept telling her and telling her, I suppose, till she believed it herself, and there was no one to tell her any different. She was all alone in the big city. It was different then, in the eighties, like. Ireland and England were different worlds.'

She looked at him appraisingly, 'You weren't . . .?'

'I was a child in the eighties – I didn't have much idea what was going on.'

She nodded, satisfied, and things went quiet for a while, but he could feel the story going around and around in her head, puzzling itself out. As they watched, the boat went out of sight behind the cliff. It was heading in to land, towards the little bay in front of Grace's cottage. The girl spoke as if to herself and this time her voice was so quiet that he had to step forwards a little to hear what she said above the rising sound of the incoming tide.

'When she came back, she wouldn't say boo to a goose – she shuffled and all, walked with her head down, talked to herself – Mum says it was awful, you'd cry to see her at it. Pulled her hair out, shit like that.' She shivered a bit. 'I can't imagine her like that – can you?'

He shook his head.

'They kept finding her half dead, you know, when they least expected it.'

'Jesus.'

'I know, poor thing. You can see it in her eyes sometimes, still. That's why I come down a lot. She jumped off the cliff over there, once, didn't end well.'

She pointed at the cliffs to the left of the bay. They were dark and steep with a jagged, nasty edge to them and nothing below but sea.

'Christ.'

'I know. Broke loads of bones, I can't remember which, but didn't die, obviously. Did all sorts else. They put her in the mental after that and fried her with electric shocks. That's why her hair's so frizzy, I think.'

The girl tucked her own wiry hair behind her ear without irony.

'She didn't plan it out, do it properly, any of the times. I would have. I plan things. So I think she didn't actually want to do it.'

'Just a cry for help?'

She shrugged, 'Yeah – from someone who won't take any.'

There was nothing left to say.

They watched the sea for another while. Evan heard the small thump of Luca's stockinged feet on the floor behind him as he climbed out of the hammock and then the quiet crackle of a biscuit packet, a deaf boy trying to be sneaky.

Evan played the game – stayed still, looking out, until the crackling stopped and there was peace again, only the quietest munching noises coming from the swinging hammock at his back.

Chapter 25

—

THE BUCKET WAS HEAVY as she hauled it out of the boat and set it on the firm wet sand. Dog was already chasing what was left of his tail, delighted to be on land, racing up to see her with his ragged teeth all on show, then wheeling around and away again as if she was chasing him, then squirming on his back with his legs a-wriggle to scratch and dry himself on the gritty beach. She held the gunwale as it lipped up and down and watched him being happy for a moment and wished it were that simple.

The townie. He wasn't happy, either. There was something so dark in those eyes it called to her own depths – brought up things she'd rather have forgotten. It was getting to be a nuisance, actually. No one else got the time of day out of her mostly, but he and his skittish little boy and his dead girl were on the edge of her thoughts always now, colouring them grey.

She shook herself and set to heaving the boat out of the water, the hardest part of the whole enterprise. It always resisted, pulling back like a bad horse, and pitting all its weight against her as if reluctant to leave the water. Today it was particularly troublesome, and she swore as it dragged her one step too far back into the waves, and a cold wash of seawater filled her boot.

A flash of colour appeared beside her and there was Abbie on the other side of the boat, that lovely face, that bright hair, that flash of a smile, the hem of a beautiful frock floating unregarded in the water around her shins, those strong familiar hands gripping the boat and ready.

'Christ!'

'Nah, just me, dear Aunt.'

Grace felt her face widen in a smile. She hadn't hoped to see the girl for months. 'What're you doing here?'

The boat was coming forwards already under her young, strong grip.

'Helping you – and not before time either! You nearly lost her there. Here, shift over and give us some elbow-room and we'll get her moving.'

'I had her, don't you worry, Miss Smart-arse!'

'Stop talking and pull, woman, will you?'

Between them it was no chore making the little craft swim up out of the water, and soon it was tucked up and slumbering under the fringe of the grassy lane, no more fight in it, and only the gutting of the fish left to be done.

'Have you a blade for me or will I run up for one?'

Lovely Abbie, always ready to help. Grace handed her the bigger knife, the one with the wooden handle, the one that made the job easy.

'Where's the wee one? You know I like it better.'

'Ach, you're a townie now, you've no skills. I daren't trust you with the wee one now you're living up in the city with all those idiots.'

The girl's face darkened instantly, and she took the proffered knife and turned away, picking up the bucket and heading for the gutting block. 'Yeh. I wanna talk about that some time.'

Grace rubbed her back and felt the gloom descend again. Abbie too? This new sadness was suddenly everywhere. No one was safe from it, if it had *her*. It seemed to come ahead of the new virus like a vanguard – the silent part of it, the terrible part, the part that opened you up to the other physiological bit, made you vulnerable, took away your fight. The donkey's call came over the rocks as she joined her niece and wordlessly selected a fish to gut. Mournful and lonely, the sound echoed around the rocks and ran off out to sea. They worked in silence for a long time, letting all the dark thoughts work themselves through. There was nothing to be heard but the swish of the water and the scolding of gathering gulls on nearby rocks. There was nothing to be seen but the parts of life made to hide in darkness being brought out into the light – the deep purples and greys, the browns and clotted whites of the fishes' innards, rich and pungent.

'They call me Sofa,' Abbie said quietly and made a long, deep incision on the silky belly under her hand, almost too deep, risking nicking the bowel, spoiling the meat.

Grace nodded once, to show she'd heard, and went on slicing and scraping. It didn't make sense to her, but then she had never understood how people thought, what inspired their many cruelties.

'I didn't know. Didn't even think they'd noticed me.' She sounded ashamed, as if she'd done something wrong.

'Thought you were top of your class.'

'Yeah. Maybe that was the problem. Anyway, I'm not going back, when they open up again.'

Grace nodded again. It wasn't her business. The quiet drifted back in.

As they finished and scraped the guts onto the beach, raising a huge rasping flight of white bellies, grey wings, yellow beaks, Abbie said, 'Can I stay here, with you?'

'Yep. Have to be in my house, though, not the rental. I've got tenants down there.' She shot her niece a sharp look. '—You can share Dog's basket.'

She grunted, lifting the bucket, and the girl knew better than to try to take it from her. They trudged up the beach together, the word 'sofa' stuck sharply in Grace's mind like a stone in a shoe. At the lane, she plonked the bucket down beside a thick clump of dock leaves and clapped her hands together to clean them. The scales and slime made them sticky and uncomfortable.

'Here,' she said, lifting four neat fillets out, pulling a big broad leaf from the clump at her feet to wrap them. She held them out to her niece. 'Take these down to the rental, will you. They wouldn't know good food if it hit them in the face, those two.' Her forehead creased. 'See if the wee fella would eat a good mackerel fillet. He's awful thin.'

'Luca,' the girl said, smiling and wiping her own hands back and forth on the long tufts of shiny grass where the lane ended and beach began. 'They gave me lunch. They're nice.'

She held out her hands for the fish. Grace sniffed, and gave the parcel over.

'I thought they were lovely,' Abbie said. 'And you don't give anyone else your fish, dear Auntie, so what's up? Making friends at last?'

'Hardly,' sniffed Grace again. 'There's something going on with him, the Da, that's all.'

'Yeah, a dirty great hangover,' said Abbie. 'Christ, the smell of drink off him – whew! Worse than you in the bad old days.'

'Well. He says that's it.'

Abbie looked at her. 'That's what?'

'With the drinking.'

'Oh. Right.'

Abbie's head was tilted to one side, regarding her, and it was irritating.

'Get along with you, if you're going, young lady,' Grace snapped, pushing herself up the short step to the lane and hoisting the bucket again. 'I'll go ahead and throw some straw down for you in Dolly's stall, sure. With that sharp tongue you'll only hurt yourself, inside.'

Abbie snorted and strode off in the direction of the rented

cottage. Grace put down the bucket and swiped a boot at Dog who tried to stick in his nose, and watched the girl go.

Sofa.

The child was beautiful. Such a lovely frock, just what she'd pick out herself on a rare visit to the big town. That gorgeous hair, all golden and cloudy. That lovely skin, fresh and clear and plump. That big, generous, swinging stride. Maybe too generous altogether for city-folk. Frightening for them, the pussy-footed nasty bastards.

Sofa.

If she found the fuckers, she'd use this knife.

Dog whined at a distance. She must have growled aloud. She clicked the knife closed and slid it into her pocket and lifted the bucket one more time to carry it home.

Chapter 26

———

IT SEEMED VERY EARLY when Luca stood beside Evan's bed, poking him gently with one finger. The little room was dark and musty, and he was deeply asleep, without dreaming. When he opened his eyes they wouldn't focus, full of sleep mist, but the boy was standing ready with his glasses and began to push them onto his face for him, poking him in the eye. He sat up, pushing him gently away.

Stop! What time is it? Why are you waking me?

Can I go fishing?

What? Are you kidding? Evan groaned and flumped around, already losing the thick warmth of sleep. He closed his eyes again. Maybe later, leave me alone, it's too early.

Poke-poke-poke. A little finger in his shoulder.

'Oh for god's sake, what?' he said aloud, and sat up again. —What is it, Luca? I'm not going fishing at dawn, for god's sake.

Not you. The fat girl. She says we can go in the boat. If I'm allowed.

Evan rubbed his eyes. Don't say the fat girl, he told his son slowly, her name is Abbie.

The boy shrugged. Can I?

Wait a minute. Let me get up. Where is she?

188

The boy's face was twisted with urgency. She's gone to the beach already – her beach – to the boat. Quick! Can I? Can I?

Evan shook off the last of the sleep and swung his feet over the edge of the bed, which creaked wildly as he moved and bobbed gently under him like a boat at sea. He was starting to get used to it now, since the boy had come, and the little noises and scratchings around him in the room at night were almost comforting.

Wait, he told his son with a frown. Just wait a minute. Let me think.

The boy moaned and bounced on the balls of his feet, already working himself up to tears, those nerves already singing, the frustration already building.

Evan frowned at him sharply. Don't start, Luca. Get a grip. I mean it. Or you definitely won't go.

He watched the boy bite his lip to hold back the feelings, and he stretched out and put a hand on the thin arm.

You'd need a jacket. A special thing for the sea, to keep you safe.

With a sudden watery grin the boy bent down and picked something from the floor at his feet, and waved a faded orange lifejacket at him triumphantly. It was hers, when she was my age. That's why it looks so old.

Evan laughed. It looked the right size, as far as he could tell. Wait, he said, again. Let me see what the sea looks like.

He pushed himself off the bed and went into the main room, the boy skipping anxiously at his heels, following the bright shine of the morning sun to the big window. The sea was like glass, the still air of summer lulling everything already, the little fat-headed pinks on the rocks nodding only slightly in the breeze.

Bring me my phone.

Luca groaned and flumped across to the table, found the device and brought it to his father, who checked the forecast. Fair with a light breeze.

Tap-tap-tap on his hand. Look, the boy said, and showed him his own phone, an icon of waves and some numbers and graphs. It's a good tide, too. Please?

Evan looked at him quizzically. You know how to read that?

The boy nodded, proudly, and stuffed the device back in his pocket. The fat— Abbie showed me. It means the water will be moving slowly and only a little bit. OK? Can I go, now?

OK. OK, Evan signed, sighing. Let's go and see her.

Luca squeaked in excitement and Evan damped it with a warning hand.

It's not good to be excited on a boat. The sea is dangerous.

He thought wryly of his own adventure. But the boy was already at the door, hopping from foot to foot as if the floor was hot, poking his arms into the lifejacket which hung down around his shanks, the crotch-strap trailing. Evan grabbed a couple of apples and a banana from the bowl by the window, a towel from the back of the chair and the small jacket slung on the sofa, and followed him out into the yellow day. It was early, but the seabirds were already busy about their business and the whole of the summer world had been up for hours.

Eat this, he told his son, as they scrunched up the lane, and passed him a banana. The boy needed to remember to eat, he thought, watching him despatch it in a few hungry bites, and then toss the peel far into the weeds and run ahead. He could see the string of muscles in the thin legs, however, and a looseness in his movement that was new.

Around the corner to the bay in front of Grace's cottage, he saw the little boat already flipped over and ready, as if sailing on the sand. Abbie was sitting beside it, legs stuck out at angles and busy with a bucket and some kind of string. Today she wore purple and white stripes but had tucked all that hair behind a scarf, the better to see her work. She looked up at the sound of their approach and smiled.

'Morning!' he called. 'You sure about this?'

She smiled up at him and he saw she held a little rod, and it was fishing line she was using, stringing the line through the eyes, and tying little fluttering silver ribbons along its length. Luca skidded to a seat beside her and saw too. He reached out a quick hand, but she was there before him and drew the rod away, waving a warning finger.

Gently pulling one of the little ribbons aside instead, well out of reach, she showed him that underneath was a curved, sharp hook. The boy drew back as if he had been hurt by it and she shrugged. Luca looked at her doubtfully and asked, Is it for the fish?

She understood and nodded, opened her mouth wide and snapped it closed, tapping her finger gently on the point of the hook for him to see. Evan stood at a little distance, watching his son realise what would happen. He was pleased when the boy turned to him for advice, his face an open question, full of doubt. He shrugged in response, and said, That's how you catch fish, Luca. And then you have to kill them, too.

He spoke it aloud as he signed it, so that the girl could hear.

'—And cut them open, and pull out their guts,' she said helpfully, but he didn't repeat this.

Luca's head turned slowly back to his friend, who had resumed her work, and then looked at his father once more. Kill them how?

Evan shrugged again. He didn't know. 'How d'you kill them, Abbie?'

She smiled at him like a movie villain and lifted a rubber mallet from the bucket. There was a scattering of spangles on its thick black snout already, gleaming pearly in the sunlight. Fish scales. Luca's eyes were as wide as saucers as he looked at it and there was a long, thinking pause. Evan wasn't sure if he would want to go, now, but when he turned back, his face was shining.

Can I do the hammer, Dad? Ask her!

Evan laughed and Abbie looked at him, her face a question.

'He wants to know if he can do the hammer on the fish,' he told her, and she laughed too, and shook her head.

'Tell him no. He can do the fishing and sit still and behave himself or we're coming straight back in. And tell him not to bounce. It's a wee boat, and I'm a big girl.'

Her face reddened slightly as she said this, and she put her head down over the line as if doing something very tricky, although her fingers were still. Evan smiled sympathetically at her bent head, then relayed the message to Luca and added,

You must be very still and good on the boat, Luca. Don't get excited if you catch a fish, OK? Give the rod to Abbie and she'll bring it in for you, and deal with it.

Luca made a bored face in return and rolled his eyes.

Abbie finished with the rod and held it up for him to see. He didn't grab for it, remembering the tiny hooks, and she smiled in approval and tapped the side of one eye, telling him to watch. Without moving, her broad legs still splayed on the sand and her toenails gleaming cherry red, she drew the rod gently back over one shoulder, the line loose and trailing, all the little ribbons fluttering, a little round weight at the end holding it all straight. Then with a deft flick, she cast the line and they watched it sail in a slow, whistling arc through the air. They saw the weight land with a little whump in the sand a fair bit ahead, and Luca squeaked and wriggled and held out both hands for the rod, to have a turn, but she moved it out of reach and spoke to Evan over the boy's wavy curls.

'Don't worry, I'll do that bit for him, and then he can hold it and jig it in, this first trip.'

Evan nodded and sat on a rock to watch, as she gave the rod to the boy and steadied his hand on it. She taught him how to flick the keeper over on the reel, how to turn the crank and wind the line back in, how to pause every three turns and wave the rod out to the side, jigging, making the ribbons flash to emulate the stop-start movement of sand eels underwater, to trick the fish. A dry scrap of seaweed snagged on a hook and he reeled it in and lifted the line so that it twisted in the breeze.

'Yay!' Abbie called, clapping her hands. 'You've caught something! You're a natural!'

His face glowed as he wound his catch in, and turned to show his father. His teeth gleamed white in his browning face and the silver ribbons twinkled in the sun and suddenly something ached in Evan's chest. The day was still and warm and perfect. The boy was happy and healthy and excited. Everything was perfect. Perfect. Evan held his breath for a second to keep the feeling in. It was almost as sharp as pain.

'Perfect,' he said aloud.

He hardly dared move. Hardly dared breathe, just felt the joy and relief of it leaping inside his chest like a fish trying to get free. Suddenly he was grounded. He was planted fair and square on the shifting grains of the beach, with his son, with that smiling face, with the sun warm on his shoulders, content. He wanted it to stay like this for ever, and never change.

'We won't go out too far,' said Abbie, clambering to her feet and breaking the spell. 'But he'll need a coat or something. It's colder out on the water, you know.'

He stood up and passed her the jacket in his hand with a smile.

She pulled the boy to his feet and worked at zipping up the lifejacket. The salty zip was sticking so that she had to go up and down, up and down a few times to free it, and Luca could hardly stand still. She laughed and shook the jacket so that his head waggled. Evan stood where the boy could see him.

Stand still, you fool, he said, and Luca stood still.

'Will you give me a hand hauling the boat in?' Abbie glanced at his trainers. 'But you'll need bare feet, and roll up your jeans.'

He did what she said as Luca kicked off his sandals and

danced around the beach, a bright orange bubble. When he came her way, Abbie handed him the rod and a bucket from which the mallet handle stuck like a knuckle. He danced on. Evan tapped him on the shoulder and gave him a stern look.

Be careful, he signed.

To his surprise the boy set the rod and bucket down gently on the beach, stood back up and looked at him, straight, with almost an adult expression of exasperation on his young face. I am so fed up with people giving me that sign, he replied, slowly and deliberately.

Evan stared at him.

This place is different from home, the boy told him angrily. You don't have to tell me to be careful, careful, careful all the time. I'm OK here.

He put his hands on his hips and glowered at his father, while Abbie tactfully pottered with the boat, popping in rowlocks and stowing things out of the way. Looking down at his son, wiry and brown, Evan was strongly aware of the wide-open sea nearby, the high treacherous cliffs behind him, the sharp jagged hooks on the fishing rod, the very little boat, and he laughed. They were a world away from home and all its rules and restrictions, sure enough. What the hell could go wrong?

You're right. I'm sorry, he said, and watched the boy nod sharply at him, pick up the rod and bucket and stride off down to the water's edge without looking back. He shook his head ruefully and turned to the boat where Abbie waited, her hand on the gunwale. It looked as if she'd tucked the voluminous skirts of her clothing into her underwear, and her legs were thick and strong and pale in the sunlight and she stood in easy unselfconsciousness and waited for him to give a hand.

He stood in the shallows for a long time, watching the little boat make slow and steady progress out to sea, Luca perched high on the prow, his face turned out to where the water covered everything. After a time the tickling fronds of seaweed washing over his feet brought Evan's attention back to himself again. The water on his feet and shins was perfectly comfortable now, not cold at all, and he could feel the sand shift and erode under him with the flow and suck of the little waves, and everything was very still and very calm. He was aware again of that deep quiet within himself. He thought about it, trying to give the sensation a name. It was an absence of fear, he realised; a peace and a sense of space that had crept in on him unnoticed all the time he'd been in Ballybrady, in the little cottage, locked down. Becky would have a proper name for it, no doubt, he thought with a grin.

He stood for a while longer, watching the little boat get smaller and smaller, feeling the water move over his skin, letting his heart beat, until the space inside him became hunger and he roused himself and left the sea and climbed back up the beach, heading back to the cottage for breakfast with an appetite.

The living room was more than usually dark as he stepped in from the glare of the sun and the laptop sent a bright blue light into the gloom from the little kitchen table. Luca must have been playing on it earlier, he realised. As he felt around in the gloom for the button to turn it off, he noticed he had mail.

Hi Evan, I'm sorry I haven't been in touch before now but things have been mad, crazy here, you've no idea. This city is horrible atm. Masks everywhere you go, no one speaking to anyone else, staying inside, looking out the windows at each other or hiding in their back gardens. I've been in charge of sourcing the PPE – gowns, masks, the works. Would you believe that little handbag factory we used to laugh about has started churning out masks for us because I asked, and now we're getting face visors from another place in the South that I found. They've saved our lives, I'm telling you.

It's been exhausting, honestly, you've no idea.

Well, no. I read that back and it sounds rude. Of course you know what it's like. You used to work these hours before Jessie died. There, I said it. She died.

I haven't been too busy to get in touch at all. Let's be honest, I've been enjoying the time on my own. I've been using it to get my head around things, around what happened, and I want to say sorry before we go any further. Its really hard to put this down on paper but all these weeks I've been meaning to, and I'm going to do it tonight. Right.

I never told you but that night, when I came in from the restaurant and saw you both asleep on the chair, I knew I should wake you but I didn't. I was so afraid she'd wake when we moved her, and Id had a few glasses of really nice Prosecco and I was really tired, and I didn't. I didn't wake you. I couldn't face it. Instead I sat on the coffee table and looked at her, sleeping there on your shoulder. It wasn't a sight we saw often, was it, her sleeping? And she was so lovely, so small and warm there. I reached out and took the throw from behind me and, holding my breath, I draped it over you and tucked it under your arm, under her chin. At least I think I tucked it under her chin. I don't know, Evan. I cant remember. It may not have been tucked in properly, It may have been over her little mouth, or been loose somehow, and made its way over her face in the night, I don't know, I don't remember, I cant stop thinking about it. Wondering. If only I'd woken you, if only I hadn't gone on in to that big, lovely, empty quiet cool bed and left you both there. And you never asked. You never said, where did the blanket come from? When the medics came and everyone was fussing and talking and passing her around, remember, it was so awful – you took all the blame, and have done ever since.

And I blamed you, I'm sorry. Shamelessly, I blamed it all on you and it's made me miserable. I've blamed you for what happened as if you planned it, as if you wanted it, and that wasn't fair.

And here's the thing, Evan. I blamed you for Jessie dying because I was already blaming you for Luca. Not his disability, of course, but your coldness to him, the way you look at him when you think I don't see, as if he's wrong, broken, as if he doesn't belong. I should have pulled you about it long ago of course, but I don't think it would have made any difference would it? So maybe this time together has been good for you both. Or maybe you've strangled him by now? I'm sure Id have heard ☺.But then youre always so quiet, you tell me nothing, just give me that look. You know the one I mean.

No, I hope he's OK. I hope you're both OK.

I didn't mean to go on and on like this, but its just coming out of my fingertips so Im letting it flow. Ill correct the typos later or maybe I wont bother ☺ I just wanted to get this off my chest so maybe you'll understand where Im at, now, what's up with the two of us maybe, why I want what I want, now. Why we cant go back to the way it was. Anyway, things are a bit calmer here now. I'll come and take him off your hands again, Im sure youre ready for a break and he needs to keep up with his school work over the summer or he'll fall behind, you know what he's like. Thought Id come at the weekend. Anyway talk soon, see you soon, L X

Evan blew all the air out of his lungs in a long hiss and read the email again.

He stood up slowly and crossed to the window. He could see the little boat as a dark speck against the water but couldn't make out the shapes of those on board. The images of Lorna flickered through his head. Her hair, sliding across his face as she sat astride him in the early light of a weekend morning. The smell of her, passing him fresh from the shower, demurely towel-clad. The quick scissor of her legs in her work-clothes, slim, smooth, fit. The twisted anger on her face as she looked at him before he left. The exasperated shake of her head to his every suggestion regarding the boy. Her smooth white teeth biting into an apple. The pointed shoulder turned away from him night after night. The cold eyes she fixed on him in the bathroom mirror. Lorna.

The calm peace of the beach had gone with her first words, and in its place was the old burning. He wasn't hungry any more. He wasn't tired, he wasn't thirsty.

Fuck it, he thought, the sparkling water beguiling as it crept up to high tide outside his window, the burn of her blame and her rejection and her sorrow a thing that must be dealt with, needing a short sharp shock. I'm going for a swim.

Chapter 27

FROM HER VANTAGE POINT on the top of the hill behind the lane she watched the peregrines hunt. She'd seen the flip-flap of their casual flight become that wondrous stoop not once but three times while she'd been here, the little martins evading them each time of course, nippy and alert. The raptors were only playing, she knew, like bored louts in a playground, throwing their weight around. They were waiting for the real food, for the slow and sleepy pigeons that would clap their way out of the wind-ragged copse sooner or later and be brought home to the hungry peregrine young as a scruffy tangle of feathers and gore.

She'd loved this pair ever since she'd seen them take out a townie's drone in mid-air a few summers ago. The little male peregrine had let the female do most of the attacking that day and she'd stormed the machine with her great wicked claws time and time again until it had spun out of control like a sycamore seed and tumbled down into the sea. Grace laughed aloud at the memory. She hoped the thing had cost a lot of money. It pleased her to imagine the chagrin and impotent rage of the moron at the controls – swearing, red in the face maybe, perhaps getting a close-up view of talons and then seawater on his stupid screen, and then nothing ever again. Excellent.

She lowered the binoculars to rest her eyes a moment, and the dog lifted his head beside her and whined at something or somebody to her right. Turning her head, she saw the townie leaving the cottage below, swathed in a towel, his bare feet scuffed into running shoes with the laces flapping loose.

'Going swimming, that's all. Calm yourself,' she told the dog quietly. 'But let's just hope he's better at that than kayaking, because I've no boat to rescue him this time.'

On the word, she raised the glasses again and located the little craft. It was the real reason she was here of course, although she'd never insult her niece by saying so. Doing well, Abbie was, and so she should be, the amount of hours Grace had spent teaching her to handle the tricky cross-currents at the mouth of the bay. The boy with her was doing well, too. He sat still and intent with the rod in his hand, jigging it carefully, turning to Abbie often in case there was an instruction. They'd been out at least an hour and still he wasn't bored.

Grace smiled through the binoculars. He hadn't had a bite yet, but Abbie had the jig-line, and she'd pulled in a couple of decent fish, and he'd squealed and clapped his hands as they'd curled and gleamed their way out of the water but kept his seat. Good boy. The second time, she was sure she saw him taking a turn with the mallet, raising it high above his head like an avenger's axe, and wondered how that had gone – the slippery crunch, the manic flippering, the running blood and loosened eyeballs.

Her stomach rumbled and she thought about pulling some new potatoes from her carefully rationed drills, to have with the fresh fish that night, and hearing from Abbie how the trip went, what adventures they'd had in the strange silence of the boy's deafness.

'It's nice having her around, it really is,' she confided to the dog. 'No offence, mutt, but your conversation is a little sparse, sometimes.'

The dog butted her elbow with its twisted snout, and she

rubbed its head absently, watching the townie again without the aid of the binoculars, resting her eyes. He was on her beach, not on his own, barefooted now despite the pebbles. She guessed he wanted to be there when the boy came in. They were better with each other, now, she'd noticed. Easier.

'Oh. Here we go,' she said comfortably as the man approached the water and dithered with his towel, turning from side to side and finally draping it on a low rock at the edge of the water.

'Tide'll have that, sure it's coming in, isn't it, you idiot?' She lifted the binoculars again. 'Better not be one of mine.'

She watched him slowly raise his t-shirt, drag it off over his head and fold it neatly, taking his time, looking around him quickly once or twice, as though he felt her gaze on him, on his naked chest and arms.

'He's not looking forward to this, is he?' she remarked happily. 'He's stalling, Dog. Doesn't fucking fold anything in the rental, and that's a fact.'

She laughed softly and she didn't lower the binoculars, although she knew she should.

He was a long, slim shape, if a little flabby at the hips. The body of a runner, maybe, or an athlete of some kind, once upon a time, but no longer. Still, his shoulders were strong and shapely, the muscles visible and neat under the pale skin, and she let the binoculars follow the faint line of his spine past the shoulder-blades and down the curve to the two little dimples of his hips, and into the purled elastic of his shorts.

'Naughty Grace. Bad Gracie,' she whispered, smiling, and the dog nudged her elbow again. This time it was ignored. The townie's toes were already in the seeping water, and now there was no more dithering to be done, if he was going to swim at all. She watched him rub the tops of his arms and imagined the millions of little goosebumps on that pale skin, chased up by the chill of the water and the little breeze that always lingered at the water's edge.

'Betcha a fiver he chickens out,' she muttered, and the dog sighed and put its head on its paws.

He began to inch out into the water, letting it creep up over his knees, ease up onto his lower thighs, icy.

'Any minute now, watch,' she said to the dog. 'He'll start splashing it up around himself like a dickhead, give himself the heebie-jeebies, and it'll be all over.'

She felt a space beside her, some sort of emptiness, and glanced away from the binoculars, but the dog was doing no harm, just sniffing and piddling around over at the hedge, so she let it go. She looked quickly back at the beach with anticipation. It was nearly time to separate the men from the boys. When the ice-cold seawater hit their balls, they tended to stop walking. Their faces would register the pain and shock. Some screamed and some did not. Out they'd mostly come again – quicker than they went in – walking funny and asking loudly if there was any more coffee in the flask.

But not this man, she saw. He was doing what she did, what you had to do to get in at all – going just deep enough, and then, whoosh, pushing himself forwards into the water, hitting with the chest first, keeping his head up, letting the gasping and the panicked breathing take over for a while, getting the cold-water shock quick-quick-quick, like a burning on the skin, like a zooming in to the core, like a wonderful rush, the best bit and the worst bit, all at once.

She felt her own breath tighten and quicken, watching him. It looked lovely, the water, like silk on his skin.

There – he was swimming properly now. Well, well, well, he was doing all right, she thought, and she kept watching, although she knew she shouldn't. He swam a sketchy breast-stroke, craning the head up for the sake of his glasses, getting the breath back under control. She saw the white gleam of his legs frogging underwater and the purple blur of his shorts and the strong working of his shoulders, up and down, up and down. He was settling and getting a rhythm going. The ache would be lessening in his hands and his feet, the body adjusting. The water was relatively warm – thirteen degrees the last time she checked.

He looked confident now, and it was good to watch, nice.

She let the kind breeze stir her hair, stroke the skin of her face, and let the steady rise and dip of the man, swimming, steady her breath where she sat, spying down on him.

Suddenly his stroke faltered. She saw him stop and tread water as if he were watching something a little distance away. She lowered the binoculars to pinpoint what interested him and saw only the dark shape of a cormorant bobbing up and down in the gentle swell where the rocks protruded out to sea and stirred up sand eels from the seabed.

'What's up?' she said aloud. 'Cramp?'

She peered through the binoculars again and the dog came close, sensing her interest.

But he was swimming again now, towards the big black bird. His stroke was cautious. She could tell he was unsure. As he approached, she expected the bird to duck smoothly down under the water and disappear – its own singular magic trick. But it stayed on the surface even as he came closer and didn't swim away. He needed to watch out – he was well out of his depth now, she noted, but he kept on going. The bird was very still – unusually so – she realised, and as she peered at it, she saw its neck was at a strange angle, and it regarded the swimming man from a red eye sharply tilted to one side.

'It's caught on something,' she said. 'How the hell did he spot that, the specky bastard?'

The townie was touching distance from the bird now, treading water still, unsure about reaching out to it. He glanced back to shore and she could see the surprise on his face as he registered the distance he had come.

'Make up your mind time, I think,' she said quietly.

He didn't turn back for shore.

'Stupid bugger,' she tutted, but she smiled to herself, nonetheless.

Instead, he stretched out his hand to the bird, slowly, slowly, and still it didn't duck underwater, didn't move away, although she could see its neck straining to keep him in sight, to keep that large prehistoric beak pointed at him on the ready. Now his hand was on its feathers, on its back, pulling it towards him and it made a feeble attempt to peck at him, but whatever held it was strong, and the neck was braced and immobile, and the wings were pinioned.

'You'll never be able to free it out there,' she muttered. 'You'll end up getting yourself caught, if it's fishing line, and then there'll be hell to pay. Come on dog!' she said loudly, gathering herself. 'Better go down, see what the bonehead's at. Haven't rescued him for a day or two, have we? Bound to be due, right enough.'

She was on the beach in a couple of minutes, shading her eyes with a hand to see what was going on. He'd left the bird and was treading water nearby, thinking or resting, she wasn't sure. She shrugged off her jacket and reached into a pocket for her little penknife. Kicking off her boots, she hesitated a moment, and then pulled down her cotton trousers in a firm, smooth movement, and stepped her bare legs out onto the sand. In a few quick strides she was in the water, t-shirt and knickers and the knife in her fist, and then she was swimming, feeling that lovely ice-grip, coming alive, and swimming out to where the man still trod water, at a loss but reluctant to abandon the bird to its fate.

She was a good swimmer and strong, and in no time at all was beside him. He flinched as she appeared and blinked in surprise. She saw he was already very cold, unused to the water and staying too still. She said nothing but went to the bird and felt around. It watched her with its red eye but didn't struggle.

'Fishing line,' she confirmed over her shoulder.

He was beside her now, breathing hard.

'Stay back,' she said sharply, 'Fucking line could be any length, and we don't want you getting strung up as well, for fuck's sake.'

'What'll we do?' he asked, and she could hear his teeth chatter behind the words.

'Best to cut him loose and take him in. We can see better there, what the damage is.'

She could feel the thin cord coming off the rubbery foot and running back through the water.

'C-couldn't we just l-loosen its neck first?' he asked behind her. 'L-looks so unc-comfortable like that.'

'Aye, and have it peck bloody holes in my hand all the way back to shore? Don't think so,' she retorted, making a deft slice through the line and feeling the bird come loose with satisfaction. It sensed the slight freedom and began to wriggle but the line was tangled right around its head and beak. It had swum fast into the thing while hunting under-water, probably, and had done well to get back to the surface as it had.

'Head for shore,' she told the townie, 'you've stayed too long as it is.'

He nodded gratefully and started back, and she followed behind, towing the bird like a swim-float behind her and watching with concern the man's slowing movements, his weakening strokes. She checked behind and out to sea in case Abbie was coming back in and could give him a tow, but the boat was nowhere in sight, the small wavelets obscuring her view.

She went a little faster, came alongside him and glanced at him quickly.

'I'm all right,' he said, 'don't worry,' and he smiled hard at her, keeping the water out of his mouth. 'You won't have to rescue me again, honest, I'll make it.'

'Good,' she said, her voice sharp, but she stayed beside him now, giving him silent encouragement with her steady side-stroke, the fishing line and the knife tight in her fist and her feet kicking strong. She spotted his towel floating gently in the shallows and the white gleam of his t-shirt washed up on the shore with the incoming tide. They were both breathing hard. There was the sand beneath her tiptoes now. The man was standing already, just that little bit taller, making for the shore quickly and shivering badly. She swam further in until she could wade out comfortably and then turned for the bird and lifted it up. It was weightless in her arms, a fluff of feathers and hollow bone and air, almost done, almost gone. She bent to hook the sopping towel with one finger and drag it with her too. It was one of hers, right enough.

When she glanced up, the man was on the beach, watching her, so cold, standing and shaking as if having a fit. He'd never make it back to the rental without full-blown hypothermia, and she shook her head in resignation.

'Go up to the house,' she told him. 'Behind you. The door's open. Quick.'

He nodded gratefully with his jaws locked and trotted off up the beach, the purple shorts clamped to his grey skin, his every move jerky and painful. She followed behind with the bird, checking it over for tangles and knots in the line.

'Jesus,' she said softly as she reached her front door and followed the wet footprints inside into the warmth. 'As if rescuing one lame duck wasn't enough, now I've got fucking two.'

Chapter 28

___

HE WAS NEVER SO AWARE of his nakedness as when she stood there in the doorway and looked at him. His muscles were jerking and firing of their own accord, right across his body, trying to warm him. He couldn't even speak, but she didn't seem to notice his discomfort as she brought the bird into the big light room and kicked the porch door closed behind her with one foot. He saw her bare white legs, strong, wiry, and her sopping t-shirt tight to her body and her small knickers, dark coloured round the top of her thighs. Her breasts were small and low and distinct under the t-shirt and she was a long shape in the torso, not like Lorna, and he looked down at his feet that were the grey of the dead.

'Towels in the hot-press in the hall,' she said. 'Bathroom's beside it. Set the shower cool at first or you'll be in agony, and warm it up in stages.'

He didn't argue. The thought of trying to get back to his own cottage with this ague was unbearable. Worse than the knowledge that she'd rescued him again, that he was intruding on her, again, that he was a useless dickhead, standing dripping on her rug and should be shot.

'Thanks,' he said, and juddered away, fetching coarse bright towels from a neat stack and finding the bathroom with a shaking hand. It was sparsely furnished, no knick-knacks anywhere, but it was spacious and spotlessly clean. A shower stood in one corner. Hastily he turned on the water and let it heat until it steamed, and stepped in. There was sudden unbearable fire in his hands and feet and his body crackled.

'Jesus!' he said and jumped back out onto a bright woollen rug. He let the shower run a little cooler and got back in. Better, just like she'd said.

He let his body warm slowly and stood under the streaming water until the terrible shaking eased. When the water stopped, he stood a moment under the last slow drips and rested his forehead against the wall.

A minute later he put his sopping trunks back on and replaced his glasses on his nose and felt a little better, a little less exposed, a little less ridiculous. Wrapping a large towel around his waist and another across his shoulders to catch the last intermittent shakes, he stood a while with his hand on the doorhandle before he took a breath, shot the bolt back and left the steaming bathroom to face her, clad in two large towels and a pair of lurid purple Simpsons trunks that were really only boxers, a Christmas present from Lorna years ago, a joke, back when both of them were laughing.

He almost tripped over a pile of something thick and soft that had been left folded at the door. Bending, he realised it was the big poncho that she'd lent him the last time she rescued him. OK, he thought, with a wry smile, but of course it was just what he needed. Gratefully he shrugged it on and felt the same scratchy hug that had enveloped him when he'd worn it in the boat, and it reached all the way down to his knees. He turned and dropped the discarded towels gratefully in the wash-basket behind him, and with a little more confidence went to find her, the poncho swinging loose and his feet beginning to warm on the wooden floor.

She was there in the big room, in a beautiful voluminous kaftan all the dusty colours of the desert, and her damp hair was wound up on top of her head in a big careless pile. He could see the way it would loosen and lighten and puff itself up as it dried. There were already wisps escaping and falling around her face as she leaned over the table, attending to the bird, intent, like a great bird herself, all angles and piercing eyes.

'Stick on the kettle, there, and make some coffee,' she said, without looking up.

'Thanks for the – clothes,' he said.

She flashed him a quick unexpected smile and the sharpness of her features softened with it. 'Gonna start charging you rent for that poncho.'

'Yeah,' he said. 'Sorry.'

She had scissors in her hand and had been snipping patiently away at the filament binding the quiet bird but she stopped at this and looked up at him and there was definitely something of the bird in her own gaze now, as she cocked her head to one side and regarded him.

'It was a good thing you did, to help this creature,' she said. 'Not like last time. That was self-destructive. This was self-generative, I think. So, stop worrying.' She nodded sharply and went back to her task. 'Stop beating yourself up. Leave that to others, for fuck's sake, you can always rely on them.'

He smiled a little and asked, 'How bad is it? Can you get it off?'

He came closer to the table and the creature shifted uneasily. He could see the head and neck were still bound. Behind him the kettle rumbled and clicked off and the last of the shakes ran through him at the sound. Coffee would be very welcome indeed.

'It's a right mess,' she said, deftly snipping. The thin line was entangled around flight feathers and legs and pretty much everywhere. A small pile of strands sat at her elbow and there were a couple of curved hooks in there, too. He looked around for coffee, mugs and milk. All were at hand, so he poured water and stirred and carried the steaming mugs to the table, the scent filling his nostrils. Once again, the bird flinched.

'Cake,' said Grace, her head almost on the table as she looked under its belly for a hidden hook or snaggled line. 'Abbie's got a sponge going, up there, under the bowl.'

He found it quickly, a big lopsided delicious thick thing of cream and jam, and cut two big slices. Opening cupboards, he found plates and slid them on. Forks. Brought it all to the table, and Grace sat back with a sigh, and put the scissors down.

'At least one a year,' she told him, looking at the bedraggled bird sadly.

She looked so much easier, so much more relaxed in this bright, book-lined room. For all of the fishing line on the table the bird seemed as entangled as ever. Evan looked at it as he forked in delicious soft cake, and felt the sugar run through him immediately; he chased it down with hot coffee and started to feel a whole lot better. He leaned closer, to see what she was doing, aware of the tang of fish and brine which surrounded the bird like an aura. It was a huge thing, up close, this bird, all dark sleek feathers and latent energy.

He was glad he'd saved it. Even if it did mean he had to be saved himself. 'Abbie can certainly bake,' he said.

'There's a lot that girl can do, would surprise you,' was the answer. 'She's not all flowers and foolishness, you know.'

He smiled to himself and ate some more.

Grace was back at work and silent again, tutting now and then as she found another snaggled barb. He watched her hands, strong brown things with square nails, lifting tiny feathers, exploring underneath for hooks, finding them clear, snipping away the line. Each movement was neat, careful and precise. He remembered Maggie telling him Grace was a needlewoman, making quilts or something. She looked as if she'd be good at that tiny kind of work, that fiddly stuff. She put down the scissors and sighed again, saw he had finished his cake.

'Here, I'm going to wash my hands. You take over. Check for hooks before you pull, OK? Follow it along with your fingers to the next hook. Go slow and easy, that's the trick.'

He nodded dubiously.

'Whatever you do, don't release the head until the last. That beak's wicked. He still has a bit of fight in him, my boyo.'

She smiled at the creature and pushed back her chair quietly so as not to spook it. After a quick hesitation he slid across into her seat. He felt the warmth of her from the chair and blinked and put a hand out to the bird, cautiously. It felt as though it were made of cloud and twigs. He'd expected the feathers to be slick and oily, but they were dry and light under his hand. He checked to see if she was watching, for reassurance, for guidance, but she was gone. There was water running in the bathroom.

'Sorry, bird,' he said, and bent his head to see what needed doing. He heard Grace moving around in another room now, humming to herself quietly.

Following the loose line that ran under a wing he found a hook embedded tightly where the bird's armpit would be. Remembering the evil little barbs that had shone on Abbie's line earlier, he didn't pull at it but gave it a tentative wiggle instead. The bird's eye stared at him, unnervingly. He wiggled the hook again to try to loosen it. It came away in his hand and a short length of line with it, and he breathed again.

'Right,' he said, and picked up the heavy scissors.

Grace returned as he worked and sat quietly beside him. He heard the chink of china and fork and forgot her again in the intricacies of the tiny filament that enwrapped the bird. It was like a puzzle, following the line into delicate feathers, careful not to snip the creature by mistake. He knew without being told that to cut feathers would mean trouble for the animal and after all this effort he wanted, with a deep, full passion, to have saved it, to have restored it and perhaps to see it free and swimming again. He worked on in silence, feeling the coffee and sweet cake run through him, heating him up from the inside, and keenly aware of the warmth of her at his elbow, watching him work. Now and again, she'd point at something she'd noticed, or say, 'Wait,' and pull back a set of flight feathers to reveal a nasty hook. He was aware of the silence and the comfort of the place, and the stillness around him, and the steady breath at his shoulder, and it felt good.

'Right,' he said, after a while, 'unless you want me to snip the bits on the head, I think we're done.'

'Aye, we'll do the last bit at the water's edge,' she agreed, and leaned across to lift the bird which sat still and resigned in her hands, unaware of its near-liberation.

'They're not very bright,' he remarked, following the flow of her colours to the door.

'They hunker down inside when they're hurting. Takes someone else to set them free.'

The air seemed chilly outside after the cosy warmth of the cottage and he rubbed his arms for heat as they processed to the water's edge. Just where the bay disappeared into the sky, he could see the little boat with Luca in it, bobbing and skipping its way back in to shore, and the prickly edges of the poncho tickled his legs.

'Right, fluffy-brain, let's get you away,' said Grace, setting the bird on the pebbles right at the water's edge and squatting beside it with the scissors. It scented the briny water so close to its feet, and wriggled, but still its neck and head were held fast. Evan hung back, letting her organise things until she craned her neck to look back at him, and said, 'It's your rescue, come on. You get to cut the cord.'

She grinned and held up the scissors and he crouched awkwardly beside her, his feet warped and painful on the pebbles. She pointed to the lead line holding the bird's head down. 'Here,' she said quietly.

He put the scissors around the line and glanced at her to check. She nodded encouragement and smiled again. Her breath smelled like coffee. The bird seemed quite large, suddenly, and the beak grey and pointed like bone. He held still. She nodded encouragement and he could see a bright light in her eyes that matched his own, an excitement that was almost joy. He snipped the line and instantly her fingers were there to disentangle the last strands and pull them away from the beak, from the feathers. The bird's head came up on a surprisingly long neck and it shook vigorously, opening its mouth in a silent gape. The wings came out clumsily to flap and curl back, and immediately the bird was moving away, flat-footing it over the last few pebbles towards the sparkling water, dragging its behind like a toddler, the tail-feathers splayed and ugly.

'They're not great on the auld feet,' Grace remarked, with love in her voice.

With two more ungainly steps the bird was in the water and moving out as though engine-powered. Bending its neck like an angular swan it put its whole head underwater and he could see it looking from one side to the other.

'Washing his eyeballs,' Grace said, and he glanced at her and laughed. She stayed intent on the bird.

Then with one quick dip it disappeared, slipping neatly underwater, and Evan laughed again in surprise with a quick, keen pleasure, as the skin of the water healed and it was gone, quite gone.

He looked at Grace and she was smiling too, out at the flat water and the boat in the distance.

'Just watch,' she said. 'He can stay under for over a minute, but he'll come up somewhere out there, again.'

So they stood and waited and watched the boat approach in Popeye fits and starts, until, sure enough, the bird appeared again, a good distance out and its gaze fixed straight ahead.

Chapter 29

———

SHE DIDN'T STAY TO SEE the little boat run in onto the beach, after all. She could feel the townie watching her from the corner of her eye, and everything he did was a spiky irritation suddenly, disturbing her peace. He said nothing as she turned and stumped back up towards the cottage, and this irked her more.

Inside, the door to her workroom lay open, a silent recrimination, so she cut herself a generous wodge of cake and went reluctantly inside. The laptop sat open and dark on her little table in the corner. She glared at its dead face and turned away, sitting down heavily at her worktable, stroking the bright fluttering yellow of the fabric spread there. She picked at a gleaming thread on the raw edge and sighed. The colours and clutter failed to soothe her, to draw her in as they usually did.

Instead, she absently began to eat the cake, slick and sweet, looking out the big picture window opposite, to the rocks and the waving marram grass beyond.

'Yoo-hoo! Give us a hand with the boat?'

It was Abbie calling in through the door, back onshore with the boy, who wouldn't be much help pulling it up the beach right enough. She should go. But she stayed where she was.

'Leave it where it is,' she called over her shoulder. 'The tide's going out anyway, sure,' and she went on poking at the cake and staring out the window.

Silence returned, and she thought the girl had gone back out, to lift the oars and rowlocks, make the boat secure. She should get up, give a hand, pull the thing up to the lane, safe, but she couldn't move. She didn't want to move. Then a board creaked behind her and Abbie was there, quiet for once, pulling out a chair and sitting down.

'What's up?' she said as she sat.

Grace glared. 'Why should anything be up?'

The girl raised her eyebrows in that irritating way she had, and folded her arms, sitting back and staring at her, as if she could read her thoughts.

'You look just like your mother when you do that, you know,' she said nastily.

Abbie laughed, a short, round sound. Her teeth were white and even and a dimple sat in her cheek. 'Boy, you surely are in some form this evening. What happened while we were gone?'

'Can't I sit in peace and quiet in my own bloody house, if I want, without nosey questions or bother?'

She went to push back her chair, to leave the room, but the girl set her hand on top of her own, and the gesture was so unusual between them that it held her in place, and she looked at her niece for a short second and then dropped her eyes, knitting her lips together tightly.

'Och, Auntie Grace,' said Abbie quietly. 'It's not like you to be out of sorts.' She paused and took her hand away again. 'Am I in the way? It's been a few weeks right enough. D'you want me to go?'

'No!' she said. 'No,' more quietly. 'It's just ...' Grace felt around for the reason and said, 'I can't handle the work, is all.'

Abbie waited, watching her.

'I'm feeling old and done, I'm afraid. I'm feeling old and done and useless, that's all, honey.'

The girl's face creased in concern. 'Christ almighty woman, you're only fifty, not a hundred and ten, would you listen to yourself?'

But Grace shook her head slowly. 'Oh love, look, you've done a brilliant job setting up the websites for me, showing me how to do it all, but I can't manage them myself. I just can't. There's orders coming in every day now it's lockdown, and I can't keep on top of it all.'

She sighed, realising this was at least part of the truth, feeling a little relief at having said it out loud, and looked at her niece.

Abbie was fiddling with a rejected swatch, turning it over and over in her hands, as if searching for the way forwards. 'Maybe I could stay on,' she said quietly without looking up from it, 'after the lockdown, after the summer, I mean. I could look after the orders and stuff so you could get on with this.' She moved a hand over the colours and shapes strewn on the table. 'I could do the online sales, too, if you like. We could be partners.'

Grace looked at her. 'What about uni?'

'Ach, what's that for?' her niece asked bitterly, pushing herself up from the chair with a swish of skirt, and going to the window to look out. 'What the frig's a degree in engineering and technology going to teach me that I don't know already, that I can't teach myself. Do you have a degree in marine biology? Or textiles? I don't think so.' She huffed at the window crossly. 'Anyway, our lectures'll be online mostly anyway, they're saying. I could do them from here – in the pub maybe, for the Wi-Fi, if I had to.'

She turned to look at her aunt, and Grace felt her heavy mood lift as if the girl had taken it on herself. She thought for a moment. 'Have you still got the car?'

Abbie nodded, 'Up in the village. Same old banger but it still goes. More than you can say about your quad anyway.'

She turned away from the view altogether, and rested her

behind against the windowsill, excited now and looking very young.

'You could do the runs to town,' Grace said, slowly, watching her. 'Answer the emails?'

Abbie nodded, smiling and biting her lip. There was silence while they thought it through, and Grace felt a new energy fizz in the room. 'You'll need to tell your mother. About the online thing, the lectures, at least.'

Abbie nodded, fast.

'It'd keep her from having a conniption. God love her, she's determined you're going to be the next Bill Gates or something. We could see how it goes.'

'I don't need to see how it goes, Auntie Grace,' said the girl, coming back to the table and sitting down again, leaning forwards in her eagerness. 'They call me things, no one talks to me.' She looked down at her hands. 'I hated it,' she whispered. 'I swear – I would have done something stupid if I'd had to stay there, if I hadn't had you to come to. I mean it.'

When she glanced up at Grace, there were tears in her eyes and she looked as she did when she first started coming for the holidays, when she was just seven or eight and fighting with her mother already. She blinked them away and said brightly, 'I didn't realise things had got so busy, that's all, or I would have offered earlier. You're a right success! You can show me where you've got to on the orders and I'll take it from there.'

She patted Grace's hand like a tattoo. It was the most they'd touched each other in years, and it was starting to sting. Grace drew her hand away.

The girl didn't notice. 'I'll start tomorrow, OK? It'll be great! OK, partner?'

Grace pushed herself up and away, briskly. 'Deal,' she said, and nodded. 'Thank you, Abbie.'

There was a second or two of silence which filled the room, and the girl smiled shyly.

'Well, it's time for my couple of drams,' Grace said.

She headed along the lane towards the village, passing the little boat on the beach which was keeled over to one side with the oars still poked in, but she shoved her hands deep into her pockets like a recalcitrant child and left it as it was. She jingled coins as she stumped up the hill, enjoying the pull on her heart and in her legs, her thoughts on her niece and all of the things she could do to make herself useful.

Abbie could live in the rental if she wanted, have her independence. It would be good to have those townies gone, she thought with sudden vehemence as she breasted the hill and saw the darkened huddle of buildings ahead. Hassle, they were, and interference, like all the rest. A flickering picture of the man in the water desperately paddling and gasping and smiling beside her was pressed away briskly. She could do without having to rescue somebody, for god's sake, morning, noon and night.

'Looks like rain,' she told Brendan Curran as he let her in.

'Just in time. Pretty soon we'll have the tourists back again, they're saying,' he replied glumly, and Paddy straightened up from behind the bar and put a bottle on the counter as she approached her stool.

'Last one, gents,' he said. 'Oh, and ladies. Evening, Grace.'

'Last of the John Powers,' Mickey Flanders said with reverence.

'Lockdown'll be over in a week or two anyhow,' said one of the old gits. It was hard to tell them apart.

'Not a whole pile of locking-down you did,' said Mickey. 'In here every fart's end, far as I can see, and you the age to be at home praying for a happy death.'

'Well, you're one to talk,' came the indignant retort. 'You prop up this bar day and daily – worse than Maggie Gill at the altar-rails, isn't he, Paddy?'

The barman turned his back and joggled the heavy bottle into the optics and said nothing.

'Yes, well, I'm an official alcoholic,' said Mickey with slow pride. 'I'm entitled to be here. It's medicinal.'

Grace sipped her drink and let the quiet banter flow over and around her like a comfort blanket. Outside the world was sick and dark and lonely, but within these doors was steadiness and companionship, people she'd known from childhood, faces melting and sagging with the years but softened by the warm yellow light from behind the bar. No one spoke directly to her. They were used to her ways, and could tell by her shoulders that she was in no mood for chat, but she felt included, nonetheless. She let the time pass without comment, and it was with a slow reluctance that she drained the last of Number Two, feeling the warmth creeping through her like a magic snake.

At least she had Abbie at home, and the dinner ready, probably, she thought as she slid down from the stool and sorted herself to leave once more.

'Headin' on, Grace?'

Paddy was always one for stating the obvious. She didn't bother with a nod, just moved past the rounded backs on the barstools into the dark back room where her hat hung in state on its hook.

'They tell me the townie's taken up swimming, now,' said his quiet voice beside her in the gloom.

She glared at his narrow back as he went past her without further comment and began sliding back the bolts on the door.

'Do they now?'

She lifted her hat and jammed it on her head.

'Thank Christ lockdown's nearly over, and they'll go back where they belong,' he said softly to her passing shape.

'Time you married that nice Becky-girl and got your big nose stuck into your own business for a change, don't you think?' Grace declared without turning.

She found herself growling slightly as she went back down

the hill towards home and wasn't sure if it was in her head or a real noise, so she held her breath a second until it stopped. Rain was falling at last, refreshing after the long dry spell, light on her face like a blessing. The whiskey fuzzed her thoughts nicely, so she let them flow wide as the rough tarmac of the road became the pebbles of the lane. She thought about Abbie as a child and her wild abandoned screech as she'd pile out of her parents' shining car and run towards her, arms wide. The only person Grace had ever hugged, that was Abbie. She thought about Dog and his radar senses and how he slotted himself into her moods as if he were part of her. She thought about her sister, Marcella, Abbie's mother, up in the city, a rich widow, and miserable no matter what she said, chasing her children into professions all day long.

And then she thought of the man in London who'd kept her, and how he was probably dead by now and how good that would be, to know that he was gone. She thought of the men she'd had, fleeting and strange liaisons of bumping and soft cursing before they went home to their wives and never made eye contact again.

She didn't think of the townie until he came pelting around the corner, dishevelled and distraught, and then she knew she was in for it again.

'Have you seen him? Luca?' He stood with his hands on his hips to catch his breath but all the while he looked around and behind and up the straggling banks of grass to the high cliffs above and around.

She shook her head blankly.

'He's gone. Shit! He's fucking run away.'

Part Three

Chapter 30

———

HE WAS OFF, LOPING UP the hill towards the village, his head craning right and left as though a clever small boy would sit on the hillside or rocks in plain sight in the rain, waiting to be found. There were a million places to hide, if someone wanted to be hidden. She'd found that a lot as a child, herself. She watched him until he was gone around the bend. The sun was a lemon circle behind thick cloud.

Luca would be home in an hour when he got wet and cold.

She marched on over the scrunching stones, looking again for the wide sweep of thought she'd been enjoying, but somehow the whiskey buzz had dissipated. She found herself peering up the banks to her right, and across the rocks and slick grasses to her left, just as the townie had done so foolishly. Just in case. Should have asked what the kid was wearing. She passed the rental and the door flapped open in the freshening breeze, so she pulled it closed. The lights were on inside already because of the rain but they didn't make the cottage much brighter. It was always a dark and mean little place and she walked on past it, quickly.

Abbie should stay with her, instead, she decided. She wondered what she'd meant earlier, about doing something stupid. She hoped it wasn't – that. She hoped it wasn't fucking genetic, the despair.

She went on around the corner towards her own little bay, her own cottage, the lights yellow in the windows, and stopped.

The boat was gone from the beach.

She stood a moment and looked at the place it had been, scraped up on the pebbles at the top of the beach. She looked at the place where it should be, turned turtle in a green hump against the bank, but there was nothing there either.

She stepped down onto the beach from the lane and went to where the boat had been sitting just that short time before. She looked around in disbelief and horror, her heart thumping, as if it would be hiding somewhere, grinning and peeping from behind a rock.

It had been above the tideline, of course, but only a little. It wouldn't have been a great distance from the water when the tide had been full in – what, an hour ago? But it had been safe, she'd seen it herself pulled above the tideline when she went up to the village. She remembered the oars, still in place, poking up like the V-sign in her memory. The boat wasn't light, but it had been on the slope, the beach slip behind it, and the sea not far away, ready to lift it, to take it, to bring it, to have it, and anything else aboard it.

She scanned the bay. It looked back at her, innocent and empty. Small waves perked the surface, but it wasn't rough, yet.

She turned and ran. 'Abbie!' she bawled, before she was even within hailing distance. 'Abbie!'

The girl appeared at the doorway, a flutter of polka-dots, holding a spatula, and the dog charged out behind her, glad to be free, and capered around her legs.

Grace found she couldn't speak, whether from running across the shingle or from fright, she couldn't tell.

'The boat!' she managed, after a second of staring.

Abbie looked behind her, alarmed, and her face creased in concern when she saw the empty beach. 'But I pulled it up over the tideline, Auntie! I did! And wee Luca helped me.'

She was right out on the lane now, on the stones in her bare feet, craning to look around as Grace had done, as if it were a prank that someone had played.

'He sat in it for ages practising his rowing before he went off home with his fish.'

'The lad's disappeared too.'

Abbie looked at her, the smooth face emptying. 'Oh. Shit.' The words were very quiet. Just as her aunt had done, Abbie scanned the bay, and then looked at Grace again, fear in her eyes. 'What do we do? What do we do?'

Grace pushed past her into the kitchen. 'I'm ringing the coastguard. Get your shoes on and find the townie – Evan. He was heading up towards the village, looking. Tell him. Get him back here. And get the neighbours out. We're going to need a hand.'

Abbie lapped away out of the house as Grace lifted the phone. She made her voice calm as it rang once, twice, three times and then the despatcher's voice began at the other end, asking which service she required and putting her through. They asked question after question – age, clothes, location, type of craft – and she did her best to answer them, wishing she'd even glanced at the child that morning, to see what he was wearing.

There was someone coming, she was told. Would be there shortly. They'd take it from there.

Just as she hung up, Evan came, breathless, to the door. 'Oh my god,' he said, and swung around to look out at the bay, now a dirty grey colour although only a little lumpy yet. 'Christ,' he said, sinking down like a bent angle on her doorstep and fluffing his hair. 'I've lost another one now, haven't I? He's out there? On his own in a boat? Oh, my fucking god. I've lost them fucking both.'

'Now's not the time to be a drama queen,' she told him curtly. 'Did he take the lifejacket?'

He looked up at her, staring. There were beads of rain on his dark hair and his face was white, his lips grey. 'Shit. The lifejacket,' and as quickly he was on his feet and racing down the lane towards the rental to see.

The boy wasn't stupid, not at all. He'd have taken the jacket for sure, but his dad needed something to do. That was the worst of it, she thought, standing there in the doorway, her hands loose at her sides, listening to her own breathing. Not being able to do anything. Not knowing, and not being able to do anything. She'd have been out on the boat like a shot, looking for him, if he hadn't taken the fucking thing already. The image of the old kayak flickered in her mind, but she dismissed it immediately. It wasn't the evening for it, and it was a nasty fucker in itself, so she stayed where she was, thinking.

The tides were faster at the peak of flood and ebb and would whirl a little craft like hers right out into the Irish Sea if he'd set sail at the wrong time. If it were a little later, when the waters had settled, he maybe had a chance. She stepped out onto the pebbly beach and felt the wind with a wet finger. Sou'westerly. Christ. That wouldn't help. Wouldn't help at all.

A big white jeep pulled up at the top of the hill, the last turning point before the lane, and two people in red overalls got out. Grace watched them point and orientate themselves towards her, and then dip out of view as they came down the lane. Abbie rounded the corner just behind them, and with her Maggie and Frank, Eamon and Carmichael, Paddy and Becky, running. Holding hands, those last two, she noticed, but hurrying fast towards her, towards the empty bay and the empty sea. She turned quickly and pushed the reluctant Dog into the bedroom and closed the door on its ugly snout.

The coastguard was impressive when they reached her. A

man and woman who spoke through facemasks and wouldn't come inside. They looked at the bay and at the space she indicated where the boat had been. They noted that the missing child was deaf, and that he wore an orange lifejacket faded to pink. They tried to check things on their devices but found they couldn't get a signal. Grace told them the state of the tide – ebbing, neaps – brought attention to the outblowing wind, and they nodded. The woman gave in and came inside to use the landline just as the townie reached them.

'I'm his father,' he said to the coastguard. 'He took the life-jacket, at least. What do we do now?'

'The Hinch lifeboat's been scrambled, sir,' said the man, who had been stolidly noting things in his black-bound book. 'It's on its way. Meanwhile, we can get a search party organised and moving along the clifftops.'

'Clifftops? Why?' The townie's face was stretched and panicked, although she knew he understood.

'Evan,' she said, and put a hand on his arm to keep him from flying off. 'You were in the currents out there. Chances are he's in the water, now, maybe along the coast here.'

He swore, and she kept the hand on his arm and squeezed to ground him and make him listen. People were gathering behind, fastening coats and pulling on hi-vis waistcoats and hats, and there was a muted buzz of voices.

'He's wearing the jacket,' she said quietly. 'He'll float and he should be easily enough seen. There's a few hours of daylight left.'

The townie nodded at each statement, drinking them in like a child, believing anything she said as gospel. She nodded at the people gathering behind him, getting him to stir himself. There were groups of five and ten coming towards them down the hill as the word got out.

'Come on, we need to get started. We've done this before. There's folks here to help.'

He gulped and she could see him pull himself together,

straightening up and nodding. She hoped he didn't remember how cold the water was, earlier. To distract him she felt in her coat pocket and found a tissue, scrunched and tight. Wasn't sure if it was clean, but she gave it to him anyway.

'Wipe your specs. You'll need to be able to see.'

He took it with a jerky nod and did as he was told. His skin now had a greenish tinge and she thought about shock.

The coastguard had waited nearby quietly, and now he was joined by his colleague who removed her face covering and began the briefing.

'Dublin chopper's on the way,' she said, and the small crowd murmured in satisfaction. This was what they knew. This was a good thing. They were ready to help. Grace saw the faces, all eyes and ears intent on what the coastguard was telling them, and felt such a rush of love that her eyes prickled. These were her people, her family. The boy would be found. He'd be all right. She checked back up at the sky, darkening with more rain, and listened to the woman's calm voice. Groups of three at all times, moving together as a larger group at first until they had covered the immediate area, then spreading out to cover as many of the myriad inlets and bays on both sides of the cottage as possible before dark. The Search and Rescue team and other agencies had all been scrambled and were on their way, but there was no time to lose.

'You'll need torches, at least one per group,' she said, and hands raised torches. 'Binoculars if you have them,' and these were lifted from around seasoned necks. 'And whistles are very useful if you have them available to you, but only until the dogs get here. My name's Jade and I'll make this cottage—' she looked at Grace, who nodded '—the search base. Any questions or findings bring them here as quickly as you can or call them in if you can get a signal.'

Grace had heard it all before. She watched the male coastguard coming out of the cottage and setting up a briefing table just behind her, her little laptop table utilised, and she wondered if he had gone through all her rooms in search of it. He spread a map out which lapped over the edges and flapped in the breeze and began to orientate himself, making marks with a pencil and muttering under his breath as patters of rain wet the surface. She saw Abbie, pale and quiet, inviting him back inside, donning a facemask he offered with clumsy unpractised fingers, carrying his bag and coat as he lifted the table, grateful to be out of the weather with it, after all. Other groups were forming, little threes with earnest faces, muttering, and then behind them, coming down the hill, more people, more and more, not instantly familiar. Coats and walking sticks and rucksacks and wet gear.

Becky saw where she was looking and called to her, 'It's up on Facebook, Grace – there'll be loads of people to help soon,' and she made a reassuring face from her place by Paddy's side.

Now the female coastguard was speaking to her quietly, separately from everyone else, as if she were very sick or delicate. She tried to pay attention. Jan or Jane or something, she was called. She was peeking up under Grace's big hat right up into her face. Grace held her breath to keep the smell of whiskey in and made a smile-shape with her mouth. She tried to keep her mind on the pleasant young face and out of the panic. She tried not to think about the grey sea at their backs, about the little boat somewhere out there, somewhere wrong, with the little boy inside, perhaps peeping over the side, frozen-fingered, helpless with the oars lost, bobbing in the sea.

Wait a minute. The girl was telling her she was to stay here at the cottage. She wasn't to go looking along the coast with the others. She was suddenly one hundred per cent present, paying full attention. What?

She wasn't to guide a search group like all the other times before.

She wasn't to show them Lignabaw or Crushkeen, or any

229

of the other deep bays where the tide ran in and brought its junk to float about.

She was to stay behind like a little old lady and make a thorough search of her own house and outbuildings, while several other groups were assigned to do the same up in the village and over the nearby hills and rocks.

She listened with growing outrage. Nobody knew the place like her. Nobody.

Abbie coughed to get her attention. Grace looked at her where she stood behind the girl and saw her raise warning eyebrows, touch her finger to her lips. The coastguard was in charge here, she was saying. They wanted help, didn't they, so behave, Auntie, she was telling her.

Grace shook her head but said nothing, grunted and nodded at the coastguard-girl as she turned away. She'd let the bloody dog out, do her own thing as soon as she could get away from this pack of idiots. The boy needed to be found, and quick.

'Here, I'll show you where the tea-things are,' Abbie called to the coastguards. 'And I can get set up for coffees and stuff at the door, for the volunteers maybe. Would that help?'

'Trust you to think about food at a time like this,' thought Grace nastily and was instantly sorry. Things were wrong. She was frightened. She saw the girl smile at Abbie and say she'd love a cup of tea while she waited for the others – she'd been on another shout before this one and hadn't had a bite since breakfast. Abbie offered her a slice of cake, and the girl accepted gratefully, as if it was a bloody tea-party, as if a child wasn't drowning out there, right now.

Grace pushed rudely past them and went back in through the narrow doorway to let the dog out. As it barrelled past her to sniff the newcomer's legs and make her jump and squeak, she went into the bedroom and checked the wardrobe and under the bed – all the ridiculous inside places a child might hide. Did the same with the bathroom, the workroom, the washhouse, the spare room, diligently, just as she'd been told. The house was clear. He wasn't here. Of course he fucking wasn't. He was still out at sea on the little green boat, still waiting for the lifeboat to get here, still lost, still gone. She looked at the coastguard, who was talking in a clipped efficient voice on the phone with a steaming mug in her hand. Abbie was digging out the wake-kettle and finding stuff for sandwiches, but her face was tight and pale with fear. She was dealing with it, best way she knew how. She was a good girl. Always had been.

Grace tutted and headed outside. She had to do the outhouses, then she could fuck off like she wanted. She had a fair notion where the current would have taken him, if he was still on the boat. She needed to get up there on the cliff and spot him, get a fix on him for the lifeboat when it ever came. Maybe hail the wee crátur and let him know help was on the way. Sometimes that was all it took to keep them safe. She pulled her raincoat from the hook at the back door and gathered the storm torch and binoculars from their shelf beside it. The little black phone lay quietly on its charger beside them and looked at her in a friendly way, so after a pause she reached out and took it too, shoving it deep into her pocket to keep it dry. Stopping at the back door in the fresh rain she made herself count ten slow breaths. The whirr of a helicopter was on the air and getting louder. She was wasting time, but she stood there anyway, to get a hold of herself.

'You're scared, Gracie, that's all,' she muttered. The dog at her heels whined. 'You're doing that thing you do when things are out of control – and you know that shit doesn't work. Just let it go, will you, you dimwit, and get on with what you have to do. And stop talking to yourself or they'll think you're mad as well as geriatric.'

She yanked the raincoat on and fastened it up, made sure everything was stowed safely in the huge pockets.

'Come on, Dog,' she said.

It was already away and ran ahead of her with its stubby tail jerking as they scrunched across the wet grass to the outhouses, the shed and the stables, to look for the boy who was lost at sea.

Chapter 31

——

DOG BARKED AND WHIRLED AROUND, making her jump.

'Christ the night!' she said and aimed a boot at it.

The townie was behind her, out of breath, with a new face on. He looked determined and grim. He bent and touched the dog's head absently and it waggled its stump.

'Grace, they're making me search the fucking house,' he said. 'They're keeping me out of the way – I know it. I need to be up on the cliffs, looking for him properly. I can't hang around here. Can I go with you? You know the place better than anyone else.'

'But they've grounded me too,' she said. 'I've to check the sheds and stuff because I'm fucking old and useless.' She paused. 'I'm giving them the once-over and then I'm bloody going.'

'Right,' he nodded, and jogged to the big shed doors to haul one open. It resisted, trailing itself over the long grass.

'Fucking waste of time,' she said as she joined him. 'Youngster couldn't open these doors. Fucking Hercules would struggle.'

He didn't answer but helped her to haul the doors wide to let in some light, and they went inside together. It was dry and quiet out of the rain, with that rich smell of animal and time that she loved. Everything stood and sat patiently around, orderly and relaxed, waiting for her, and she knew it all, every stick and tool and complicated thing. The floor was dust and earth, and their feet sank a little into it as they stood and looked about.

'See? Only my footprints,' she said, pointing. 'No one else's. No kids.'

The townie didn't answer. His head was tilted, listening. The sound of a chopper overhead, *whacka-whacka-whacka*, and she knew his guts were twisted with the need to be out there, looking and finding. She lifted what she'd really come inside for – the long coil of rope – slung it over her shoulder and headed for the doors and daylight.

Suddenly an unearthly groan filled the air and the townie jumped and dropped his torch. 'Jesus!'

She turned to see his wide eyes staring at her. Did everything alarm him? What must it be like to live a life in constant apprehension? A wave of pity swept over her, washing things up from her own memory, her own experience of drawn-out fear.

'It's Dolly,' she told him, and would have smiled if it had been any other time. 'Donkey. Stable's next door and she hears me. Come on. We need to get to the cliffs.'

He nodded hard and followed her out, his face creased with strain. They left the big doors open behind them as a sign the place had been searched. Grace hesitated and then she bent and tore a thick handful of sweet wet grass and quickly opened the top half of the stable door beside her. The bolt scraped and protested as the townie waited behind her, moving from foot to foot. There was the soft and fuzzy nose of the donkey, a quick comfort that she needed just at that moment, and the smaller shadow of the cross old goat behind, just a rustle in the straw at the back.

'Ah Dolly,' she said, and offered the grass to her lip, but the donkey felt the rain on her nose and dropped her head back inside.

'Scared of the rain,' Grace said over her shoulder, letting the strands of grass fall to the floor inside, but only the dog was listening.

She closed the half-door over again as the donkey turned back into the darkness, and wished she could do the same.

'Will you hurry up?' she said over her shoulder. Dog was way ahead now, following some urgent olfactory message. She should have brought something of the kid's. Maybe the dog could have tracked it. Maybe it wasn't completely useless.

'I need a signal.' The townie stopped dead and looked at her and then back at the phone, distractedly. 'I haven't told his mum yet.'

'Good,' she said over her shoulder, feeling the bite of the salt air in her lungs as she started the climb. 'Don't.'

'What?'

'We'll have him safe and sound in no time, no need to upset her. You seem to go out of your way to bring trouble on yourself. Cause grief for yourself.'

'Grief!' She saw he had put the phone away at least, and the fresh air was bringing colour back to his cheeks.

They were quiet then, saving their breath for the climb up to the clifftops and readying their eyes for the sight of the sea. She wondered again how his daughter had died and how that would feel. She could imagine nothing like it. She wondered how it would feel to have lost your son at sea, too, and knew the answer instantly, because she'd felt it herself when she'd seen the boatless beach earlier – a ragged, searing hole in her chest and a breathless fear. It was still there, just underneath the skin, too, as well as a constant hope that she'd see him, a little shape on the water, when they got to the top of the hill, when they looked out over the waves. She wondered for a moment if that was how her mother had felt – that searing pain, that desperate wishing, as she searched for her through the foreign streets of London all those years ago. The thought was strange and warming and distracting, so she pushed it away. Just let us find him, she thought, and felt it deeply, pushing on her thigh with both hands to get herself up the last step of the stony slope which was slippery with the rain.

She parked her hands on her hips to get her breath and peered out over the water for something – anything that would tell her the boy was still afloat. She raked the grey expanse for a flash of the pink lifejacket or the black band of the boat's gunwales. Those were two good colours to look for, that stood out from the shifting sea. Her eyes dragged backwards and forwards, backwards and forwards, and came back empty each time. There was the sea, a staggering spread of grey, dizzying at first and then just there. She could see nothing else.

She lifted the binoculars next, settled them on the bridge of her nose and angled them slightly down to shield them from raindrops.

'See anything? Can you see anything? I can't see anything,' the man said hoarsely at her shoulder but she pushed the sound away and homed in on the points of sight down the tubes of the binoculars, the tiny areas of sea within the scope.

The townie was silent as she took a long slow sweep. The sea was empty and massive and deeply, deeply silver under the rain. It looked back at her with cool innocence. The waves were muted here, under the throb of the helicopter. She could see the wash of the dark raincloud moving over the sky, long smoky tendrils of rain still falling from its underbelly. The child would be wet and cold if he'd stayed in the boat, but he'd be floating at least. She hoped he'd had the sense not to jump in and try to swim for shore, and she thought he had.

'Luca!' the townie shouted in a raw voice, but she didn't ask why. 'Lucaaaaa! Lucaaaaa!'

The dog barked and waggled its tail, excited by the noise.

The helicopter was to one side of them in the distance, scouring the water to the east, and the sound of its blades came to them only weakly now, against the rising wind. She lowered the binoculars slowly. There was no boy and no boat in the water.

'Lucaaaa! Lucaaaa!'

The townie's face was wide open with all the pain coming out as sound.

She put her hand on his arm, on the wet sleeve of his sweater, and gripped it until he was quiet. She took stock. There was definitely no boat, no boy, out there in front of them, but she could see the sea-witches scurrying across the surface of the water and stirring it up from satin to silk, and the current running fast along the cliff edge, too. The weather was changing all right. They needed to keep looking, to find him – fast.

She glanced behind her and could see bright dots of yellow and pink all along the eastern clifftops – the crowds of people searching. So many! Beneath the cliffs a big red life-boat bounced. It was combing the area methodically from the shore to sea, checking the smaller inlets near the bay first before it would come out into open water, and she relaxed a little. There were more than her, here. There were others who knew what they were doing.

'Come on,' she said, pulling the arm now and making the man move. 'First place he'll have blown if he got out of the bay is Lignabaw. It's not far.'

He nodded and they hurried along.

The sight of the sea was disconcerting when you were looking for something lost in it. It made everything else so small, and the boy was smallest of all. The ground was treach-erous, summer grasses disguising the pits and falls where the sheep churned it up in the wintertime searching for the sweet grass not salt-burned. It was difficult to walk and look out to sea at the same time. She stumbled badly once, and he shot out a hand to grab her arm and stopped her falling. She pulled it away without speaking and concentrated harder on her feet.

There was nothing on the slate-grey sea to give them even a moment's hope. No little dot, no flash of colour, not even the sleek head of a seal closer in to give them pause. It was like searching a sheet of paper for an invisible message. She read it as best she could. She was sure she was right about the next place. The tide had been ebbing, so he'd have been washed quickly out of the bay and around the corner – just look at the run of the current – and then off the line of it into a gap in the rocks, with any luck, if there was any god at all, at all.

There was only room for one to walk at a time on this narrow part of the headland so the man gave way to her. She listened for him following and he kept close and kept pace and his breath was loud. The lifeboat smacked the water, moving further away, working in tandem with the helicopter above, taking the obvious route, but they didn't know the waters like she did, not here.

'I just don't get it, Grace.' He was in that head of his again. '—I told him his mum was coming, that's all. She wants to come down at the weekend, did I tell you? She's missed him.'

'Save your breath,' she said sharply.

'They're so fucking close, you've no idea. The two of them against the world, it feels like. And everyone else outside.'

He kept talking and she walked on. Lignabaw was just up ahead. She was afraid of the disappointment she'd feel if the child wasn't there, watched where she was stepping and tried not to think ahead. Place was treacherous, eroding away year by year.

'I don't get it, like.' The man was wambling on. 'He just looked at me when I told him. Didn't look delighted, I can tell you. Didn't smile, even. Gave me that dead-eye stare instead.' He laughed softly, 'Wee bugger.'

He must have stumbled because she heard an oof and then he was quiet again.

'We're going to have to climb down a fair bit,' she warned.

'The land juts out in places, over the sea – we have to go down to check he's not in there, washed in underneath. Don't know if you'll manage.'

'I was a climber,' he said, behind her. 'Rock climber. When I was younger.'

She grunted. That's where the boy got the monkey-genes from. She stopped for a quick moment to look back and see what the chopper was doing, and the man did the same. It was further out now, criss-crossing the water just outside the bay, low. They were looking for the boy now. Not the boat any more.

The rain dripped from the brim of her hat and she shook it off and walked on.

'How long would you survive? In the water, I mean?'

The townie had seen the change in the search pattern, too.

'You were in it, earlier,' she said shortly. 'What do you think?'

'Oh god. The stupid wee fool.' His voice was high and frightened again. 'Like, why couldn't he have talked to me? Running away like I was a monster? Could have told me what was wrong. I'd have listened. Don't you think I'd have listened?'

She said nothing, but took the coil of rope from her shoulder and looped it over her head and under her arm, out of the way for climbing. The seagrass at the edge of the inlet was thin and slick with rain, and hung in long tatters in places where the earth had fallen away.

'Down here,' she said, and took her hat off, set it on the grass. The air was instantly lighter around her without the broad shade of it on her head. She shed her jacket next, folding it deftly and putting it on the crown of the hat, off the wet grass. She wanted to have a boy to wrap in it, when she returned. She wanted that very much indeed. Nodding at the silent man she turned to go feet first down the slippery slope, taking great handfuls of the strong grass in each fist as she stepped backwards down. He stayed still, watching.

239

'Give me space and then come after. It evens out to a ledge again in a minute. Sheep track. Rest of it fell into the sea but the important bit's there.'

She smiled despite the situation, despite the weather and the sick dread in her stomach. She loved this place.

The townie peered over her head to the water far below and nodded without speaking. The black rocks were stained with long splatters of guano, and seabirds watched them warily from little ledges here and there, shifting on their broad orange feet. The dog stood close to the edge and whined at the top of her head. She ignored it and concentrated on moving each foot, getting a snug grip with the toe before moving the next. Below her she heard the chuff of soft waves meeting land, a friendly sound. There was no bumping, scraping sound of a wooden boat against rock, but they were still too high, maybe.

'Well?' she said, glancing upwards. The long shape of the man blocked the sky.

'We used ropes,' he said shortly and then he shrugged and pushed up his sleeves and began to follow her.

The first bit was the trickiest, always, but she was pleased with the way he climbed, carefully but without dawdling. They worked in silence for a few minutes, taking their time, making their way down bit by bit. She heard her own breathing mixed with the sound of his. After a while her feet found the old sheep track which wound in among the grass of the bank and the exposed rock points, and allowed her to stand again. She waited for the townie to join her, greeting him with just a nod. When he was ready, she moved on, leading the way along the narrow track with one hand wound in the grass at all times, and a dizzying drop to the left. She liked the way he trusted her implicitly, asking nothing but following silently.

'Don't lean out to look down,' she told him over her shoulder. 'There's no point. Can't see the edges from here. Hoping he's below us somewhere. We'll see better from further down.'

There was no answer.

They came to where the grass stopped altogether, starved of earth, and the naked rock began to descend gently in a moderate slope, a series of natural steps. She'd gathered gulls' eggs here as a child, while it was still a good thing to do, the yolk of them thick and blood-red in the pan, and the route was familiar and welcome. It was a simple matter to scramble across and down, using hands and feet like an ape. The sound of the sea grew louder and louder, and the tangy briny stink of the place filled her nostrils. She kept going, hand to hand, making her way over the points and jags of the rocks, ever downwards, the sound of the man's breathing just behind her, the noise of the water getting ever louder.

There.

There was the large natural rock ledge just beneath her, the sea lapping at its borders – journey's end – and she held her breath and jumped the last bit, looking around into the water before she had even landed. The man hit the ground beside her neatly and they both looked. There was silence for a while. The sea was black in here, under the shadow of the looming cliffs above, and it was a solid thing, unbroken by the shape of any little boat, any little face.

'Oh my god, Grace,' he said beside her. 'What am I going to do? What am I going to do?'

Chapter 32

———

HE COULD TELL BY THE SHAPE of her shoulders as she climbed back up the slope that she had lost hope. The thick dread in his belly was almost overwhelming, but strangely he found that the physical effort of following her up that ragged cliff path eased the pain a little, so he kept going.

'Where's the next inlet?' he asked quietly when they stood on the headland again. She was shrugging herself back into that awful old coat and brushing grass from her hat. She put it on her head, pulling the string to hang under her chin, and looked out to sea without speaking.

'We have to keep looking for him. We can't just stop, Grace.'

'He should have been there. I was so sure.'

'But he might have blown further. You said so. We have to check.' She looked at him and shrugged but there was nothing in her eyes except sadness. He kept talking to keep the panic back. 'Maybe they've found him, anyway, right? The helicopter? The lifeboat?'

He could hear the slap of the lifeboat not far away and the thrum of the helicopter as a base note underneath. His boy was still at sea, alone and frightened. He couldn't give up yet.

'He isn't dead yet. I'd know,' he said. 'Please Grace. Help me. Help me look for him.'

She clicked for the dog and moved off without speaking, heading further away from the cottages and the village, towards the second inlet. He checked his phone for a second before he followed her. No calls. No messages. Lorna hadn't heard – yet.

His head was spinning here on this fragile headland in the rain and he thought he might just let himself step off the edge and fall. It might be easier all round, it might be best. If they didn't find Luca in this next place, he decided, he would send Grace home and keep on going, keep on looking, further and further away and never, ever come back. The thought gave him some comfort and he hurried to catch up with her.

'Run away a lot, does he?' she asked without turning, when she heard him arrive breathlessly behind her.

'Not usually. He prefers to stay and fight, actually.' She made a humph sound and they walked on in silence for a while, but her question made him uncomfortable, so he said, 'It's his deafness. It frustrates him. He can be hard to reason with, sometimes.'

'You don't have to explain yourself to me. It's none of my business.'

He kept his head down and watched her strong legs in their sturdy boots marching steadily ahead. He thought of Luca's pale, mute face and its expression as he tried to make himself heard, understood, effective, in his own world, where every decision was made for him. A clever boy like him, kept on a leash night and day.

'His mum suffocates him,' he said aloud, and realised it was true. 'She won't let him breathe, half the time. Won't listen to me, when I tell her the kid needs a bit of space. He's deaf, I tell her – he's not simple, but she shuts me out.' He paused, as a thought occurred to him. 'I think she actually likes it this way.'

'Munchausen Syndrome by Proxy.'

'What?'

'Look it up. Here.'

She stopped abruptly so that he almost walked into her. The cliff at this point seemed in much worse condition, than at the last. The drop was sheer, and it wasn't obvious how they were to get down.

'We don't have to get down into this one, only a bit closer to the edge,' she said, seeing his face. 'We'll be able to see from there if there's anything washed in. There's a path down a bit further on, if we need it.'

He could be here, then, down below, right there, bobbing about in the boat, waiting for them. The rush of hope and fear was powerful, like a cold wind blowing up over the lip of the cliff.

He stepped forwards immediately and went to lean over to look down.

'Wait,' she said, grabbing his shoulder, 'can't you see it's perished there, you fucking idiot? We have to go across and round a bit, for god's sake – just follow me again.'

The dog barked, sharply, from a little way ahead, and trotted perilously close to the cliff edge too, looking down into the sea. Grace didn't call it back, just looked at it and stayed very still and turned her ear to the wind. Evan held his breath and did the same.

Yes. A small sound came from the rock-bound bay far below. A percussive bump-bump-bump. Something was running against the rocks with the movement of the tide. It was. It was the boat. It couldn't be anything else making that noise. His face went hot, and he was suddenly full of fire.

'Quick!' he said hoarsely. 'Show me!'

She had heard too, and threw her hat to the ground. She sat on the grass with a plump and slid herself forwards and down the sheer slope to where a straggly bush hung itself high on the cliff edge, and held this and pulled herself around it and out of sight. He followed her quickly. They came out onto a big black rock that sat like a stage on the edge of the cliff. He got to his feet carefully and didn't mind that Grace held his elbow. All his attention was fixed on the edge of the rock and what would lie beneath.

They inched forwards together, feeling the exposure, and looked down into the black water below. At first he could see only darkness – the water and the sheer rock the same, no seabirds to break the dark blankness. Then he saw a bowl of white. The inside of the little boat, gleaming up at him from one corner of the inlet just under his feet, moving up and down a little on the incoming water but going nowhere. His heart leapt. Then with the next beat he realised. It was empty. There was no boy inside. No Luca. He wasn't there.

The boat was empty.

The cliffs were sheer. There was nowhere for a child to climb up, out of sight or out of the water. He wasn't on the cliffs anywhere.

Evan strained to see right out where the sea came in, but there was nothing there. No one.

They hadn't found him.

He was lost, and worse than before.

Luca. Poor Luca. I'm so sorry, he thought.

He felt the weight and awfulness of it all like a blanket thrown over his head, and dizziness rushed up on him from below. His foot moved in an attempt to steady him but found only emptiness over the very edge of the ledge and his body tipped forwards.

'Oh no you don't!'

There was an arm across his belly, pressing him back hard, so that he stumbled and fell down onto soft, wet grass, away from the drop and the water and the darkness. He lay there and let the clearing sky move overhead, and the despair work its way through. He thought about things, and how empty it all was, how much it hurt and how cold the ground was underneath him. When the hissing stopped in his ears and his spinning head stilled, he opened his eyes and there was

Grace, standing in her wide hat, looking down at him. Her eyes were very bright.

'Third time lucky,' she said, but he didn't feel lucky.

She didn't tell him to move, or even extend a hand to pull him up. It seemed that there was no hurry, now, after everything, and he was tired to the bone. He felt her sit down beside him with a sigh and her familiar scent puffed out from her and wrapped him. A mixture of baking and hay and washing powder, he thought idly. The gentle rushing of the sea was calming, and for a moment his mind was empty and idle. He would have fallen asleep if he hadn't felt suddenly chilled, so cold that his body tensed with shivering. He felt her fumbling around and heard the subtle clicks of a phone being dialled. Funny, he thought, he'd never pictured her with a phone at all.

He listened in and out as she talked to that lovely girl, Abbie – told her what they'd found and where, telling her to get the coastguard to set the lifeboat combing the cliffs all the way in from the seaward side, in case the boy had somehow managed to negotiate the currents and swim to shore. In case he had climbed out of the water, the wee monkey he was, and was clinging wet and cold to the rocks somewhere, waiting for rescue. After she ended the call she sat there for another while, quiet.

'You don't think he's there, do you?' he asked.

'No,' she said. She didn't tell him why, but that was enough.

'He will always do the exact opposite of what he's told,' Evan said and felt again the deep rage that the child could call up in him, with just a blank face or an insolent stare. 'He is just so damn smart.'

The woman snorted beside him. 'I don't call this particular adventure very smart. Do you?'

It was his turn to sit still and say nothing. There was nothing to say, after all. He let his mind drift away from this horrible place and float somewhere else. He had stopped shivering and was deep-down cold instead, as if he would never move again.

'Come on. Up with you!' She was gripping his arm and pulling. He tried to stand and got his feet under him. She pulled and he pushed up, weakly, like a baby, and stood. His head reeled. 'That way.' She was pointing back behind him, the way they had come. He remembered. Luca wasn't here, wasn't anywhere, it seemed, and it was time to leave.

He took fistfuls of grass and used them to pull himself back up and around the straggling bush. She was behind him, so close that her shoulder bumped his leg if he tried to stop to think about things, so he kept going. He waited at the top for her to grab her hat and cram it on. The lifeboat churned by, out at sea, all the orange helmets turned to face the cliff, and the noise of the helicopter was becoming a hellish racket overhead. He should go and stand at the edge of the cliff and look down for a flash of orangey-pink, or a little face, but he didn't trust himself to come back again when it wasn't there.

'Can you walk?' she asked.

Of course he could walk. He looked at her, dazed, and nodded.

'Come on, then ... Dog!' she shouted, and set off at a gentler pace along the headland. There didn't seem to be any hurry now. He hesitated a moment and looked in the opposite direction, away from the noise and the searching and the village and all of the people. The clifftop seemed to go on for miles and miles and miles into the cloud. His sweater was soaked and stuck to him, chafing hotly under the arms from walking, and the rain was running off his hair.

He didn't want to go that way.

Grace was standing still. She was waiting for him, and he thought she looked quite beautiful under the rain, tall and strong and wise and kindly. Her hair fluffed out from under that hat despite the rain, and her jacket blew a little around her in the breeze coming up over the clifftop. Her two long legs were planted solid on the ground as if she grew from it and she looked at him with those bright eyes, waiting.

His foot caught a tussock of grass just as he reached her, and he stumbled badly and fell forwards, but she was there. She held him up for a moment with the warmth and the softness of her coming all through her arms like an energy, and then to his surprise she drew him in. She didn't say anything, but she put her arms tight around him and brought his wet face into her shoulder and kept him upright while her warmth flowed through from her body to his. Her old jacket was as soft as rabbit-skin against his cheek. That scent of hers was strong and hot and familiar, and the beat of her pulse was slow and steady and calming against his neck, so he wrapped himself around her and breathed her in and held on tight against her, feeling everything acutely and letting it pass.

They stood there a long time, still and sensitive, until the tick-tock of her heartbeat receded like the helicopter in the distance. She was pulling away. He lifted his head to look at her. They were just the same height. She didn't speak. Up close, her eyes were flecked with dark, dark blue in the grey. The lines around her mouth and eyes were a lighter shade than the skin of her face, and her body against him was hard and strong and warm. He didn't let her go. There was no expression on her face as she looked at him, so close he could kiss her mouth if he wanted to. Her breath was warm and biscuity on his skin and he breathed it in.

'Grace,' he said quietly, 'your name suits you.'

She looked at him for another heartbeat and the dog whined at her ankle, tired of the rain. Then she kissed him, lightly on the forehead, as one would kiss a child, and held his face in her hands a moment.

'It's never as bad as it seems,' she said. 'Never, and I should know. Now come on.'

She let him go but it was all right. He had some strength again, so he could follow. The place where her mouth had been was warm for a second on his forehead, and then washed away by the rain. She turned her back to him and clicked for the dog and headed back, and he kept pace behind her, just as before.

He kept his eyes on the grass as he walked and tried to notice it, to keep from thinking. Brown and yellow and green it was, studded with little round-petalled yellow flowers – the summer bursting out even through the rain. He didn't look up. He kept his feet moving, one-two-one-two, bringing him back towards the rented cottage, the crowds of bright good-hearted people, the buzz and the fuss, the tragedy of a lost child, the clattering and calling and, probably, Lorna.

He wasn't bringing Luca back with him. They hadn't found him at the inlets – sorry, everyone.

He couldn't imagine his angry little boy in this growing darkness, freezing and juddering in the huge and empty water, left alone because they couldn't find him, so he didn't. He looked at the grass again instead, hard, and at his feet, and felt the trickle of raindrops down his back and on his skin and running over the end of his nose and thought about Grace and her own sad story and her ugly dog and her delightful niece, and kept away the shadow of Luca, pale and angry in the dark, mute and upset and lost because his mum was coming to take him home, and his dad was going to let him go again.

Chapter 33

———

THE LANE WAS TEEMING WITH PEOPLE, the feel of a party, as they rounded the bend. Her worktable was still at the front door but now it was laden with plates and boxes and cups and flasks. People were offering platters of sandwiches, tins full of cakes and biscuits. She realised she was hungry. She didn't know anyone in the crowd. Faces swivelled to watch them as they approached, and elbows nudged. She had to get the townie inside before he was recognised. He would bolt like a bad horse if these people crowded him. They'd accost him and cluck and fuss at him, trying to find out what it felt like. She wished she'd taken off her hat. As it was, she stood out, instantly recognisable as the madwoman neighbour, and they were all turning to her like flowers to the sun.

'Have you all forgotten about social bloody distancing?' she demanded loudly.

Those closest to her looked sheepish. A couple fumbled for facemasks and there was a general shuffling apart. Sandwiches were tucked back under paper and lids discreetly clicked back onto cake tins. She glared for a second more and then turned and took his elbow. He didn't resist. Still in la-la-land, then.

'Quick,' she muttered, 'get inside.'

They pushed through the whispering crowd and in through the front door of her cottage. It was quiet there. Abbie sat at the table, legs wide, flip-flops pointing east and west, twisting a tea towel in her hands and looking at the floor. The table was spread with charts and notes and papers to every corner. The male coastguard was poring over these, marking invisible lines with his finger. He glanced up as they came in and crinkled his eyes over his mask in recognition.

'Who the hell are all those people out there, Abbie?' she demanded, ignoring him.

The girl ran her hand under her nose. 'Facebook,' she sniffed. 'No luck then? Oh god Auntie Grace, I can't believe it.' Then she saw the townie standing in the shadow of her aunt and stood up quickly. 'Oh, poor Evan,' she said. 'You're absolutely soaked. Oh, you poor thing. You poor, poor, thing. Come in – come in and get warm.'

Her eyes filled with tears again, and her red, shiny face was all puffy with crying. She must have been dripping like a tap as she served the tea to the hungry hordes outside. Very hygienic under the present circumstances. Grace tutted. She had always been too soft, that one.

'He needs a blanket and something to eat, not more water, for god's sake,' she said aloud, hanging her hat on its hook and taking her coat to the back door to shake the rain off. The dog was nowhere to be seen, but it would come back in its own time. When she turned, the girl had put the townie in the soft chair by the Aga and was draping the bright checks of the throw-blanket from the sofa over his shoulders. He was quite still.

Grace parked her bum against the counter and alternated swigs of coffee with bites of sandwich, thinking.

The boy should have been in that first bay. The weight of the boat and its load should have swung it around in Duckers Hole just before, washing it in. Or was she losing it altogether? Had hope blinded her to likelihood and made her think things that were false? She was genuinely at a loss. The big brown clock ticked in the quiet room. Abbie wiped surfaces aimlessly, one eye on the man in the chair. The dog barked outside, disliking all the people, all the fuss.

Then there was a woman closing the front door and standing just inside it. Birdlike, beautiful, and distressed in pale blue jeans and a tight-fitting t-shirt, elegant sandals and car keys looped in her fingers. She looked around a moment without speaking and then came right in, her hair glossy and straight and shining under the light, sparkling with raindrops. She went over to the townie and knelt at his feet.

'Is it true, Evan? Mairead called me. Is it true? Where is he?'

Grace watched the man shrink further back in the chair, and Abbie leaned in with surprising deftness to rescue his coffee before he spilled it. He didn't speak. The woman showed straight white teeth as she took his shoulders and shook him slightly.

'Evan! Is Luca out there somewhere? Talk to me, for god's sake!' She looked up at Abbie who was hovering nearby. 'What's wrong with him? Why won't he answer me?'

'Shock,' Grace said across the room, and set her cup down on the counter with a click. She took a pile of the sandwiches from the box beside her and wrapped them in a long strip of kitchen towel.

'I heard,' the woman said in a high voice, still holding the townie's shoulders but looking up at her, 'that my son was lost. On a boat? Is that true? Is that true?'

Grace nodded. She should say that they were doing everything they could. That they usually found the drifters within a few hours. That the coastguard and the RNLI and half the country were out there looking, bound to turn up shortly, only a matter of time, but she didn't like the woman, and all she could see was her own darling little boat, empty and incongruous in the rock-clad bay, and the pale-faced boy, his eyes wide, watching a crab scuttle across her hands, afraid and delighted all at once. She stared at the lovely woman without speaking and saw that her eyes sloped down elegantly at the corners and were the deepest richest brown, like chocolate, like the boy's.

'Oh my god,' the woman said now and blinked slowly, and her eyes filled with tears. She looked back at the closed front door, where behind it the people milled about and the camera crews set up, ready for the long haul. 'Oh my god.'

She put her hand over her mouth as if her distress were poor manners. Grace watched as she sat back on her heels, full of questions but unable to speak, and liked her a little better.

Abbie held out a tissue. 'Here,' she said, and the woman took it with a shaky smile of thanks, and dabbed at her face with it. Abbie crouched down by the woman, her dress a bright spotted circle on the floor, her head tipped to one side in honest concern and pity. She'd sort it out. She'd bring her up to speed.

Grace went quietly to the back door, unhooked her wet coat again and let herself out into the garden. She pushed the pack of sandwiches deep into a pocket as she shrugged the coat on, chilly against her skin. The clouds were clearing, and the sun was a warm yellow as it sank behind the distant hills. Everything sparkled brightly after the long-awaited rain. The hum and chatter of the people outside the high wall rose and fell. Someone laughed. Another called a greeting to a new arrival. People moved away to begin searching and others returned; asked where the coffee was; clattered and banged around.

The dog barked again out there among the hubbub, looking for her, and Grace pushed herself upright and crunched along the little path to let it in through the side door.

Outside was a mass of fluorescent yellows and greens and pinks like a tree full of parrots, and no one seemed to be doing anything much but standing around and gossiping and eating. The group nearest to the door turned to look at her curiously as she stuck her head out, but she ignored them and called, 'Dog!'

There it came, scampering up with its teeth showing and its tongue lolling, from where it had been scratching at the cottage door. The group parted quickly at the sight of it and let it through. She held the garden door wide to let it bound into the garden, slobbering wetly and making small jumps at her legs on its stubby, ugly feet. She closed the door on the inquisitive faces and shot the bolt loudly, nodding at the blank wooden face of the door as she did so. The dog whined and she knelt right down on the wet ground to hug it.

'Oh, Dog,' she said quietly, rubbing its coarse back and smelling the stink of wet animal and something it had rolled in. 'Oh Dog. Oh Dog.'

The animal groaned as she scratched a good spot and panted gently as she stood up again, consoled. The people outside had gone straight back to their chattering and laughing. Someone with excellent diction said, 'Och yes, and the poor wee thing's simple, as well, you know. Probably can't find his own way home, the wee pet. They've no hope of finding him, really, have they?'

A buzz of other voices answered in indistinct murmurs like hens crooning in the roost. Grace bent quickly and lifted a handful of gravel from the little path and lobbed it over the wall like shrapnel. There was a chorus of horrified 'Oh!'s and the sound of people scattering.

'He's not fucking simple, he's deaf,' she bawled. 'There's a huge fucking difference, you cretin. Now fuck off and look for him, or go the fuck home.'

There was a scandalised hush and then the sound of boots receding down the lane a little, but it didn't make her feel any better.

'Useless fuckers,' she said.

She stooped again and picked up the padlock from the grass,

slipping it back on the loop of the bolt. As she'd expected, it was quite badly rusted. She couldn't get it to lock.

'Oil,' she said to the attentive dog. 'Can't have that pack of yahoos coming in here for a nosey, can we?' and it trotted happily after her as she headed across the grass towards the shed, keeping herself busy. She could hear the crackle of the coastguard's radio among the crowds out in the lane, and a repeated request to 'Keep your distance, please,' and 'Head on home now,' but all the while the chatter continued unabated, and the bright blue lights of the media had come on while her back was turned.

'Bastards,' she said under her breath. 'Bored and nosey is all they are. As much use as tits on a boar.'

As she went across the garden, her boots squeaked loudly on the wet grass and the cross old goat came running towards her in the field, a long string of buttercup hanging from the corner of its mouth. It was hoping for pony nuts, no doubt. She stopped still and looked at it, at its tattered pelt and its one twisted horn, as it reached the gate and blinked at her from slotted eyes, expectantly.

She forgot about the shed then, and went to the stable instead. The top leaf of the door was as snugly bolted as she had left it, but the bottom half was unlocked and opened easily under her hand as she pulled it wide. The donkey snuffed out at her curiously, bending its stubby neck to peer from under the top door, checking for rain. The goat in the field bleated loudly when it saw the donkey's nose appear and pushed roughly against the gate, making a rattling sound. She turned and saw that this was unlocked too, with a thick gap between pillar and gate, and that only the goat's stupidity kept it inside.

She paused and looked quickly around and behind her. The garden was empty.

Inside the cottage she could see the lights were on, a warm yellow colour in the increasing dusk, and people moving around in her kitchen were just shifting shapes and colours like a kaleidoscope, the bright red and white of Abbie a repeated pattern back and forth, back and forth. Biting her lip, she checked all around once more and then ducked in under the top door of the stable, pushing the dog back gently with her boot to keep it out. It sat on the grass and whined quietly as she disappeared inside. She pulled the bottom door tight behind her again and held it for a second to make sure it didn't swing open of its own accord.

She breathed in the silence and the dark and stretched her ears with listening.

Everything was quiet. She felt the donkey lipping her hair as if it were hay and pushed its head away.

She needed to be able to find her way around, so she stood a second to let her eyes adjust to the dim shapes and shadows illuminated by the tiny crack of light that sneaked in through the half-doors and the loosely clinkered walls. Her nose was full of straw-dust, so she nipped it with two fingers so that she wouldn't sneeze. The donkey groaned softly at the unexpected company and she felt around with her hand in the darkness for its nose, and from there found its spiky mane, its knobbly back, its sloping haunches, and so navigated her way to the back of the stable, to where the straw lay thick for the donkey's bed. It groaned again and shifted away from her, uneasy now, until she stood in the darkness alone.

She pushed into her back pocket for her phone and allowed it to light up and shine brightly on her face. There were only two names in her contacts list. She selected the one she needed and typed,

Evryones looking fr u

She lowered the phone and let its face go dark and she waited.

The pile of hay rustled again in front of her. There was nothing else for a while. She braced herself to catch whatever might bolt, but all was still. She waited again. Then suddenly there was a dim glow just in front of her, low down against the back wall, as if another phone had switched on.

A flare of bright joy filled her so that she smiled to herself in the dark.

She typed another message.

Ur dads worryd sick

She waited some more.

There was a subtle ping and her phone showed:

So

She didn't move but sent:

Cn I sit down

Pause.

Ur stabl

She pushed off her boots one by one and they made a thick swooshing sound as her feet came free of the sodden insides. She pulled off her socks for good measure and stuffed them in the boots so that she stood in her bare feet, looking down at where the boy hid, snug and well, and enjoyed the moment. The stable floor was soft earth and almost warm, and the scent of sleepy animal was one of her favourites in the world. With exaggerated creakiness, she eased herself down to sit against the adjoining wall, where she could see the pile of straw and keep an eye on the little light which still shone out from it like a tiny sun. After a moment she texted,

I thot you were the goat

That thick chuckle came from under the straw, and then a sneeze, and then Luca pushed his coverings away and looked at her, a little defiantly, with straw sticking up from his hair here and there and his skin green in the light from the phones. She couldn't help smiling at him.

Sory i had to put him in the feeld he kept pushing me with his hed

She nodded.

He does that

I took lumps frm the barel outsid and he folowd me
Tht ws clevr he luvs ponynuts
😌
That was clever with the boat too, she told him.

He nodded, and they looked at each other like conspirators.
Im a good hider
U are indeed
It had been a long day, fraught and challenging, and she was suddenly very tired. She rested her head back against the wall and looked at the darkness where the roof would be. Her hands dangled loose from her knees and she felt herself breathe for a while, sucking in the happiness of being there with him, safe, like a golden secret that she'd tell when she was good and ready.

Her phone lit up.
I dont want to go away
She looked at him, keeping her face calm and blank.
I want to stay here
She sent:
I think ur mum only here to visit, and shrugged.

His thumbs raced across the screen of his device:
U don't know her she wont let me stay she wont let me do anythin
There was a long pause, and the boy picked straw from his hair and let it fall strand by strand onto the pile on top of his knees.
Why don't u want to go home
He put his head down.
Its 💩
She laughed.
Is that wot I think it is
He nodded, grinning. She had to hunt quite hard for the same picture but found it eventually.
Why 💩?

Her reward was his smile. Then his face fell straight again and he typed fast.

Cant do wot I want. dad not hapy. Mum not hapy. Nobody hapy any mor

She nodded.

The straw rustled loudly and, in the dim, green light, she saw him get up and come to sit beside her, close. He was lovely and warm and felt as if he had just woken up, all loose and floppy. She would have liked a boy of her own, she thought suddenly, leaning back on him a little. She would indeed.

Cn I tell u a secret

He had sat this way so she couldn't see his face, she realised. She concentrated on her phone instead, looking for the picture she needed.

😖

He nodded greenly, and sent:

My sister died

She nodded back.

He put his phone down carefully on the straw and from the corner of her eye she could see him pull at the edge of a scab on his knee. He'd got it climbing after a gull the other day. She'd seen him slip and slice it on the sharp barnacles on the rocks. He hadn't cried, just examined the cut and then climbed on, although of course the gull was already long gone. He hissed through his teeth now as the scab proved too new to pull away, and picked up his phone again. Her bum was going numb. She readjusted to ease it and he cuddled back in to her new shape and nodded for her to look at her phone.

I kild her. I kild my sistr

OK, she thought. There was a long pause.

He scooched forwards a little so that he could see her face. He was frowning.

I kild jessie. I did

Ok

How is it ok

The skin of his face was pulled back tight over the bones as he stared at her to see what she would do. It almost hurt to look at him, to see so much anxiety in the young face, so much pain.

Tell me what happend

He stared at her still, but he was seeing the scene playing over again behind his eyes. After a moment he bent his head down again and began to text.

She alwys cryed. Nobody cared about me. so I kild her.

Ok

He growled at this, stretching his eyes wide, and she shrugged.

So tell me

It took a while, and she watched him bite his lip as he pressed send, and rock back and forth until the text came in to her. His eyes were fixed on her face as she read it.

Dad was sleepin in th chair. She wuz lyin on him. I put my hand on her mouth and her nose

Y

Saw it on tv it kils them

Ok

Wel so she opend her eys and lookd at me

He took a break and pushed some straw around with the toe of his trainer. She waited and thought about the townie, fast asleep in a big soft chair, exhausted by the screeches of a new-born, oblivious to the pain of his other child, oblivious to everything, those bloody glasses askew, that wide mouth relaxed, the lips parted, maybe snoring.

Wel I dint want her to dy then so I took my hand of. It ws all wet. She smild at me and bubles came out f her mouth.

What did u do then

Wnt bak to bed

He scuffed the floor with his toe.

Ok, she typed.

Yeh but

He looked at her helplessly.

She nodded, and sent:

💩

Yeh 💩, he agreed.

They both sat quietly for a while, then, and she felt him snuggle his hand into hers. It was small like a bird, and warm. She held it gently, as if it had a broken wing. It was difficult to text like that, but she stuck her tongue between her teeth and wrote:

DId u tel yr dad

The hand was removed. He scooched forwards again and stared at her, the fear written all over his face.

No and u cant too. It's a secret

😖 Like I sed

Ok

Ok 😐

She could see misery all over his face, a huge sad loneliness that made him seem old, not eight, and she couldn't leave it like that.

Cn I say somethin

She waited as he fiddled with his phone and then nodded at her to go ahead without lifting his eyes.

Don't think she died bcos of ur hand

?

U know ur dad thnks he kild her too

He shook his head. She could see thoughts scurrying across his face. He was a clever boy.

She sighed.

Sometimes 💩 happns nd its nobdys fault

He shook his head.

She typed more.

Yes. Sumtimes babys just dy. Its tru. Look it up. Called sids

He was staring into her eyes now, trying to read the truth in the dim green light of their phones, to see if she was being an adult or just being honest. She made her eyes wide as she could and didn't blink despite all the dust. This mattered, that he believed her, now. At last he looked away, down into the straw. She shifted again to find comfort and a familiar scent reached her nostrils. She sent him:

U like egg n cress

Wots cress

Green stuf

I like egg

She nodded and fished in her pocket for the paper towel. The sandwiches inside were pretty squashed but she calculated he had been hiding there for at least six hours, and boys got hungry. She heard the donkey snurf with interest as she unfolded the towel and flattened out the food inside as best she could, and its dainty hooves scuffed the floor as it tried to turn to see what goodies she had. She held the damp towel out for the boy to take one, but he put his phone down and lifted the whole thing and grinned at her again. She watched him bite and chew hungrily. She could see why mothers fed their sons so obsessively. It was a perfect happiness.

I beter tel them ur ok, she told him and watched his phone light up on the floor. He read the message with his mouth full of bread. He stopped chewing and looked at her. His cheek bulged.

U stay here for a while ok

He nodded, looking nervous.

She smiled at him and reached out to pat his knee through the straw. On an afterthought she shrugged out of her jacket and put it around his shoulders, and he snuggled into it luxuriously.

Promis u wont hide somwher els

He nodded again, and she believed him.

'Right. Move your big arse, Dolly, I'm getting up,' she said, and hauled on the donkey's tail to pull herself to standing. It blew air through its nostrils and moved away grumpily as she dusted herself off. At the stable door she peeked out carefully. The dusk had crept in and hung like smoke in the garden, intensified by the glare of huge lights over the ridge of the house where the operation continued, the search at sea for the lost, drowned child.

There was no one in the garden except the dog, patiently waiting in the half-light and panting as though it were smiling at her. She glanced back one more time at the straw-covered boy against the back wall, and he raised a sandwich to her in salute, his hair still stuck with straw like an Indian brave. She smiled at him and waved a finger – stay there, now – and sneaked out onto the grass, carefully closing the stable door behind her, feeling a little cold through the light sweater she wore. The goat bleated and scraped its bent horn on the wood of the gate. On an impulse she lifted the lid of the bin at the wall and took a huge scoop of the pony nuts from inside.

'You deserve this, you cantankerous old bastard,' she said gently, as she scattered the treats over the gate for the animal. She leaned on the soft, splintered wood for a while and watched it lip up the nuts from the ground delicately, while the last of the light faded and the summer night came creeping over the grass with a faint chill. The noise from over the wall was fainter. People got cold and bored. People went home. She shivered and pushed herself back off the bar of the gate. It must be almost midnight.

The dog huffed and a bright yellow pool spilled out into the garden as the kitchen door opened. The townie came out, furtively, huddling the blanket around his shoulders and closing the door softly behind him, much as she had done earlier. He didn't see her standing there in the shadows, but the dog ran forwards and snuffed at his socks, making him jump.

'Jesus!' he said, and looked around for her, squinting into the darkness. 'Grace! You there?'

She came forwards slowly, letting her hair go every way it wanted to in the breeze, watching the man smile wanly and bend to stroke the dog's head as if it weren't ugly. She didn't say anything at all, just let him come forwards to her in his stockinged feet, the blanket shifting and curling around him in the rising wind.

'Oh Grace,' he whispered. 'Grace.'

'I want to show you something,' she said firmly, taking his hand as if he were seven.

Chapter 34

———

IT WAS LATE, but he couldn't sleep.

God knows, he'd slept on the rickety old sofa many times, and he had some catching up still to do after the craziness of Tuesday, but tonight he was full of a crackling energy that wouldn't dissipate. Grace would blame it on the moon, no doubt – the huge white-faced stranger in the sky outside. At the thought of her, all sleep scattered. He sighed, stretched, and sat up, patting the floor beside him for his glasses and pushing them on. The hammock hung still and full in the shadows across the room, his boy safe inside, and his wife slept in the bedroom and was leaving in the morning, alone.

Kicking the tangle of mismatched blankets from his feet he stood up and went to the window. The moon whitened the thin curtains, and he drew them quietly back, looking out onto a still black sea paved with a silver moon-path, but his thoughts were elsewhere. His face heated as he remembered how Grace had towed him by the hand away from her cottage that strange night, away from the dying search and towards darkness and the shed and the stable.

He'd held tight to her strong hand and followed her, of course, but as she pulled open the stable door he'd hung back, looking over his shoulder at the house where the second shift of coastguards were planning the next phase of the search for his boy with divers and drag-ropes, and his wife paced the floor twisting her hands and avoiding his eyes, silent and grim.

'Grace!' he'd said in a hoarse whisper. 'What—'

Her face had been alive with laughter and lit up by the light from the house as she turned to him. He could see her as a girl, suddenly, tearing through life and pushing away boundaries and constraints, escaping to London from the stifling silence of country life.

She'd squeezed his hand.

'Trust me. Haven't you learned to fucking trust me by now, all the times I've saved your neck?'

He remembered ducking in awkwardly under the stable door, not wanting to offend her, and the pungent smell of the place and the darkness and the big hot shape of the donkey taking up almost all the space, and the question of what in the world she wanted to show him, right then, in that place, in the dark. It never occurred to him.

A light had appeared in her hand – her phone – and they'd looked at a pile of hay or straw or something, heaped up at the back of the stable for the animal. She'd let go of his hand and he began to understand with a racing heart as he came alongside her, pressing up against the flimsy wall and straining his eyes into the darkness. He hadn't dared to ask in case the answer wasn't yes, so he'd held his breath instead, and waited to see what would happen. He had learned to do that, if he'd learned anything at all.

Nothing moved for what seemed like an age and he'd had to let his breath go and take another. Grace had texted again, and they stood in the light of her phone until it clicked off and they were left in pitch darkness. His very skin was alive with hope, now, and he hadn't moved a muscle, hadn't blinked, was busy trusting her with all his heart.

A second light had shone then, dimmed by a covering of straw.

He remembered how Grace had put a hand on his arm although he hadn't moved, and they'd waited until her phone had made a muted ping. She showed him:

Ok 😶

'His majesty has agreed to a parley,' she'd said in a low smile. '—I'll leave you to it,' but he'd held her arm, *no*, while all the amazement and relief and surprise rushed through him.

'Don't go.'

She'd looked at him curiously and let him keep her there.

He'd laughed nervously as they watched the straw which rustled vigorously now.

'You're not afraid of your own son, are you, you big jinny?'

'No! No. But—'

Her face had been pushed up close to his in the cramped stable and he remembered the smell of her – the sensation of her warmth as she spoke to him.

'Listen. He ran away because the pair of you couldn't communicate. Time for a *mano-el-mano*. Now or never. Clear the air. Before he has to face the music in there.'

She'd nodded sharply in the direction of the cottage and the cameras and the assembled crowds.

'OK, but stay, Grace, do,' he'd pleaded. '—Just for a minute. I need you to hold the light so we can sign – and he'll behave when you're here. I don't want him running out of here as well.'

A dark head had appeared as he spoke, stuck all over with yellow straw like a bird of paradise, and Luca had looked at his dad from under his eyebrows, surly. Evan's insides had turned to water with the joy of it, and he'd been unable to move or speak or think. He'd just looked.

Grace had huffed a laugh at the sight of the boy, flipped her own wild hair back over her shoulders, and made a big scene out of easing herself down almost on top of the boy, who squeaked and punched her gently on the arm to make her move over.

Evan had stood there awkwardly. He could feel it again, now, as he stared out of the window at the unmoving sea – the strain of trying to connect with the child, his own son, who wouldn't even meet his eye.

'I don't know what to say,' he'd said aloud to her in the darkness.

'Start with a hug,' she'd replied.

'We don't really hug,' he'd said and felt like running away.

'That's OK, neither do I,' she'd replied. 'But you could start by getting down here, too, then. You're not the bloody Lord High Chancellor in here, you know.'

He'd scuffled to the other side of the boy, with one hand carefully on the coarse pelt of the donkey, pushing it gently out of the way, aware of the hard hooves at the long end of its legs, and sat down like a yogi. The boy had been examining his phone, studiously ignoring him, but looked up at a tap on the shoulder and a pointing finger from Grace, as though he'd been unaware of his father's presence until then.

We thought you were in the boat, Evan had signed, holding his hands clear of the straw.

The boy didn't respond immediately but had tinkered with his phone some more. Evan had had to push down his irritation. In the cottage back there, he'd promised never to lose his temper with the boy again, ever-ever-ever, if he could only be found safe and well, and there he was, only a matter of seconds in, and he'd wanted to shake him. Hard.

Suddenly a huge light flared out from Luca's phone, and he handed it to Grace with a little smile.

'Ah,' she'd said, smiling and nodding. 'Torch. Good batting, thinkman.'

She'd held it aloft, and it was as if a lamp was lit in the dark space. He could see long thick cobwebs hanging down behind her head and dark shadows under his son's face. It was very late.

It's very late, he'd signed.

Sorry Dad.

The boy had looked at him for the first time, and at last Evan could feel the relief and love at the sight of that face, those dark eyes, those flashing fingers.

I was so frightened, he'd told his son. I thought you were in the boat and we would never find you.

The boy had frowned. I'm not that stupid. Did you think I was?

Evan had laughed, and he smiled now at the memory of the warm buzz between them.

Luca, he'd said, do we always have to fight?

The boy had put his head down and Grace had patted his knee where it poked through the straw. Sorry Dad.

Evan had reached over and put his face and his hands close, speaking aloud as he signed, for emphasis, the shadows moving over his skin in the light of the phone. I don't know if you know this – but I love you, Luca. I always have. I promise. He'd nodded slowly as he spoke and held his gaze, willing the child to believe him, and then he'd gone on. I'm sorry. I don't really know how to be a good dad. I'll try harder, I promise.

'Careful. That's a lot of promises,' Grace had said wryly but he'd ignored her, and held his son's gaze until it dropped again, and small fingers pulled at a flaking scab on a bare knee.

There had been a silence for a time, where the boy had bitten his lip and looked young again and Evan had adjusted his position, trying to find some comfort on the dusty earth of the stable floor.

'Watch out for that pat beside you,' Grace had warned quietly, and he'd seen that his hand had narrowly missed a large pile of donkey-droppings, and flinched quickly away.

The boy had laughed.

Do you want to come outside? Out of here? Evan had asked him hopefully.

The boy's face had clouded again. Does Mum know? Is she here?

269

Evan had nodded. Do you want to tell me why you ran away? Before we go out? She's in the house. In Grace's house, trying to find you.

Grace switched the phone from hand to hand and the light dipped and rose.

'Sorry,' she said, wincing. 'My arm went to sleep.'

Evan had smiled at the shape of her, the glow of her behind the light, a bright fizz.

I told *Grace* why.

So tell *me*.

The boy had made a face, trying to organise his thoughts and tell them on his fingers. I don't want to go back home, Dad.

It was Evan's turn to nod. He'd understood completely. He'd felt a surge of pleasure as he realised that at last he was not one guy all alone against the united forces of his wife and their strong-minded son.

Tell me.

He'd waited.

I like it here. With you and Grace and Abbie and the donkey and the crabs and the beach.

The boy had blown his fringe up with a puff of his breath. Evan had savoured it. Luca had said he liked it here, with him. He was first in the list. He blinked sympathetically at his son.

You know this was just a long holiday, though, don't you? Because of the sickness. The virus. None of us gets to stay here for always.

The boy had pouted. Grace does.

Well, except Grace. I mean you and me and Mum.

Luca had pushed his feet out straight in frustration. I'm not ready for it to be over. Why did Mum come here and spoil it? Why does *she* get to say?

She didn't get to say anything. You ran off before she even got here.

Luca had laughed then, and he'd felt like he was winning. He'd reached out and squeezed the boy's foot through his trainer.

Anyway. She doesn't always get to say. We're a team, right? The three of us.

Luca had shaken his head. You always say that but she still gets to say. Like the operation.

?

They're my ears. If I want them fixed why can she say no? Why don't you stop her, if you love me? I hate these stupid ears.

He'd tugged them hard, as if trying to pull them off, and Evan had had to reach in and take his hands back down.

How do you even know about this, Luca? I didn't think you knew.

Dr Campbell signs when he talks to Mum so I can understand too. *He* thinks I'm smart enough. *He* wants me to have the operation too.

Evan spread his hands helplessly. So do I.

Luca's signing was sharp and angry. But you won't *tell* her! She says no so that's it! And now I'm stuck at that stupid school and stupid sign-classes for more ages. Why wouldn't you tell her we are a team? Tell her it is yes sometimes? You'd tell her it was yes if it was *Jessie*, I bet.

Evan didn't know what to say for a moment.

His daughter's name had dropped like a stone into the connection between them.

Is that what you think? he'd asked, astounded.

But anyway she was perfect not broken like me so it didn't matter. Well now she's dead and I'm glad and so there.

Then the boy had been crying, loud hard *boo-hoos* that threatened to blow their cover before they were ready. Evan had quickly moved in and gathered him onto his knee, cuddling him and soothing him even before he had time to realise what he was doing, or to fear being rejected or pushed away.

To his amazement, the boy had let him do it, going soft and pliant in his arms, not fighting or resisting. Evan had held the hot head close to his chest and let him cry, looking helplessly over the top to where Grace tactfully lowered the phone so that the light was dimmed against the pile of straw at her side. She said nothing, but smiled slightly, so he smoothed the child's hair and pulled him in tighter as though he were a baby again and the two of them, friends.

It had been a lovely time, just them, in the warmth and the dark, like a new start. A new thing being made out of all the old and painful stuff, like the best kind of alchemy.

He jumped as the bedroom door opened with a snick and Lorna came out, looking frightened.

'There's knocking,' she said.

'What? Knocking?'

'Yes. At the window.'

'The window?'

'Would you stop repeating everything I say?' she snapped. 'Yes. The window. Someone's knocking.'

He laughed softly. 'I hardly think – maybe it's a branch or something.'

He was halfway across the room and she'd turned away, back towards the bedroom. She hadn't looked at him properly at all, since she'd arrived. At the door, she hung back, hiding her hands in the sleeves of the big jumper she wore over her nightdress, and let him go in first. He looked back at her questioningly and she pointed wordlessly to where the little window gleamed light against the back wall. She looked like a little girl, balancing one bare foot on top of the other to keep it off the chilly floor. He smiled at her and went across to the window. He pulled back one of the curtains which stuck and resisted on the old plastic rail, and looked out into the moonlight. It must be about midnight, again, he thought.

Witching hour.

He was secretly relieved to see no one outside.

'There's no one there,' he said, without turning. Then something caught his eye. A bottle, lying on its side on the windowsill, just below the frame.

'Wait!'

Quickly unlatching the window he pushed it gently open so as not to dislodge the thing and brought it in. There was a little note tied to the neck with string.

He grinned at her.

'Yum! Irish Mist! Look!'

She creased her forehead.

'Who the hell's leaving you bottles of whiskey at your bedroom window? What sort of place is this?'

He shook his head and pulled the note from the bottle.

Glad the wee lad's OK. Have one on us to celebrate. Pat & Mickey

Laughing, he held it out to her.

'It's the boys from the pub,' he explained. 'Closing time about now.'

'How on earth do you know them?' she asked in a high voice, not taking the note. 'Aren't the pubs all closed here? Why are they leaving you bottles at the window? Why not use the door like normal people?'

'They're anything but normal,' he smiled. 'But they were here with the rest on Tuesday night, searching. They're good lads, Lorna.' He shook his head and reread the note, delighted.

'You haven't been drinking again, Evan . . .' Her voice was low and pained.

'Yes, I have indeed, just the once, but I did it right.' He was still amused. 'Come on, Lorna. We can't refuse their good offering. It'd be rude!'

He was twisting the cap off as he spoke and heading for the door when he realised she wasn't following. He stopped and looked at her, the still, calm beauty of her, the face he had kissed so many times. 'Ah come on, Lorrie,' he wheedled. 'Let's at least try to talk to one another. It's the least we can do, after all that's happened.'

She lifted her head at the pet name and smiled sadly.

'Remember that rockface in Chamonix?' he asked quietly. 'Remember how you couldn't find a hold, and you were getting tired? Dare I say it – panicking?'

She laughed softly and shook her head. 'Don't bring that up again, for god's sake,' but her cheeks were a nice pink.

'Remember how you didn't even know my name – we were just on the same bus together?' His voice was teasing now, and she was smiling slightly. 'Remember how I held out my hand and told you to take it?'

She waggled her head *yadda-yadda*. 'Trust me this once, you said, and then you'll never have to speak to me again,' she mocked. 'And I did trust you. OK, OK, and you got me off the rock. So what?'

'Well,' he wasn't smiling now. 'Have a drink with me, this once, just like that.'

'I ended up bloody married to you, you fool!' she laughed.

'Exactly,' he said, and he took her hand and led her through into the dark little living room where their son hung like fruit from the roof and the white beam of the full moon lit everything up like the day.

Chapter 35

——

'I'LL LEAVE THE LIGHT OFF, will I?' he asked. 'The moon's enough.'

Lorna shrugged and smiled slightly, flicking that sleek dark hair back over her shoulder, and he sat down across from her and smiled back.

Her hand curled around the glass, slender and fine, but she didn't take a drink.

'It's been nice having you here,' he said.

She smiled a little more. 'It's been nice having a break,' she said.

'You could have done without the heart attack on Tuesday, of course.'

They both laughed softly and glanced towards the hammock.

'Little shit,' he said gently.

He sipped his drink and watched her over the rim. Her face was pale and still in the moonlight. She hadn't been able to sleep, either, then.

'It's been tough, has it?'

She nodded, and absently sipped from her glass at last. 'You've no idea, miles away down here, honestly. You're cocooned from the worst of the weirdness, I think.'

'Oh I don't know about that,' he laughed, thinking of Big Frank, of Becky, Mickey Flanders. 'There's plenty weird going on down here, believe me.'

He reached across the table and took her hand. 'Sounds like you're making a real difference. And maybe you're happier? You seem happier.'

She shrugged and smiled sadly, 'You think you'll never get over it. And you don't. I know I'll ever get over it, over my Jessie, and I don't want to.' She took her hand away gently. 'But it's just another weight you carry. The guilt. Thinking, if only I'd woken you when I came in that night and found you both sleeping in the chair, instead of sneaking off to bed for that greedy few hours' sleep.'

She shook her head and he let her talk. This was the first time, after all.

'The horror.' She shuddered. 'The feeling of her when I lifted her, dead like that in the dark, when my milk came and woke me, and she hadn't cried for it and her face was empty, nothing there any more.' She took a shaky breath. 'No. You don't get over it. You just keep going, don't you?'

He nodded and waited for her to continue.

'But our ways are different, Evan.'

His face was still as he tried to hear what she was telling him.

'I mean – this has made you happier – being here, quitting the job, having Luca to stay, hasn't it? I mean, I can see it in you, in both of you. You look so well.'

He laughed ruefully. 'Well, I didn't think so at the start – definitely thought I'd die in this horrible old dump, Lorna, or that Luca'd be the death of me.' He nodded. 'It got better. I've loved having him here, Lorrie. Really loved getting back in touch with him again.'

He shook his head, seeing the boy wave at him from the rockpools, and scamper along the top of the rocks, waving at him to hurry up, catch up; shovelling food into his mouth at the end of the day, ravenous and sun-kissed and happy across the table.

'It's been a while,' Lorna said meaningfully.

'I know. I know.' He met her eyes squarely. 'We lost each other somewhere along the way. I—' He almost said the words. Almost said, 'I'm sorry.'

He closed his lips tight and didn't let them out. It wasn't all him. It hadn't all been his doing.

'—He's kept me busy, anyway. He's an incredible little scientist, you know. Reads the most difficult books. And I've been sleeping a lot, as well.' He was blathering now, but he didn't care. 'Catching up, I suppose, when I get the chance.'

She was smiling again. 'Sleeping? Good for you. We didn't get much of that, when Jessie was around,' she said.

'No,' he agreed, and their eyes met.

They listened to the silence for a while, the shush of the waves outside and the occasional creak of the hammock as the boy shifted.

'You're right,' he said with a little surprise in his voice. 'It's been good to me, this place.'

He moved a bit on the hard chair and took time to pour a little more into his glass. He offered the bottle to her, but she shook her head, so he put it down gently and traced a slow circle on the table with his finger, waiting to see what happened next. There was a silence in the room, and he remembered the despair she'd called up in him, the self-hate, the self-loathing.

'Luca wants to have the operation,' he said.

There was a moment's hesitation. 'Yes. He told me.'

'I want him to have it, too, actually.'

He went on, watching her face carefully, but she stayed calm, almost distant, and he waited, holding his breath.

At last she nodded, one neat finger picking at a tiny splinter in the old table, making it worse. He wished she would say something, look at him, even. 'All right,' she said.

'It'll set you free, a bit, as well,' he said, tentatively.

Her eyes were sharp suddenly as she looked up at him. This was the way she ended their discussions, with that look, a cool blank stare to keep him out. 'That's fine. I'll let Dr Campbell know when I get back, although I'm sure everything's on hold because of this . . .' she waved her hand around.

'I think knowing it's coming will make all the difference,' he said gently.

'What happened to you here?' she asked, almost wistfully. 'You've changed.'

He smiled at her, but let the long silence swell and grow and didn't bother to try and fill it.

After a quiet while, she yawned theatrically. 'Well, Mr Mysterious, good talk. Honest. Now. *I'm* going back to bed.' She stood up and came around the table to him, smiling gently, to plant a kiss on the top of his head. She let him wrap his arms around the narrow reach of her and hold her close for a while. Her smell was everywhere, and his face pressed into those wonderful small, firm breasts of hers through the outsize sweater – little pockets of something like muscle, his favourite part of her. He groaned very quietly and turned his face into her like a child squeezing her close and tight, expecting her to pull away as she always did.

To his surprise she softened instead, and stayed, and he knew he just had to move in that certain way, to stand and slide his arms up behind her, to meet her face and her lips would part, they would kiss, they would give in, they would make love here in this gloomy little kitchen with their son a few feet away, and it would be wonderful, that last time, and seem to mean much more than surrender.

But he remembered that smell on their dead baby, too, that scent of Lorna as he came groggy out of sleep that night, and he remembered how she had torn Jessie from him and shaken her so that he was frightened at the little head jerking and jumped up and tried to take the baby back. He remembered the horrible tug of war for a short, short time, her nails cutting deep into his hands and the sense of what she was screaming lost in white noise, before he realised what was happening, and let go, and she fell back, hard, onto the wooden floor, holding the baby to her chest regardless, and screaming as she sat rocking back and forth, back and forth, back and forth.

He let her go, and she stepped away, tucking her hair back where it had fallen, sexy, across her face, a little hardness back around her mouth.

'Well, goodnight, then,' she said.

'Night,' he said and squeezed his legs tight together and watched her go away into the little bedroom and close the door neatly behind her. He heard the ancient springs saw as she climbed into bed and felt the whiskey warm in his belly as the silence returned and the moon climbed over the top of the house and out of the window frame.

Chapter 36

———

SOMETHING CALLED HIM to the window.

It must have been well past midnight now, and the moon was over the ridge of the roof and lighting up the beach and the sea like a spotlight, round and full. There wasn't a breath of wind. The whole expanse of water was as still as a mountain lake, and as black, and as magical. Far out on the horizon tiny pinpricks of a denser light were fishing boats and cargo ships heading for the rest of the world, but everything here, at that moment, was still and taut, as if waiting.

He went back to the table and lifted the squat little bottle and his empty glass with one hand and then opened the front door as quietly as he could with the other, checking behind him to see that nothing stirred. He paused on the threshold, barefoot, his skin prickling, and scented the air. It was full of the thick sweet scent of late summer hebe and honeysuckle, all mixed up with the tang of the sea. The light was blue and grey and silver, and every object under it was black. He shook his head in wonderment and felt the warmth of the night on his face, and then he followed his instinct out into the weirding light to see what would happen.

The stones of the lane were prickly underfoot but not painful, and he crossed them quickly and scrunched onto the dry and powdery sand. Feeling a childlike wonder at the strangeness of the night and his presence in it, he made his way slowly to the low rock at the edge of the bay, a favourite seat, and settled himself, pouring a small dram and then wedging the bottle into the sand at his feet. Things scurried from the rock and out of sight as he moved but he paid them no heed, and somewhere a night-bird peeped. He sipped and sat and looked and felt everything keenly, as if his skin was thinner under the moon.

A small sound caught his attention.

Nothing more than a shift in the air telling him something had changed, something was moving nearby. His ears hissed with listening and he sat very still. He felt the hairs rise on his arms and across his back.

He set his glass down carefully, in the shadows at his feet.

Time passed.

He relaxed a little.

Then, something was indeed moving across the little beach from the far side of the bay, but he couldn't make it out. His eyes stretched to see. Too heavy for a fox or a badger. Something larger was coming down the beach towards him.

Then a shape began to appear as the night-visitor approached the water, moving out of the cover of the surrounding rocks. The sharp shape of a head and shoulders, a daguerreotype against the sea and the sand, then arms and legs, a torso clad in something voluminous, flapping gently as they walked. Nothing otherworldly, of course, of course, but human, and he felt the relief as a kind of joy running through him, and he knew, too, of course, who it was.

He almost called out but stopped himself in time. If he had been alarmed by someone walking across the sand, how much more would she be, by a disembodied voice from the black rocks? Then it was too late anyway, because Grace was pushing off her footwear and shrugging one arm, then the other, out of her wrap, just as he'd seen before. With a rush of acute embarrassment he realised she was going to swim naked again, but this time he was right there, with her, on the beach.

Oh my god, he thought, and sat on.

She was undoing something at the front, at the neck. He could see her elbows poking out as she worked blind. He should definitely go. He looked around at the cottage behind him, twisting on the damp rock, and his foot clinked against the whiskey bottle, the tiniest sound. He froze, but Grace showed no sign of having heard him and didn't turn in his direction.

So he sat, transfixed and embarrassed, waiting until she would be swimming and the water-noise loud in her ears so that he could sneak up the beach unseen and away to the rickety old sofa-bed, where he should have been long ago. In the meantime he watched with shallow breath as she pulled the wrap right over her head in one smooth movement and dropped it on the beach.

She was a strong shape, all power. In her black silhouette he could see wide shoulders and solid torso and broad hips and long mannish thighs with the quads bunched a little above the knee, but not much more. She lifted her arms to secure the thick bunch of her hair behind her head, and he saw low breasts lift, the nipples erect in the night air, then droop as she dropped her hands again.

She took a few steps down to the silver line of the water and waded in, and it was as if her feet and lower legs disappeared into quicksilver. He shivered. His skin was alive with watching her. The moon gleamed now on pale skin and gave her a silvery sheen like a selkie, like a mermaid. The long tangle of her hair ran down her back like a shadow, almost to the cleft of her buttocks which were a deep curve of darkness moving away from him into the water.

She turned then, gracefully, and looked straight at him, where he sat, black, among the rocks. She said, 'Well, are you going to sit there all night, or come in? The water's lovely.'

'Christ!' he muttered, and, 'No, you're all right thanks!' he called. 'You go right ahead. Enjoy!'

It sounded inane even before he said it but the words were gone before he could take them back.

He thought she was smiling but he couldn't be sure. She didn't wait for an answer. Instead, she turned away and the silver skin glinted, and she put out her arms in front to slice the water and bent her body so that the round hips rose up in front of him, and she pushed off and into the water with only the smallest intake of breath audible on the still summer air, and then she was swimming away, away, away, moving sleek and ice cold through the midnight water, the sea marbling the skin of her back.

'Christ! Shit!' he said aloud, now.

He should go. He should really go, for fuck's sake. But he sat on, watching the slow rise and dip of her head as she swam a few yards, then ducked her head under and flipped her feet up, and disappeared altogether.

Now that the sea was empty, he looked at the glass in his hand.

He didn't want any more whiskey.

He wanted daylight and Becky and her firm convictions and a cup of her grassy tea.

He wanted a wall in the sunshine and Luca beside him, swinging his feet and chatting with his fingers.

He wanted more than he had, and he wouldn't get it by sitting like a sad pervert in the darkness.

He found himself on his feet, moving towards the water, using his hands on the slippery wet rocks between him and the sand.

There was a splash. He looked up.

'Evan!' She was on the surface, just a shining head, the water streaming, and her voice was thick with laughter.

Before he knew it, he was at the edge of the sea, pulling off his t-shirt, his pyjama bottoms, throwing his glasses carelessly down on top of them, until he was standing naked there in the light in front of her. She was still, in the water, a little blurry now, her eyes on him. He spread his hands wide as if to say, *Well, here I am, all of me*, and she laughed softly. There was kindness in the sound. He pushed his shoulders back and felt the air on his skin, an unaccustomed tickle, and felt better. He became aware of a wonderful buzz of whiskey under his skin and of the summer sea air over it.

He laughed. He was insane and it was OK.

She was laughing too, he knew it, but it was OK.

He felt like beating his chest and roaring, suddenly. He was alive. He was awake again, at last. He was going in. He was going fucking *in*.

Before his brain could catch up, he strode forwards into the water, keeping his eyes on her. There was no shock of cold, yet. He waded further, the weight of the water against his legs a surprise, little squishy things skating away underfoot. He didn't think about anything, didn't anticipate the shock, just pushed off into the water as she had done, as he had done before, no problem, and felt the intense cold grip his chest and squeeze, lacing the back of his neck with ice.

She was patting her hands together in silent applause as he gasped and doggy-paddled, as his body acclimatised, and he found himself smiling broadly as the breath returned and his body settled down and he began to swim.

There was a different texture to the water in the darkness, he found. It was more solid, more substantial, and he felt the surge of its energy under his skin. He swam for a while, alone, pulling in sensation, wondering at the resistance of the sea to the push of his hands that was surely not as strong in the day. The moonlit surface was a single plate of silver, but he broke it every time he sank and thrust forwards, and knew it healed again behind him. The cold was receding and in its place his body throbbed and burned, doing its thing, adjusting without his input to the new environment, remembering. The only sounds were the small bubbles of his movement, the small puffs of his breath, and, if he paused to listen, the small bubbles of her movement, the small puffs of her breath somewhere beside him.

Turning to look at the land from the sea, he saw the street-lights of the village flare like a string of cheap beads along the top of the headland. A single plane flew overhead, a rarity now, its red and green lights flickering among the white stars, and there was a new flame of joy in his heart in the place that had been hollow, before.

'We must be nuts,' he said quietly.

Grace nodded, treading water beside him, her hair wet and dark as weed on her back, tamed by the water. 'I know I am,' she said. 'Dunno about you, yet.'

They let the silence fall again and stayed close, without touching but aware of the heat and the proximity of the other through the shifting water. Then without a word they turned, and began swimming towards the shore together. Her stroke was surer, stronger, and he lagged behind, but she didn't look back.

Perhaps she'd get to shore far ahead of him, and step out and walk away, her night-time adventure over, her swim swum, and that would be that. Perhaps she'd disappear into the darkness as she'd come, just those slow and scrunching steps, leaving him behind on the sand, and he'd have to face the walk to the cottage, the juddering after-drop of cold in the sofa-bed, alone. He didn't want that.

She was further away now, the water lower on her body, her broad shoulders clear of it, and then she was wading, her feet on the bottom.

He called, 'Wait!' in a high unfamiliar voice.

She was almost at the shore, but she turned.

She stood and looked at him a moment, flipping a long twist of wet hair back over her shoulder as if she were a young woman, as unconscious of her nakedness as if she were a child.

He couldn't believe it when she dipped in once more and she swam back to him. He trod water, waiting until she reached him in the deep water and took his head in both her hands and kissed him full on the lips, warm and cold at once, and salty. He slid his hands around her and felt softness, give, and plenty, where with Lorna there were ribs and muscle. It was marvellous, generous, chilled and lovely. He gripped her and kissed back, hard. Their legs bumped and tangled, and salt water seeped into the corners of their mouths so that they broke apart and laughed quietly as though the night required them to keep their voices low.

'Come on,' she said with a direct look. 'It's getting cold.'

Chapter 37

———

SHE DIDN'T LOOK BACK as she walked up the beach, but slowed her steps just a little, pulling her wet hair up into a draggling bunch and fastening it with the elastic from her wrist to keep it out of her eyes. She heard his footsteps scatter sand as he ran somewhere behind her, and then he came alongside with his clothes dragged on shapelessly, and as she glanced at him, he grinned, shivering, and held up a dark bottle.

'What is it?'

'Irish Mist. Appeared on my windowsill this evening.'

She smiled. 'Ah, the magic bottle. Nice one, Paddy.'

At the edge of the beach there was a sharp step up onto the lane where winter tides had taken bites from the land. She hitched her robe to step up and felt his hand on her elbow, gentle. She didn't snatch it away. She liked the courtesy of it, now, the kindness.

It was all a dance, really, she thought, and this part as important as the rest. She stepped up onto the lane and waited for him to follow, and they walked on together, the sensation of his hand still warm on her chilled skin although he'd taken it away. As they walked in companionable silence the cold built up and made them shake and rattle and hurry along.

Their bodies were adjusting to life on land again, sharing out the stored hot blood down legs and arms, into buzzing fingertips and toes, cooling the whole, rapidly.

At the door of her cottage she kicked off her sandals and heard them thump gently against the wall. The dog looked up from its basket as she went past, rubbing the tops of her arms, and it wiggled the sad stump of its tail but didn't rise, even when the man came after. Its tongue hung out and it looked as if it were smiling. There was a good smell of bread and biscuits, and the place was toasty warm from the slacked-up Aga along the wall.

She felt him behind her, almost touching but not quite, and nodded to the sofa and the big bright throw across its back, its sunny checks a promise of cosy heat and comfort. She shivered, aware of her own teeth clenched with the rictus of after-drop, the ague that held you and shook you until your body sorted itself out from the chill of the sea.

'Throw that around you again, get yourself warmed, and put the kettle on,' she said, and went to the bedroom for her bright, snug kaftan and a hairbrush. She didn't look at herself in the mirror as she went to the dressing table and squirted a dollop into her palm of the stuff Abbie had bought her – the stuff that took away the frizz and left the curls, even on their crazy kind of hair – and was working it through the ends with the flats of her hands as she returned to the living room.

'No shower?' he asked.

He was stirring mugs of tea with the throw slung across his shoulders like a cloak, and looked up with a slight smile as she returned. He was momentarily unfamiliar, and she took a second to assimilate him with her space, her surroundings. He looked easier, affable, comfortable, as if whatever had been eating him had run out into the night sea and gone. His face was alive with interest in her.

'Later,' she said. 'Sea-salt's good for you.'

He carried the mugs across to the sofa and stood waiting to see where she would choose to sit, so she sat at her end, all worn and sunk into shape just right for her body, and curled her feet up inside the folds of her kaftan and put the hairbrush on the floor and looked up at him and held her hands out for the coffee. She could tell by the way he leaned down to put it in her hands, still smiling, that he might have kissed her if he hadn't been burdened with hot liquid and the knowledge warmed her before she took her first sip.

He sat down at the opposite end and whipped the throw around gently with his free hand until it covered his feet, and shuddered elaborately. Then he looked at her over the steaming edge of the mug.

'This smells interesting,' she said, and took a sip.

'A wee nip to warm the blood, as they say,' he replied, watching her.

'Yum. More than a nip, I'd say.'

'Medicinal,' he said.

'We must be very sick indeed.'

She smiled slightly at him, appreciating the burn in her mouth and her throat behind the hot sweet tea, letting the companionship bed in a little, letting things settle.

They sat in silence for a while, sipping and warming and feeling the presence of the other beside them, the humming connection. After a while the warmth from the Aga worked its way through the thin fabric of the kaftan and into her skin so that she loosened her legs and put her feet down on the soft woollen swirls of the mat that she had knitted when she was younger, lonelier. The colours were paler than she liked, but it reminded her of things and so she kept it. She flexed her toes and curled them, enjoying the feel of the gnarled and knotted wool on her warming skin.

He looked at them and did the same, then, letting his feet down onto the mat. Then he rested one foot on its heel and began to stroke her toes with his own, gently, idly, rhythmically, without looking at her, looking quietly ahead, sipping his tea. She was surprised by the bravery of his action, his new ease in his own skin, and even more so by her own reaction. For such a basic thing, it was electrifying. She felt all of her attention rush to the nerve endings in her foot and hang there, spellbound.

She closed her eyes. The silence grew heavy like a drop of water on the tip of a leaf, until it couldn't be borne. 'That's so good,' she said.

'You have lovely feet,' he said quietly.

'They're my mother's. The only lovely thing about her.'

He laughed softly. 'She was some woman, by all accounts.'

She looked at him, her mug nestled in her lap with her hands cupped around it, her eyes half-closed. 'I take it you've heard the stories then. London.'

He nodded, and sipped his tea, and settled his feet quiet on the mat.

'I don't talk about it.'

'I didn't ask about it. It's only your mother I mentioned. We all have stuff we don't talk about. It's all right.'

She laughed gently and sipped the tea, which was mostly whiskey, now. 'You're different, tonight,' she said.

He didn't reply, just drained his mug and twisted to set it down on the floor beside him, and sat back up again. He put his hand out and took hold of her forearm where it came out from the huge loose arm of the red and orange and golden kaftan. He turned it around so that the soft caramel of the arm disappeared, and the pale white underarm showed instead, the veins running faint underneath the skin to the wrist. She felt her skin pimple under his touch.

'See,' he said, without looking at her. 'I'm beginning to think everyone has a regular side, the side that sees the sun, gets the tan; and an underside, that doesn't, like this,' he told her, delicately trailing his finger along her forearm from the elbow to the wrist, just firmly enough not to tickle, gently enough to be delicious. 'You have to find a balance between them, if you want to be happy.'

His thumb sat firm in her palm, where he held her arm straight. She sat very still, enjoying the sensation of his skin and hers together, quiet.

'Until I came here, I was all upper-side, you know? All for show, for others to see and to rate. The job, the house, the stuff we did, the places we went.'

The wife, she thought, but didn't say.

Now his thumb was tracing a slow arc across her tender forearm and back again, over and over, and he was speaking very quietly, as if to himself.

'And it didn't work. When Luca came – he didn't fit the picture, the showy side, the way it's meant to be. He belongs to the underside of me.' He looked up at her suddenly, the flop of hair over his glasses leaving his eyes in shadow. 'So do you,' he said.

This was the moment to stop it, if she was going to stop it at all, she thought, but she knew she wouldn't. Instead she let him lean closer, felt his warm breath on her skin, saw his eyes careful and watchful and keen, in case this thing was not yet granted. In case something had changed since the sea, but it hadn't. She had decided long ago, at least when she watched him swim into danger for the sake of a trapped bird, that this was a possibility. She closed her eyes slowly so as not to startle him away, and felt his lips on hers, full and firm, and she kissed him back.

Chapter 38

———

THE SUN WOKE HIM, and a sense of something lacking, and he rolled over lazily in the big soft bed to find himself alone, the bars of sunlight falling across a bright coverlet from a gap in the thick curtains. He pushed himself up onto an elbow and blinked, but she wasn't there, and the room was still and empty, so he lay back down and pulled the fragrant duvet high up over his head and burrowed into a sharp disappointment that she was already gone. The side of the bed where she had been was cool. He would have liked to have done those things again, felt those things again, talked things over a little in this strange new closeness in the half-dark of the early morning.

For a moment he thought of what she had felt like in the dark, full and generous and soft and clever; how it had been, and then he blinked his eyes open again and pushed back the duvet from his face and looked around.

The slatted light from the edge of a curtain showed him a plain space. One wall was lined with shelves packed tight with books like the rest of the house, but the others were a calm cream without ornament or picture. The plastering was rough and old, and the paint moved in and out in gentle shadows. His hand lay on a quilt which he could see, even in the half-light without his glasses, to be a glorious thing, a complicated swirl of colour and texture in warm colours with yellow splashes everywhere. He wandered his fingers over it appreciatively, feeling raised sections and intricate stitchwork, letting the calm of the place settle into his bones. He didn't want to move just yet. Instead he lay and let the morning seep into him, the thick comfort of the night fade away.

He stretched out luxuriously. Someone was moving around in the kitchen. He heard cupboard doors open and close; the loud scrape of a pan dragged out and set on a hob. Humming. Only Abbie. It was suddenly awkward, lying there naked and alone with the young girl pottering about just outside, so he rolled over and felt around on the floor for his glasses and slotted them on and blinked for the couple of seconds it took to readjust and see clearly.

Then he swung his feet to the bare wooden boards and reached for his pyjama bottoms, all tangled on the floor. His skin shuddered as he pushed his legs into them. They were still damp and very sandy. His t-shirt was the same, and smelled of the sea, of their adventure. He'd have to walk home again in bare feet, too, like a wayward teenager. He checked the time. Six forty-five a.m. There'd be no one around to see him, at least.

A warm scent of baking flowed around the door as he opened it, and Abbie looked up from the pan, smiling, as he came into the room. She wore a white bathrobe that swung loose around her hips and left her legs cool and bare. Her glorious hair foamed around her in the morning sunlight and she mocked him gently with her eyes as she looked him up and down. She didn't seem surprised at his presence in the least.

'Morning, sleepyhead,' she said. 'D'you want some pancakes?'

'Eh, no thanks, Abbie. It's a bit early for me. I'd better be getting home, actually. They don't know where I am.'

She laughed. 'I'd say they don't, right enough.'

The heat flared in his face as he crossed the room, but she smiled quickly once more at him and then turned her attention to a creamy mixture in the basin, scooping up a ladleful and pouring it out in a long thick stream again, watching it carefully. He reached the door to the porch and she didn't look up again.

'Grace around?' he asked, as casually as he could, with his hand on the latch.

She filled the ladle again and this time let the contents out into the pan with a thick, rich sizzle, her tongue between her teeth. When she was happy with it, she said, 'She's headed out fishing, I think. Won't be back until the tide turns, probably.'

She flashed him a smile and dipped the ladle again.

'Oh, right, OK,' he said. 'See you, then.'

Abbie flipped the round brown pancake expertly and then looked at him over her shoulder.

'—Don't worry,' she said, her head on one side just like her aunt. 'She *will* be back, eventually.'

He scuffed his foot on the floor sheepishly, 'OK, thanks. Bye.'

'Bye, lover-boy,' she called after him.

He laughed a little, gently, shaking his head, as he went out into the porch and noted the empty basket where the ugly dog had been lying last night, and the sun already strong, streaming in through the window, lighting up the cherry-red geraniums all along the windowsill, making him blink.

The dew was still wet on the soles of his feet when he stepped out into the lane. He stood there a moment to take stock, the buttery scent of the pancakes still thick in the air around him. There was a steamy silence everywhere and a couple of gulls circled overhead, just hanging out. Behind the big wall at his back the hens grumbled and muttered, and the sun was warm on his upturned face and he had the sudden, steady realisation again that everything was as it should be, and everything was perfect. He thought of Becky and smiled. He must thank her sometime.

Then he stretched a little where he stood and headed back towards the cottage where his wife slept.

The rocky bank at the side of the lane began to lower as he walked, allowing him a view of the wide blue sea, and the little boat on it, not far from shore, a single figure motionless at the stern. He stood to look for a while, at the huge hat shading head and shoulders from the sun, the rest of the woman still and tall and composed, waiting. The dog would be sleeping at her feet, probably, never far away.

The boat was drifting with the tide, further from shore as he watched, and she was letting the fishing line travel light, fooling the fish with its twinkling ornaments. Soon, she was no more than a dark smudge on the bright water and his feet reminded him of damp and chill from the wakening earth, so he headed on, around the green damp corner and into his own bay, his own cottage squat and dark at the side of the lane and almost welcoming.

'Gaaah!'

Luca was perched beside a favourite rockpool in his favourite Wolverine pants and a t-shirt, waving him over. He'd had the same crab now for over five days, keeping it from the tide by careful relocation, and teasing it relentlessly with bits of ham and fish finger crumbs begged from the table. Evan went quickly across to him, loving the fact that he'd been called to see, loving the caramel colour of his son's skinny limbs and the smile on his face as he spoke earnestly to something beneath the water of the pool, loving his own sudden loose-limbed satisfied ease.

How's Mr Krabs, he asked, perching on a smooth rock beside his son.

He doesn't have a name. Grace says you don't name wild things because you can never own them.

Evan laughed but Luca didn't see him. He was busily

probing a bedraggled blob of red seaweed with a little stick of driftwood to expose what was underneath.

But look. I found this on the beach, see?

Evan followed the pointing stick to a tiny white carcass underneath, a dead crab, which was being dragged briskly towards the mouthparts of Luca's own large green pet. The boy dropped the stick to say, He's gonna eat it! He's gonna actually eat another crab!

The boy's face was filled with excitement and revulsion in equal parts and he joggled his dad's elbow to make sure he understood.

Cool, Evan signed under the boy's nose, and Luca smiled quickly up into his face.

They watched as the larger crab tugged a little leg right off, and pushed it into its own hairy, waving mandibles. Evan's belly creaked unhappily. He felt Luca tense beside him. When it lost patience and climbed on top of the limp carcass, hiding it altogether, Luca looked away, his face strained.

You know, I don't think I can watch this after all.

Yeah, pretty gross, agreed Evan. Let's go sit up on the top of the rocks and watch the tide go out, instead.

The boy nodded and stood up straight away, and then clambered like a monkey to the top of the ridge of rocks surrounding the beach where he found himself a comfortable perch with practised ease. Evan followed behind more slowly, and looked for the little dot of the boat far off to the right, before turning his attention back to the water of the bay.

Seen another seal yet?

Luca shook his head. Not since last week. But Grace says sometimes there's dolphins. He sighed loudly. I'd really like to see that.

Well, you've another couple of weeks here. You might be lucky, Evan told him.

Are you going to stay here, Dad? When the lockdown's over? When I go home again?

Evan nodded.

Are you going to stay here forever? The boy's face was alive with hope. —Because I could come and stay with you every holidays, then. Keep my crab in a tank or something until I come back. You could feed him for me, couldn't you? He likes ham. Not bread though.

Evan shook his head. I don't know. I don't think so, Luca. I haven't made any plans. He smiled down at his son's crest-fallen face. Let's just go with the flow for a while, will we? See what happens.

The boy shrugged and nodded and looked out over the water.

Is your mum up yet?

The boy nodded.

She was packing stuff when I got up. Made me have breakfast.

He made a face and then they were quiet again.

She was humming, Luca added then, as an afterthought. I felt it in the table.

Evan looked at him. She's happy then. That's good, eh?

Yeah.

What about you, Luca? Are you happier?

The boy's hand-signs were emphatic, as if he'd been thinking about this already.

Yes. I like it here. I like it with you, when I don't have to sit and learn all the time, and drive places and get poked by doctors and all that. But.

He squinted at his father, the sun in his eyes now.

I don't want it to go back the way it was. I like it when you and Mum are different, not trying to be the same.

He put his hand on his dad's arm for a second and it was warm, and then he turned to face his father full on. His eyes were that amazing deep brown like his mother's, with flecks of light in the iris.

I know I can't stay here if I want to see Mum and have the

operation and everything, if I want to go to school and all. I know I have to go back home. But.

Evan nodded. It's OK, he replied. I know now. Your mum knows, too. He concentrated, trying to get things straight, so that he could explain. Look. Things got a bit messed up when Jessie died.

At the name, the boy nodded solemnly and watched his father's hands intently.

Well, they were a bit messed up already, before she even came along, but when she died, it was like that crab down there – the way we didn't want to watch but it was hard to look away? I had to watch your mum missing Jessie all the time, and she had to watch me beating myself up for everything, and it made us both sad and angry and we both forgot to look away and watch you.

The boy shifted his skinny behind on the warm rocks, but he was still eyeing the hands, still waiting for more. Mum was always watching me, he said, with a gloomy face.

I know, son. But it was her way of coping, that's all. She was trying to deal with her feelings about Jessie and how she died, by caring so hard about you.

Luca nodded slowly, doubtfully.

You were a real help to her by being there, when I think about it – by letting her fuss over you the way she did, without complaining.

Evan paused and thought about it.

Yeah, Luca. You were a real hero, helping your mum like that. I don't know how she would've managed without you.

The boy picked at a bright yellow scruff of lichen in a crack in the rocks. There was a faint pink colour in his cheeks.

'Evan!' It was Lorna, standing at the cottage door with her bag at her feet and a smile on her face. She looked tired. 'I have to head on, here. Will you send him over to say goodbye?'

Luca had felt him twist around anyway, and had seen his mother standing there. He was on his feet and sliding down the rocks immediately, running chicken-footed across the sand to hug her waist and press himself close.

Evan made his way down more slowly, and watched them signing to each other eagerly as he crunched his way up the beach. She was telling him to be good and he was retorting that he was always good, and she was telling him to eat well and he was smiling and telling her he always ate well and Becky only gave him chocolate on a Friday for his wages and she was telling him to look after his father for her and then they were both turning around and smiling out at him from the tight group of themselves and he thought Lorna had never looked more beautiful.

'Well,' she said to him. 'Keep in touch.'

She turned to Luca again and demanded FaceTime once a week at least, to let her know how he was getting on. The boy nodded impatiently.

'You take care of yourself, up in the big bad city,' Evan smiled, keeping his distance.

'And you get dressed!' she laughed. 'Have you been sitting out on those rocks in your undies all morning, the pair of you? You must have been up with the lark!'

Evan smiled again and said nothing. Luca picked up her bag, telling her about his muscles and how he would carry it for her to the car up in the village before taking her hand busily. She went with him a few steps, laughing, and then stopped and looked back over her shoulder to where her husband stood barefoot on the shingle.

Evan looked at her and shrugged. There were no words. There were tears in her eyes, but her mouth was still laughing.

'I'll only let him come as far as the corner in his underpants,' she said. 'Then I'll send him back.'

'OK,' he smiled.

'And I'll be in touch, about school and all, whatever they decide to do, OK?'

She turned quickly to Luca, Come on, my big strong

son. Carry your old mother's luggage to the corner, and she laughed when he growled like a tough guy and yanked her forwards.

Evan watched them pick their way off the shingled beach and onto firm ground, Lorna surefooted and deft and elegant and already elsewhere in her head, Luca scuttling behind with her bag, determined to keep up.

Evan was suddenly alone. Everything was very quiet, so he heard the sound quite clearly when it came. A tiny note, not metallic, not vocal, and gone immediately as quickly as it had come. Straining his ears for it, he felt the smooth rounded pebbles under his feet as if for the first time. A slight breeze picked up his fringe and set it down again, cooler. He listened hard, but the sound of the sea was all that was left. His chest flared hot, as it had that night when Jessie slept there, and he put a hand to it without thinking and he held his breath and felt tears sting in his eyes. The moment felt like lightness somehow, he thought, feeling something intensely now, searching for a name for it, watching his family climb the hill. As if something had been sloughed away, the freshness of new pink skin underneath a wound.

A gull called behind him, a sharp cry bringing him back, letting his breath out slow and deep, and then Lorna was gone, and Luca was running, running, running, back down the hill towards him, his hair shaggy and in need of a trim, his limbs brown and all of his happiness written on his freckled face.